VIABLE

A CODY DOYLE THRILLER

Prologue

London, England - 1920

THE YOUNG WOMAN placed the basket carefully on the ground. She sat next to it, her knees hugged tight to her chest, her back to the stone wall. It was cold, the wind driving the rain, and the wall offered little shelter. The light clothes she had left in were already soaked through. She hardly noticed. There wasn't much time. By now he would know she was gone. If she allowed him to find her he would make her tell where she had hidden the child, and it would continue. She couldn't let that happen.

A sound in the distance and she looked up, her heart racing. He couldn't have found her already. But it was just a horse-drawn cart crossing the small cobbled street, the driver hunched forward over the reins, the animal's head down as it slowly pulled its load north into the city. Soon it was gone, silence returning.

She checked the basket. She had fed him before they had left and the infant slept on, oblivious. Looking down at her son, so impossibly small, so helpless, she felt an unbearable sadness, the weight of it threatening to crush her chest. What had she done? He seemed healthy but the few others that had survived birth had all been frail, sickly. Would these people take him in, raise him as their own? She had to believe they would. There was nothing else she could do for him now.

It was still raining, but she could see the clouds beginning to break up in the distance. The drops ran freely down her face, mixing with her tears as the first of the morning light found its way over the rooftops. She had to go. She leaned over the basket and the child opened his eyes, looking up at her. He had such beautiful eyes – how could they think of harming him? She took the St. Christopher medal from around her neck and placed it under his blanket. It was all she had to offer him. It would have to be enough.

She kissed her son goodbye.

1

Montgomery, Alabama - 2003

ROB DYLAN SAT IN THE BACK, staring out of the window at the traffic flowing south on 65, the Excursion's 7.3-liter diesel idling for the aircon. The *Exxon Valdez* he called it when Brad was in earshot. But today he was glad of it. He had felt the heat when Lucy May had opened the door. Had to be over a hundred, and humid as all hell.

He wished now he'd come by himself. It might have taken him a little longer in the Bronco, three days perhaps instead of two, but he could have used the time to set things straight in his head, to prepare for what he had to say. And travelling with young kids was hard time, even when they were your own grandchildren.

But they had insisted.

It'll be like a road trip, Lucille had said, *we'll have fun*.

Hadn't trusted him to make the journey by himself, more like.

At least they hadn't tried to get him to fly out here. They'd known better than to suggest that. It had nothing to do with that business up in New York with the towers, already almost two years ago now. He hadn't set foot on an airplane in over fifty years, not since the transport that had brought him back, and he'd not have got on that if there'd been any choice in the matter. He certainly had no intention of taking up with those godforsaken machines now.

They were only looking out for him of course, he knew it, and he loved Lucille like she was his own daughter. Brad had done well there. But sometimes they fussed too much. Sure he was getting on a bit – seventy-three next month – but in good shape for his years. He'd had to get glasses last fall, but only for reading and for the TV. His eyes were otherwise as sharp as they'd ever been, plenty good enough for driving.

And the Bronco might have been old, but she wouldn't have let him down. Hadn't once in the thirty-seven years he'd owned her. He still remembered the day he'd picked her up. *Come on down to the plant*, Arjay Miller had said, *meet the guys who build the cars you're selling for us, pick one out, anything you want.* He could have had any model in the line-up – Thunderbirds, Mustangs, even the new Galaxie with that sweet V8. When the president of Ford himself calls you and tells you to go pick out something you'd better believe he means it. Hell, he'd sold more cars for them that year than any other dealer in the tri-state area; he could have asked for one of each and they'd have given them to him. But the moment he'd seen the Bronco, just rolling off the production line with that candy apple red paintjob, his mind had been made up. And then something had come over him and he'd told the manager he wanted to drive it right out of there that day, all the way from Wayne, Michigan back to Texas. He smiled as he remembered the guy running around trying to get as much added from the options list as he could before the visit was over, just so that he wouldn't have to explain to Miller that they'd gone cheap on him. A CB radio, an auxiliary gas tank, even a goddamned winch. He'd never used any of it of course, not in all the time he'd had her. But it all still worked just fine. The guys in the workshop took care of that car like it was their own, even though parts were getting harder to come by each year. *Nossir,* she wouldn't have let him down. It would have been like that drive home, when he'd first got her, fresh off the line.

He should have insisted.

He saw Lucy May running back from Bruster's carrying the sodas, her younger brother in tow. Brad followed behind with a cardboard tray of ice creams. They were good boys, he and his brother Jason, he was lucky to have them. They'd been running the business for him this last ten years, since Phyllis had died, and doing a good job of it. He'd made his mind up to hand the company over to them this year. He'd tell them both when they got back.

The door opened, a blast of heat cutting through the chilled air inside the Excursion as his granddaughter climbed up into the back seat, scooching over beside him on the leather, handing him a soda. Rob Junior was taking his time clambering in behind her and he could feel the remainder of the cool escaping into the Alabama afternoon. Then Lucille was handing out the ice creams, telling the children once again to be careful not to spill any on the upholstery. He looked over at the plastic spoon overloaded with double chocolate chip already being shoveled into Rob Junior's gaping maw and thought there were two chances of that happening, and that slim had perhaps just quit town.

He shifted in his seat, looking out of the Excursion's heavily tinted windows as he slowly ate his ice cream. A bike had pulled up at the Chevron across from them while Brad and the kids had been in the store. One of those fancy Japanese crotch rockets with the garish paint jobs. *Yamaha*. It was sitting in the sun in front of the nearest set of pumps and he could make out the decal easily. *Nossir*, nothing wrong with his eyesight. Jason's eldest boy, Mikey, had told his father he was saving for one just like it. Well he sure as hell wasn't about to let

5

that happen. The boy was turning eighteen that year and he planned to bring him down to one of the dealerships and set him up with something. Nothing too fancy – maybe an Explorer – but certainly something that wasn't going to get him killed before he reached his next birthday. It was another thing he needed to talk with Jason about when they got back. But for now he needed to focus on why he was here.

He took another scoop of his ice cream. Brad and Lucille had agreed to drive him eight hundred miles across country without even asking why he suddenly wanted to attend such an event. They probably thought that he was getting sentimental in his old age, trying to come to terms with his past while he still had the time. He wondered if they would still have brought him if they knew why he really wanted to be here. Tell the truth, he'd been a little surprised that he had even been invited. He had written to each of the organizations when they had first started to contact him, years ago now, telling them to take him off their goddamn mailing lists. And to be fair most of them had. For years he had only received an occasional letter, which had quickly found its way into the trash.

But then two months ago, this.

He reached into the pocket of his jacket, checking it was still there. He didn't need to take it out. He had read and re-read it so often he knew every word on the card by heart. An invitation to Maxwell Air Force Base, Montgomery, Alabama, to a ceremony to commemorate the fiftieth anniversary of the armistice. If that had been all the invitation would have gone the way of all the others. But then he had read that the guest of honor was to be Colonel Yevgeny Grupolov, formerly of the *Voyenno Vozdushnye Sily*, the Soviet Air Force. The leaflet that had accompanied the invitation had described Grupolov, a holder of the Gold Star of the Hero of the

Soviet Union, as the greatest fighter ace of the war. He hadn't recognized the name – they hadn't known it at the time – but it was Rudy, he was certain of it.

Fifty years.

Fifty goddamned years.

He had tried to forget. But all he ever had to do was close his eyes and he would be back there, walking from the mess to the flight line, Little Bitch sitting on the runway, waiting for him, somehow ungainly on the ground. A cursed ship; slow, thirsty, guns that overheated and jammed. But that morning he had walked right past her and climbed up into Mitchell's Sabre, his mind still replaying the offer his friend had made as they had finished their coffee. A chance to finally earn a star for underneath his cockpit.

How eager he had been to be off then, like a goddamn idiot. The short taxi to the runway, their ships quivering in the blast as the planes ahead readied for takeoff, rudders flicking slowly from side to side as the brakes released and they began to roll. Slowly at first then quickening, feeding in the power, feeling the Sabre surge forward, moments later lifting free of the ground, climbing. The observation birds had spotted MiGs being fuelled at Antung earlier that morning and he had led them north over the Haeju peninsula, across the edge of the Yellow Sea, the shortest way there. At thirty thousand feet the contrail level, speed fences appearing on the wings. Then they were through it, continuing to climb, leveling out just short of the Sabre's ceiling, forty thousand feet above the Yalu. The sun higher in the sky now, shimmering off the water miles below, a majestic sight. And yet he had hardly noticed as he leaned forward against the straps of his harness, his neck craning from side to side as he had searched for their adversaries, desperate for the fight that would earn him his kill.

But the skies had been clear and for half an hour they had flown in silence, the click and hiss as the valves in his mask opened and closed the only sound in the cockpit as he led them through long, shallow, sweeping turns, patrolling both sides of the river. One by one other flights had run low on fuel and started to leave, until only they had remained.

It was Mitchell who had seen them first, calling them out. Four wakes briefly visible as they climbed through the contrail level. MiGs crossing the Yalu, turning south towards them.

His heart raced even now, fifty years later, as he remembered. Mitchell radioed that he had lost two of them, that the remaining MiGs had dropped tanks. Alone, running on fumes, two bogies unaccounted for. But he had ignored his friend's warning. The Russian pilots had jettisoned the external fuel tanks they carried, making them lighter, more maneuverable in combat. They had come to fight.

Endless moments scanning the skies until at last he had seen them. Two birds, descending to meet them head on, the gap between the two flights closing rapidly. Then surprise as suddenly the Russians had done something he hadn't seen before, breaking formation as they rolled and dove, each heading in a different direction. Without thinking he had followed, banking hard to the left, pushing the nose down, not even bothering to call it out, knowing his friend would be behind him. The Sabres were faster in a dive and they had closed steadily, full throttle in lower altitudes burning through their remaining fuel at an alarming rate. He had ignored the gauge, his world now the gun sight reflected on the armor glass, the MiG ahead tantalizingly close.

Suddenly Mitchell's voice in his helmet. More MiGs bearing down on them from above. Cold fear flooded his system as he realized the jet they were chasing had been bait and he twisted in his seat, squinting into the glare even behind his visor, straining to see. Something against the sun, then gone. Then again, glimpsed for longer this time, the scarlet bifurcated nose of the lead MiG telling him that it was Rudy, the Russian ace, who was hunting them.

If only he had reacted then. He could have dropped back, let his friend take over. Mitchell would have known what to do. But instead he had frozen, precious seconds lost as, paralyzed with fear, he sat there, the stick dead in his hand. Mitchell's voice, no longer calm now, shouting at him to break hard to the left. Rounds from Rudy's cannon already tracing bright lines only feet from his wing tips.

Then Mitchell calling out that he was taking hits. He had watched, helpless, as the hydraulic brakes on the old ship deployed and suddenly Little Bitch was decelerating, shooting backwards towards the Russian jet just as the first shells started to tear into her fuselage. An instant later the canopy had flown off, the ejector seat turning over as it arced through the air. An explosion, bright even against the morning sun, as the Russian's wingman had flown straight into the wreckage. Somehow Rudy had managed to avoid the disintegrating Sabre but his MiG was out of control, spinning towards the deck.

And then as soon as it had begun it was over, the skies quiet again, his ship the only one remaining. He had looked down to see a 'chute opening, already hundreds of feet below, beginning its slow descent to the ground. He felt his eyes burn, blinking back the tears as he remembered. That far inside enemy territory they hadn't even bothered to mount a rescue. His stupidity had cost his friend dearly.

Well he may not be able to take back what he had done, but here was an opportunity to set the record straight. He would attend the ceremony, and he would walk right up to Rudy or whatever his goddamn name was and tell the Russian what he suspected the man already knew. He might have had more kills, but there was no way he had been the better pilot. The only reason he'd managed to knock Little Bitch out of the sky that day was because his friend had switched roles with his goddamn idiot of a wingman who had led them into a trap and then not known enough to get them out of it.

He sat back in his seat. There. That was it. That was exactly what he would say. When it came down to it there was no other way to put it, even if he'd had the inclination to sugarcoat it some, which he did not. He no longer cared if he caused a fuss, if he became an embarrassment to his country in this new era of *détente*, or whatever the hell they were calling it now. It wouldn't change a thing, of course. His friend had still died half a century ago somewhere in North Korea and the Russian would still end up with his picture in the base's Hall of Fame. But it was important to him that they understood how it had *really* been. After that they could do what they pleased.

He looked up, wiping his eyes with the back of one liver-spotted hand. The kid who owned the crotch rocket was coming out of the Chevron, returning to his bike at the pump, his helmet in the crook of his elbow. He was still in the shade of the forecourt awning, his face obscured, but there was something in the easy way he walked that caught Rob Dylan's attention. He watched as the young man strolled back to his bike, throwing one leg over before sitting astride the Yamaha in the sun. As he lifted the helmet over his head the old man caught a glimpse of his face.

The tub fell to the floor, half-melted chocolate ice cream oozing slowly into the Excursion's beige carpets. Little Rob Junior began to laugh. For once he would not be the one getting in trouble for spilling food in the backseat. Today it was grandpa's turn. Beside him Lucy May was looking from him to her mother and back again.

'Mommy, is Grandpa Dylan alright?'

But he didn't hear. He was pre-occupied with opening the back door, frantically tugging at the release, banging on the window, realizing too late that Brad had switched on the child locks as soon as the kids had climbed into the back. Lucille was turning around in her seat, asking what was wrong.

He ignored her, continuing to stare across the road at the gas station, his fingers still working the door handle. The young man on the bike paused for a second and turned to look directly at the Excursion, as if something there had caught his attention, although there was no way he could see him through the heavy tint on the windows, no way he could have heard him above the traffic. Now he saw him clearly, and there was no mistake. He called out his name, screaming at his son to let him out of the goddamn car.

Brad's finger hovered over the switch that operated the child locks in the back, but Lucille's hand batted it away. She fixed her husband with a stare, the one she reserved for those times when he needed to listen to her, and listen good. She didn't know what had brought it on – maybe the heat, maybe the thoughts of the ceremony had brought back too many old memories, maybe he was just plain tired from the trip – but she was sure her father-in-law was having some sort of turn, and she certainly wasn't going to let Brad release him onto a busy road in his current state. They had passed a hospital not five miles back on their way out of Montgomery.

That was where they were going, right now, if he kept this up.

Brad complied, as he was apt to do on the rare occasions he got that look from his wife. His hand retreated from the switch. Lucille was right, something was wrong with the old man. He had never seen him this agitated.

'Dad, what in the hell's wrong?'

Across the road the young man stared at the Excursion for a moment longer before pulling the helmet down over his head, turning the key in the ignition. Rob Dylan ignored his son. There was no time to explain; already the bike was idling out of the forecourt of the Chevron. His fingers scrabbled for the switch that operated the electric windows, realizing too late that the child locks had disabled those too. And then the young man was flicking the visor on his helmet down, turning his attention to the highway. A gap in the traffic and the Yamaha accelerated smoothly away, merging with the stream of cars and trucks flowing south on 65. The old man shifted around in his seat, desperate to catch one last glimpse through the Excursion's rear window but already it was gone.

2

Berkeley, California – 3 months ago

GHOST TANGLES; hyper-phosphorylated tau protein, twisted into paired helical filaments. The silver stain showed clearly that the fibrillary material had become extraneuronal, that the host neurons were already dead. Morphological hallmarks of the disease in its final stages.

Alison Stone stood up from the microscope. It was already dark outside; once again she'd lost track of time. The last of her colleagues had left some time ago and she was alone. Which suited her fine; she liked it when the lab was quiet. She wasn't hungry, but there was enough work to keep her here for a few hours yet and she knew she probably would be later. She could wait until she got home, but she wasn't even sure there would be anything in the apartment's tiny refrigerator. She checked her watch. If she hurried the cafeteria might still be open.

She grabbed her pass, swiped out, and took the stairs. As she walked through the lobby the security guard stood up from behind his desk.

'Doctor Stone, you had a message from Professor Rutherford.'

Shit. She had forgotten she was supposed to be having dinner with the dean. She had unplugged the phone in the lab so that she could concentrate and had forgotten all about him.

'Thanks Ryan. When did he call?'

The security guard looked down at the post-it note where he had scribbled the messages.

'Just after seven. Again at seven-thirty. And just before eight.'

Three calls. That wasn't good.

'Did he leave a message?'

'Just for you to call him when you got out.' He smiled apologetically. 'I would have come get you but I'm not supposed to leave the desk. Besides, I know you don't like to be disturbed when you're working.'

'Of course, Ryan. Thanks for taking the message. I'll give him a call.'

'You need the number? Professor Rutherford made me write it down each time.' He held up the post-it note by way of proof.

'Thanks, I got it.'

The security guard resumed his seat, blushing. He liked it when Doctor Stone smiled at him.

Her cell phone was back in the lab, also switched off. No doubt Rutherford would have left more messages for her there. For a moment she considered going back up to get it, but then decided against it, continuing out through the automatic doors. It had been another perfect early October afternoon and even though the sun had set the night air still felt warm, the late summer rasp of cicadas loud after the air-conditioned solitude of the lab.

At this time of night she'd need to go to Sproul to get something to eat. She hesitated for a moment outside the Life Sciences building, choosing left, the path through Eucalyptus Grove and Grinnell. It was slightly longer but she had the time. Berkeley was famous for its blue gums and the impossibly tall hardwoods with their thick, shaggy bark always lifted her spirits after time spent studying the disease. As she made her way towards them a young man stepped out of the darkness. For a split second as he moved into the pool of light cast by the

14

lobby she could have sworn his eyes had shone, flashing luminescence in the darkness.

She froze.

Had she really seen that?

She quickly glanced around to check that Ryan was still sitting behind his desk in the lobby. But as she turned back to face the stranger whatever she thought she might have seen was gone. Of course it had just been a trick of the light, her eyes adjusting to the darkness after the harsh fluorescent strip lighting of the lab. She felt foolish for having been so skittish.

'Doctor Stone?'

The accent was hard to place. Neutral, perhaps British, but with a slight twang. Not American, but maybe someone who had lived here a while. He was tall, lean but muscular. His hair was dark brown, almost black, thick but cropped short. He was wearing old jeans and a faded khaki t-shirt. His arms and face were tanned, and he gave the impression of someone who was used to more physical activity than an academic environment would typically provide. Her father had served a tour as a helicopter pilot in Vietnam and there was an old photo of him on the sideboard in her parents' house, standing next to the open cargo door of a Huey in his baggy flight suit, squinting into the baking sun. She didn't know why but for some reason he reminded her of that. He didn't look like he belonged here, on campus.

But then this was California; she was still getting used to the fact that everyone seemed to have a tan. And many of the students at Berkeley were here on athletic scholarships, so finding someone that worked out among all the jocks really wasn't that hard. As she looked more closely she could see he couldn't be much more than nineteen or twenty. Only his eyes, which she now saw were the most incredible shade of green she thought she had ever seen, and the ease with which he carried himself seemed to suggest he might be older.

He held out his hand. Again, a bit unusual. He was respectful, but the deference that her students usually showed was missing; she felt like she was being addressed as an equal. His handshake was cool, the grip firm. She was certain now that she hadn't noticed him around campus before. She would have remembered those eyes. She found herself wondering what combination of genes had resulted in their almost incandescent hue. She really had to get out more.

'How can I help you?'

'I've read some of your research and I have a couple of questions.'

'Sure. Mind if we talk on the way to the cafeteria? I need to grab something before they close.'

'Of course.'

He walked beside her among the trees. As they entered the grove the leafy canopy closed high above them.

'It's the article you wrote on cybrids.'

Alison's heart sank. Not another one.

Stem cells possessed the ability to differentiate into almost all types of bodily tissue, a flexibility that was invaluable to medical research. But in humans and other mammals it was only early embryonic cells that exhibited that ultimate plasticity. And the status of the human embryo remained controversial. It was what had brought her to California, one of the few states where funding was still available for her work. Even in California human eggs remained in chronically short supply however, forcing a search for alternatives. Cybrids – cytoplasmic hybrid embryos – were created by transferring nuclei from human cells into animal eggs that had had almost all of their genetic information removed. A tiny jolt of electricity to encourage the egg to divide, and the resulting embryos could then be harvested for stem cells. But earlier that year a senator from Arkansas had proposed legislation banning the creation of such hybrid embryos, effectively criminalizing an entire branch of biomedical research.

And so she had written an article arguing that given its potential, the responsibility for the regulation of stem cell research was simply too important to be left to politicians, the majority of whom seemed at best ill-informed, at worst determined to frighten and confuse an already skeptical public. The article had stopped short of accusing the senator of what she suspected – that the Bill had been funded by one or more right-wing religious groups, determined to establish rights for embryos long denied to them by the U.S. Supreme Court since *Roe vs. Wade*.

She had not counted on the reaction her comments would generate. Hundreds of protesters had set up camp outside her lab the morning after the article had been published, and the dean had suggested that she continue her work from another campus until things died down. Thankfully after a few weeks the protests had fizzled out, although she still received the occasional piece of hate mail, most of it addressed to her office at the faculty. Those were easy to ignore. Occasionally something would arrive at her apartment, however. So far no-one had called in person, but it troubled her a little that they knew where she lived.

'So what was your question?'

'Mixing genetic material the way you do, it doesn't concern you?'

She paused before responding, wary. If he had read her research he already knew her views on that subject. Was he trying to provoke an argument? They were alone; there was no one else around. She looked over, for the first time noticing what looked like a religious medal on a thin silver chain around his neck. Just ahead was the culvert, the confluence of the south and north forks of the creek that flowed through the university and beyond that the Monterey pines and native oaks of Grinnell, marking the center of the wilderness that sat at the heart of the campus. She wished now she had taken the shorter route through Dwinelle, with its brightly lit walkways and bustling student center. She glanced over her shoulder. She could just make out the lights of the Life Sciences building's lobby but they were too far for Ryan to see her. She forced herself to remain calm. She was being silly. The young man didn't appear threatening.

'I can certainly understand sensitivity to the use of human DNA. But cybrids created using cells from a patient with a genetic disorder, like Alzheimer's for instance, carry the genes responsible for that disorder. That makes them invaluable in studying the development of the disease. Besides, cybrids really shouldn't be viewed as controversial. Even though they're created from animal eggs, all the DNA in the cell nucleus is human. Animal DNA is found only in the mitochondria, but mitochondrial DNA plays no part in either cellular division or in reproduction.'

'So you think we should go further then?'

They crossed a wooden footbridge, following the south fork of the creek. The old planks creaked underfoot, the waters beneath reduced to a trickle after a long, hot summer and a dry fall. The flagstone path leading to the road and civilization beyond were still some way ahead. Again she hesitated, studying the young man's face for any sign that might tell of an impending confrontation. His manner was certainly direct. But there was nothing, at least nothing she could detect, in either his expression or the tone of his voice that indicated she might be in danger.

'Well, things do get a little more complicated when you start to consider mixing cells from different organisms, either human or animal. That said, there's nothing particularly new with the concept. A person with a replacement heart valve from a pig is a chimera. But then, strictly speaking, so is anyone who has undergone a blood transfusion. With such simple procedures concerns are typically limited to clinical effectiveness and safety, the prevention of cross-species infections, that sort of thing. At some point it's hoped we'll be able to produce patient-specific tissues that are safe for transplantation into humans. That would be really useful in limiting the instances of organ rejection.'

'What about introducing animal genetic material directly into a human embryo?'

She stopped, turning to face him.

'You mean hybrids, transgenics?'

This time he stared back at her, those green eyes searching her face for an answer.

Yes.

There were some naturally-occurring examples of true hybrids – the mule, the liger – but Alison knew the use of human-animal hybrids in medical research would never be condoned, whatever the justification. However, transgenics – animals that had genes from other animals, plants or even humans, deliberately inserted into their genomes – *had* already been created. Ordinary mice couldn't be infected with polio, as they lacked the cell-surface molecule that, in humans, served as the receptor for the virus. Transgenic mice had therefore been engineered to express the human gene for the polio virus receptor, allowing them to serve as an inexpensive, easily-manipulated model for studying the disease. The real risk lay in the possibility of inadvertently creating an animal with human characteristics. Introducing human genetic material into the nervous system of animals, particularly higher order primates, was a particular concern. But nothing that aggressive had ever been attempted, or was ever likely to be.

'Well, it's a difficult area. Given the limits on federal involvement, privately funded research into human embryonic stem cells has to date largely been carried out under a patchwork of existing regulations, many of which were not designed with that research specifically in mind. Now, if...'

'Doctor Stone, I'm not really interested in the regulatory implications. I want to know what you think.'

Alison was momentarily taken aback. She wasn't used to being interrupted by her students, most of whom were content to listen intently to whatever she might have to say.

'Look, I'm not sure where this is going. It might help me to answer your question if I understood your particular area of interest. Is it the use of transgenic animals as disease models, as candidates for xenotransplantation, as bioreactors for pharmaceuticals? Or something else?'

The young man paused before he answered. It seemed to her like he knew what he wanted to ask, but was unsure whether he should trust her. Perhaps he was afraid of being ridiculed. But somehow she didn't think that was it either.

'I'm interested in the possibilities for enhancing regenerative capacity in humans.'

So that was it. Stem cell research was the latest great hope for a cure for many of the terrible conditions that still afflicted mankind. But, like radioactivity had been during the middle of the last century, it was also the 'go to' science solution for movie producers and scriptwriters who needed to justify some ridiculous sci-fi plot. He wasn't a religious nut after all, just some film studies undergrad with an idea for a screenplay. It would explain why she hadn't seen him in her classes. She felt a little foolish for having worried. This young man cared about superheroes, not the salvation of her eternal soul. She checked her watch, anxious now to get to the cafeteria before it closed.

'Well, can you be more specific? Are you talking about growing back limbs, or just above average ability to self heal?'

He hesitated again, as if considering how to respond.

'I suppose I mean recovering from injuries in a way that wouldn't otherwise seem possible. Or physical development after reaching adulthood. Improvements in eyesight, hearing, that sort of thing.'

It certainly sounded like science fiction. She checked her watch. Sather Gate, the original south campus entrance, was just up ahead, and beyond it Sproul Plaza. She could still make it before the cafeteria closed. She started walking again.

'Well, there are plenty of examples of what you're describing in the animal kingdom. Most people know that crabs and lobsters can re-grow claws. Members of the salamander species such as newts and axolotls have also exhibited remarkable regenerative powers. It's not really attracted a lot of attention from the research community but there are a few papers that argue for the axolotl as a model genetic organism.'

'Yes, I've read Gardiner and Bryant. But what about in humans?'

She was surprised. Gardiner and Bryant weren't on any of the reading lists she handed out to her undergrads. She'd studied their research but she doubted anyone else in the department had, let alone a film studies major. She forced herself to keep an open mind. She was always reminding her students that the history of stem cell research was short; that they shouldn't be afraid to question even what might seem like the most

21

fundamental of assumptions. At least he'd bothered to do some reading on the subject.

'Well, as you probably know then, regenerative capacity is inversely related to complexity. The more complex an animal the less regeneration it is typically capable of. Mammals are just too complicated; the necessary regression of a developed adult cell to a stem cell state simply couldn't occur. There are a couple of very limited exceptions. The human liver is known to have particularly strong regenerative capabilities and we have a lot to learn about the kidney's ability to re-grow. There are also a few documented cases of fingertips growing back in young children, but that's about it. The abilities I think you're describing unfortunately just don't exist for us. It might make for an interesting story, though.'

For a moment she thought he was about to argue with her but then he simply nodded, and thanked her for her time. He seemed disappointed, and Alison couldn't help but think that for some reason it was she who had let him down. As he walked away she realized she'd never even asked his name. She considered calling after him. But ahead she could see the cafeteria already beginning to close its doors.

If she hurried she might be able to grab a sandwich to take back to the lab.

3

Fallon, Nevada - Now

THE PORTION OF U.S. Route 50 that ran through the center of Nevada was one of the things he loved most about the state; after almost ten years he had never tired of it. It had been named The Loneliest Road in America by *Life* magazine in 1986 and the name had stuck. Officials from White Pine County had in the end decided to make the best of the publicity, convincing the Nevada Department of Transportation to adopt the slogan in official highway logs and to place custom milemarkers along the route, hoping to attract those who might be drawn to the area's stark, almost alien, landscape, to the prospect of travelling for miles without sign of civilization, through terrain seemingly untouched by man.

From Lake Tahoe on the western border the road followed the Carson River past Carson City, then east towards the Lahontan Valley where it merged with the California Trail, the route followed by pioneers during the Gold Rush. The deadliest part of the trail had been the Forty Mile Desert, a barren stretch of scorching wilderness within whose bounds no water could be found. It was the section of Route 50 that began in the desert he favored. To the west the highway was mostly four-lane blacktop, serving the commuter towns of Dayton and Silver Springs. But heading east from Fallon the scenery changed, occasional mountain ridges breaking up the otherwise flat landscape, the summits starting out small but steadily increasing in altitude, eventually becoming snow-capped goliaths. If he were to take it as far as the Great Basin National Park he would see everything the state had to offer, from the barren floor of the desert valleys to the hairpin turns and impossible gradients of the mountain passes that cut through the high alpine forests.

There wouldn't be time for that today though. He would have liked to have made it all the way out through the Humboldt-Toiyabe National Forest as far as Ruth, an abandoned mining town almost on the border with Utah. He had some important decisions to make and the isolation, the stunning wilderness, would help. But it was well past noon and the next selection course was beginning the following morning. The candidates would already be en route to the base and he needed to spend a couple of hours that evening reviewing their files. Never mind, he could still cover some ground. He would stop at Middlegate and gas up the bike. He could decide then whether he had time to push on further.

The winter sun was low in the sky, moving around behind him as he left the base. It was cold, and he let the bike warm up slowly as he headed north towards Route 118. This time of year moisture-laden air moving inland from the Pacific was forced upwards as it met the Sierra Nevada and the Cascades, causing heavy rainfall on the western slopes of those mountains. But by the time the weather system had reached Fallon it was often spent, with only a wind shift and temperature fall to tell of its existence.

A single jet, even at this distance unmistakable as an F-14 Tomcat, was banking around from the north, hugging the mountain ridge as it turned towards the base, vortices forming behind the angled metal of the twin tail fins, the variable geometry wings swept fully forward in preparation for landing. He almost didn't notice the lone individual wrapped in a thick down jacket standing at the chain-link perimeter fence, a pair of binoculars around his neck. He thought he had seen the man before, recently, and there was something about his stance that made him think that he was, or at least had been, military. Not that there was anything unusual about his presence. With the exception of a number of the radar installations in the valleys most of the area outside the base was open to the public. Fallon had been the home of the Navy Fighter Weapons School since it had relocated from Miramar a decade before, merging the now famous TOPGUN academy with Strike U, the Naval Strike Warfare Center, and TOPDOME, the Carrier Airborne Early Warning Weapons School. With its network of surrounding valleys checkered with bombing ranges, radar installations and simulated air defense networks the base was the Navy's primary location for aerial combat training. The Tomcats were a big draw for the area's plane spotting community.

He watched as the pilot brought the fighter in, using the flat part of the fuselage between the engine nacelles as an airfoil to slow the landing speed. He had seen countless F-14s practicing carrier landings at the airfield but it never ceased to amaze him how little space they needed to put their planes on the deck. It had been years since he had flown a fast jet and yet he found he was jealous of the skill. He didn't miss the combat, the first sickening rush of adrenaline as he would call out the enemy, the frantic rush to close before they picked up a firing solution or escaped to altitude, or even the moment when, after his adversary had done everything he could to out-think or out-fly him he had nevertheless closed his finger around the trigger, ending the fight. But stationed here, the base's hangars housing a selection of F-14s and the F/A-18 Hornets that would shortly replace them, he often longed to climb into one of those cockpits, to feel the rush of acceleration as the plane hurtled down the runway, the first giddy moment of takeoff, the exhilarating climb as the afterburners ignited thrusting the plane skyward and then the sheer freedom of flight in a fast, highly maneuverable jet. Hell, he found he even missed flying choppers. He had often been tempted to approach one of the pilots and ask them to bring him up. Despite the fighter jock swagger most of them lived in awe of the CSARs stationed on base. He was sure some of them might even have been crazy enough to let him take the stick for a while. But he had never done it. The incident with the Pave Hawk three years before had raised enough questions. Thankfully Fitzpatrick had decided to let the matter rest but he knew that the base commander had never really bought his explanation. He couldn't afford to draw attention to himself like that again.

For now the bike would have to do. It could never match the thrill of flying but if he had to remain on the ground it was probably as close as he would get. He had bought the Yamaha, his third, that summer. A special edition of the R1 the company had produced to celebrate fifty years of racing in America. Only five hundred had been made and he'd had to travel to Vegas to find a dealer with one in stock. The black and yellow racing livery was a little garish for his taste but the bike was set up with front and rear custom Öhlins suspension and a torque-limiting slipper clutch, making it a thinly disguised production racer. Including the trade-in it had cost him eighteen thousand dollars, almost half a year's salary, but he loved it. Besides he had little other use for the money. He lived on the base and the Navy provided him with his food and clothing. Most months he found he only spent a fraction of his service pay, when he was operational even less.

He turned onto 118. The bike was warmed up, the exhaust thrumming evenly, and he twisted the grip just a fraction. The carburetors have been jetted to maximize throttle response and the bike immediately shot forward, the pitch of the engine note increasing to a wail as the revs rose, the three miles to the next junction dispatched in a couple of minutes. A quick check that there was nothing coming and he joined Highway 50, pulling away smoothly. He had left his visor half-open for the ride out but now he snapped it shut.

The bike felt good beneath him. He'd had the dealership tune the engine to run slightly lean to compensate for the thinner air at the base's elevation and now it fed on the cold dense air, snapping forward at the slightest twist of the throttle. The road east of Fallon narrowed from four lanes to two, the blacktop stretching inviting ahead of him. For the next four hundred miles there were only three small towns - Austin, Eureka and Ely – and this close to Christmas he knew there would be little traffic. He savored the moment, regretting again that he wouldn't have the time to go further.

The engine note rose to a wail again as he opened the throttle a fraction more, still short-shifting, his left toe flicking up through the gears below the redline, the surge as the bike shot forward with each gear change nevertheless satisfying. The road was straight for three miles as far as Grime's Point and the base quickly disappeared behind him. The landscape changed, the irrigated farmland and marshy waterfowl areas of Carson Lake and Stillwater making way for the barren tundra of the flats. Even in the shelter of the valleys only plants that were capable of withstanding the harsh high desert climate, some shrubs, the occasional cottonwood tree, would be found. He could see Grime's Point coming up quickly, the road disappearing to the left around the huge peak. He crouched down, twisting the throttle a fraction more, hearing the engine note rise as the bike surged forward again, the mountain quickly filling his vision. For a moment he thought he saw movement on the slopes and then an instant later something glinting in the sunlight. But then it was gone and he returned his attention to the road as it swept around to the left, leaning the bike into the turn, the tarmac a blur only inches below his knee. The bend was fast but it was still sweeping around and in the cold the tires wouldn't grip as well. He forced himself to hold back – just a second or two more. Beyond Grimes Point the road was perfectly straight for four miles and if there was no other traffic he would open the throttle, letting the bike carry him to the horizon as quickly as it could.

4

VINCENT KEOGH FOCUSSED his binoculars on the corner.

Still nothing. The spotter by the gate had confirmed that Gant had left the base and the man he had sent to Grimes Point that morning with the scope had just radioed to say that he was headed their way, fast. Three miles to the east the third member of the support team had reported that the road was clear as far as he could see. He looked over his shoulder, checking again that the van was out of sight. Across the road the police cruiser was hidden behind a large hoarding announcing the imminent construction of a power plant at Eight Mile Flat. He nodded to Arturo, his squat bulk in the dark blue uniform of the Nevada Highway Patrol waiting patiently at the wheel for his signal to roll it out.

They were ready.

He brought the binoculars up again, adjusting the focus slightly. He was uneasy. He wished again that Flood was with them. They were a team, Flood, Arturo and he, had been for over twenty years, since before they had been recruited. He had served with both men in the 10th Special Forces during the Gulf War, had seen the red-haired Irishman drink muddy water from a ditch in the stifling heat of Khafji, had watched him eat things that would have made a hyena puke while they had waited for the Republican Guard in the mountains near Al-Zabr. And now the man had been laid low by some stomach bug most likely picked up from a roadside diner.

He should have stood them down of course, allowed another team to be flown in to take their place. When after the first day Flood still couldn't move from his bed he had almost done it. But then, sitting in a bar in Fallon, cursing his luck and preparing to make the call that would take them off the job, Arturo had suggested it.

The two of them could handle Gant. The bonus for his capture was a million dollars apiece, money they would lose if they let another team replace them. And who knew when another candidate might be found – this was their first in sixteen years. He had mulled the idea over while Arturo had gone to get them more drinks. It was a lot of money to give up, and no mistake. They were paid well enough, but it wasn't like the job came with a pension plan and none of them were getting any younger. With the bonus from Gant's capture they could hire a few guys, set up a security firm of their own, maybe even try to go legit.

And Arturo was right; picking up Gant shouldn't be a problem. Once they'd got him into the back of the van there was nothing to do but drive him to the drop off point. They could collect Flood on the way and *El Conde* would be none the wiser. Which was important; their employer was not someone whose instructions you disregarded lightly. Not that they'd ever met the man, of course. Even after all the years they'd been working for him they still had no idea who he was. Their orders came through the German, Friedrichs. Occasionally they worked with other teams, but that was it.

It had made him a little uneasy at first, knowing so little. But *El Conde* took his personal security very seriously. They knew what he was looking for of course; they wouldn't have been able to do their jobs without that piece of information. The rare blood group he seemed so desperate to find, together with the seemingly limitless means he had at his disposal was what had prompted Arturo to call him *El Conde Vampiro* in the first place. The name had stuck. And it had proved apt; it was clear from the work they did for him that *El Conde* had no scruples. Keogh was certain he wouldn't give a second thought to disposing of any of them if for a moment he felt threatened by what they knew.

But over the years he had come to appreciate the security their ignorance about their employer gave them. If they couldn't identify the man surely there was little reason to worry. If they screwed up, however, and *El Conde* found out they had disregarded his orders, well then Keogh was pretty sure that each of them would quickly come to wish they had never been born.

But a million dollars was a million dollars, and so he had gone along with Arturo's idea. Besides, the two of them *could* handle Gant. The syringe in his pocket was filled with methohexital, a fast acting barbiturate, enough to put their man out for at least ten minutes, more than enough time to secure him in the back of the van and sedate him properly for the drive to the facility. Then they'd pick up Flood, deliver their cargo and get paid. Another team would dispose of the bike. The helmet, dog tags and scraps of his clothing would be found in the desert several weeks later. It would look like he'd had an accident, his remains eaten by coyotes.

Vincent Keogh lifted the binoculars again. A motorbike had just appeared from around Grimes Point, the rider leaning hard into the corner. A second later the wind carried the faint sound of the engine screaming as the revs increased, a short blip as he shifted gear, quickly building again to a crescendo, louder now as the distance to them closed. The bike was really moving. Good. He wouldn't be suspicious when they pulled him over. He turned around, indicating to Arturo to get ready. He waited a few seconds longer then stepped out into the road.

5

LARS HENRIKSSEN HAD been heading back to town on US-95 when the call had come in. He swung his cruiser around and five minutes later was rolling into the parking lot of Mount Grant General Hospital, just in time to find a couple of orderlies removing a body from the back of an unmarked black van. He pulled up behind them, hauling himself out of the driver's seat, trying not to wince as he stretched out his leg. He had his mouth open to remonstrate with the nearest one but a single glance into the back of the van was all it took to tell him he was already too late. No hope of preserving the scene; the damage was already done. And the last thing he needed now was them manhandling the body back into the van in front of a crowd of rubbernecking onlookers. He took their names, telling them to come back and find him as soon as they had taken the corpse to the mortuary.

When he returned to the cruiser Jed and Larry were already pulling up behind. He set his deputies to work cordoning off the area, making sure that the growing crowd was kept at a distance while he went in search of someone who had seen what had happened. A few minutes later he was back at the old black and white sedan, reaching in to unhook the mike from the car's two-way.

'Connie, it's Lars. You there?'

A second's pause and then a burst of static followed by the familiar voice of the woman who ran Hawthorne's tiny police department.

'Sure Sheriff. What's up?'

'Well, Connie, we got one hell of a mess up here at Mount Grant. There's a black Dodge RAM crashed into the main entrance. Two men in the back, shot, one of 'em dead already. The other's taken a bullet in the gut. He's in surgery right now. Driver's away on foot, looks like he's headed west towards the reservoir. There's fresh blood on the driver's seat and door, so most likely he's also wounded. And I'd guess carrying, which is not a good combination. I doubt he'll get far but you'd best put an APB out on him. Hispanic male, well-built, forty to forty-five years old, five-eight, five-nine, dark hair, wearing a Nevada highway patrol uniform.' He paused for a moment, thinking. 'And get Duke up here with those dogs of his. There'll be a trail but the light'll be gone in an hour or so, so best tell him to haul ass. I suspect our guy'll have been spotted long before he gets here but better safe than sorry.'

'Got it. Anything else?'

'Yep. The dead guy in back was also dressed as highway patrol. He's not from Mineral County, but I'll give you his badge number anyway. Check him out will you? I'm betting it's fake, but just in case. And when you're done with that throw a call in to the base commander up at the Depot, see if he's missing anyone. The guy in surgery was wearing fatigues. No 'tags.'

'Sure Sheriff.'

'Oh, and get on to Carson City and have them send a forensics team down here soon as they can. A couple of orderlies have already done a real nice job re-arranging all the evidence in the back of the van but you never know, we may get lucky and find something they haven't touched. And Connie?'

'Yes, Sheriff?'

'When you're done with all that give Ellie a call and tell her I won't be home for dinner.'

He climbed back out of the cruiser, taking another look at the growing crowd.

Christ, what a mess.

He'd been sheriff of Hawthorne for over twenty-five years but he'd never seen anything like this. And it would get worse once the TV crews showed up. He noticed Doug Whitley, the hospital administrator, hanging back near the entrance, a look of concern on his narrow face. The hospital was small but it was the county's only medical center and road traffic accidents were not uncommon on that stretch of the highway. He went over to check with him that the emergency room could still function notwithstanding the commotion outside. Satisfied that the van could remain where it was for now he asked Whitley to post a security guard outside ICU the moment the wounded man got out of surgery.

When he was certain he had dealt with everything that needed his immediate attention Lars returned to the van. Opening the rear doors he took a moment to survey the interior. It was a mess alright, blood splattered along the driver's side, already starting to form into small pools that were now congealing on the floor. Strapped to one side panel were a couple of automatic weapons. Foreign, expensive-looking. The serial numbers had been filed off but he took out his notepad and jotted down the make. A semi-automatic pistol and a police issue taser sat on a bench seat, covered in blood. A couple of 9mm shell cases on the floor. He bent down to sniff the barrel, confirming that the handgun had been fired recently.

The other side of the van looked like it had been set up to carry someone who had been injured. In place of a bench seat there was a gurney with restraining straps and collapsible legs that clamped to the floor. At the head of the trolley an oxygen cylinder and mask and a bracket for a drip, together with what looked like a portable heart rate and blood pressure monitor, still switched on. Bolted to the bulkhead behind the passenger's seat were several custom cabinets. He opened each, taking care not to leave any fingerprints. One of the cabinets housed a refrigerated compartment that contained three small vials of blood, as well as an assortment of medication. He copied the names printed on the front of the bottles into his notepad, making a mental note to get the hospital to confirm whether the blood in the vials belonged to the man who had been strapped to the gurney. From the bloodstains on the straps it seemed like the man had been shot while he was still restrained but he could check that with the orderlies when they returned.

The single bullet hole on the driver's side looked like it was the result of a shot fired from inside the van, most likely by the man who had been tied down. The metal had been punched outwards and there was no corresponding hole on the passenger's side to show where the round might have entered. Another bullet hole in the bulkhead separating the cab from the back of the van, low down and to the right side of the back of the driver's seat. When he checked the front of the seat he found the exit hole and a large bloodstain, explaining the driver's injuries. From the spent shells in the front footwell it looked like the driver had got in on the action as well, presumably firing through the small sliding partition in the bulkhead. Probably him that had shot the man on the gurney then, but forensics would tell him that when they got here. There didn't seem to be any evidence of shots having been fired from outside the van.

As he climbed out of the back he saw that a KHNV news truck had arrived and was setting up. The crew were busy taking statements from the onlookers but when the reporter saw him she called over. Lars waved her away. No sense getting his face on TV before he'd had a chance to think this through. After checking to see how Jed and Larry were doing he went back inside the hospital to see if there was any news on the survivor.

When he got to the operating room he was met with a commotion. One of the nurses shouted at him as she ran past that the man who had been taken to surgery had reacted to the blood transfusion they had given him. No-one else was free to explain further so Lars went in search of the hospital administrator.

He found Doug Whitley in his office, sitting behind an impressively cluttered desk. The administrator waved him to a seat opposite.

'So Doug, what's happening with this guy you've got in surgery?'

Whitley had just heard the news himself. He had been a trauma surgeon at the hospital for ten years before he had assumed his current role. He knew there were only a few reasons why a patient might react to a transfusion in that way.

'Well, Lars, it sounds like they've gone and given the guy the wrong type of blood. That's unusual, though. Transfusing someone incorrectly can be fatal, so the lab's pretty damned careful about typing blood before a transfusion's given. I've never known Sue to make a mistake like that. Hold on there while I give her a call.'

The administrator dialed the extension for the lab, pushing the speaker button to allow Lars to listen in. The phone was answered on the first ring.

'Sue, Doug here. What's going on with the John Doe we've got in surgery?'

'He's definitely rejecting, Doug. I've just completed a re-type but the results are the same – O Neg – and I've double-checked with the OR that that was what they gave him. I've already started a reverse grouping but checking his serum type will take some time. Listen, I have to go. I'll call you back the moment I know more.'

Without waiting for a response she put the phone down.

Lars thought for a moment. There was something about this he just wasn't getting. He forced his mind to run through what he knew, to see if the answer might lie somewhere in that information. The man had been strapped to a gurney in the back of the van. Whatever he'd been doing there, someone had expected that he would need medical treatment. Not for a gunshot wound, though. That hadn't been part of the plan. But if they weren't treating him for a gunshot what had they been doing with him that required all the medical equipment? And the drugs? He reached into his pocket for his notepad. Flipping to the page where he'd jotted down the names he asked the administrator whether there was anything there that might be relevant. The first few didn't draw a response. When he got to the fourth name Whitley reached for the phone.

'Sue, Doug here again. The sheriff found a bunch of drugs in the back of the van they pulled this guy out of. The only thing on the list I don't recognize is something called H-Lectin. Know anything about it?'

Lars was sure he heard the lab technician swear under her breath.

'Yep, Doug it's a reagent, one used to test for the H antigen. Listen, I need to call the OR back right now. If they were carrying H-Lectin because of this guy it's likely he has a rare blood type, which could explain why he's reacting to the transfusion the way he is. I have to warn them. Can someone get me the H-Lectin from the van?'

'Sure Sue, I'll call down and have one of the orderlies bring it over. Be with you in a moment.'

The last thing Lars needed was either of those knuckleheads heading back into the van, so he offered to fetch the H-Lectin himself, telling the administrator it would be quicker if he went, he knew exactly where it was. He walked back out through reception, into the small parking lot, past the KHNV reporter who was busy talking gravely into the camera. The van had already been cordoned off and he ducked under the yellow police tape. The H-Lectin was in the refrigerated cabinet in the back where he had first found it, next to the three vials of blood. He brought the container back and handed it to a nurse at reception, explaining that it was needed urgently in the lab. Fifteen minutes later he was back in Whitley's office, listening as Sue Ellis explained what she had found.

'I'm still waiting for the results of the serum grouping but I've tested the guy's blood with the H-Lectin from the van, Doug, and he's definitely not expressing the H antigen. I've only read about this phenomenon in individuals with the *hh* phenotype. People with that blood group test as group O. But their blood produces antibodies to the H substance, which means they're not compatible with group O donors, only other *hh* phenotypes. I need to run more tests; we'll need to get the results of the serum grouping and cross match with other O group samples to be absolutely sure. But it would certainly explain this guy's reaction to the transfusion.'

'Okay, so what can we do for him? Now that we know the issue can we just transfuse him with the correct blood type and get him back into surgery?'

'Unfortunately it's not that simple Doug. This guy needs a transfusion from someone of exactly the same blood type. The condition is extremely rare, so rare that hospitals don't test for it and blood banks don't bother stocking it. There's probably only a handful of people in the whole United States who have the same blood, and no way of finding them. I'd bet most of them don't even know it themselves. I put a call in to United Blood in Carson City on the off chance that they might have stocks but they don't and they don't know of anywhere that maintains them.'

'So you're telling me there's nothing we can do for this guy?'

There was a pause before the lab technician came back.

'Listen, Doug, I'll run a full set of tests on this guy's blood to see if anything else shows up that might help us. And I'll keep ringing around the hospitals and blood banks in case anyone's got stocks of this stuff. But I wouldn't hold your breath. If Lionel's giving you other options I'd suggest you consider them seriously.'

She rang off.

The administrator called the front desk and paged Lionel Keegan, the surgeon who had been due to operate on the wounded man. A moment later the phone rang. Whitley listened, asked a few succinct questions then hung up.

'Well, Lars, it doesn't look good. This young man's in a bad way. One kidney is shot to hell and the reaction to the group O blood he was given has caused the other to pretty much shut down. Lionel doesn't want to operate on him without stabilizing his condition as he thinks he'll just die on the table. But without a transfusion of the correct blood he doesn't see this guy making it through the night.'

'Alright Doug, I hear you. But the third man from that van's still on the loose, most probably armed. Any chance he'll regain consciousness long enough for me to speak with him?'

'Probably not. Even if he did he'd be too weak for you to question him. Sorry, Sheriff.'

Lars thanked the administrator and headed back to the parking lot. As he passed the hospital waiting room on his way back outside he saw that the story had already made the local news. He stopped to watch the KHNV reporter refer solemnly to the events unfolding in Hawthorne, raising the possibility that the men who had been in the van, well armed and dressed in police and military uniforms, had been intent on carrying out a terrorist attack in the county. The reporter mentioned that although it was so far only speculation Hawthorne was best known as the home of an arms depot responsible for warehousing and distributing vast quantities of munitions for the U.S. military, the most likely target for such an attack.

Just what we need, thought Lars as he headed back to his cruiser.

The theory quickly took hold. By the time the forensic team had arrived from Carson City an hour later the networks had picked up the story and the consensus was now that the target had indeed been the depot. A senator from Alabama who sat on the Armed Forces Appropriations Committee appeared on CNN querying whether it was a good use of taxpayers' money to maintain an obsolete base that looked like it had become a prime target for terrorist attacks, suggesting that the base might now be decommissioned. The interview prompted a panicked call from the mayor, urging Lars to do everything within his power to get to the bottom of what had happened at Mount Grant as quickly as possible. Although in peacetime the depot was never fully staffed nevertheless a significant portion of Hawthorne's four thousand or so residents depended on the business it provided for their livelihoods. The announcement the year before that the depot was a potential candidate for the Army's Base Realignment and Closure list had caused consternation in the little town.

Christ, thought Lars, *sometimes we do the terrorists' work for them, making sure everyone remains good and afraid.* Whatever this was, he wasn't convinced it had anything to do with a terrorist attack. He was still hopeful that Duke would pick up the driver of the van and that they'd be able to get some version of what had happened from him.

But several hours later the driver of the van still hadn't been located. The dogs had followed his scent from the car park but it had led straight to a stream that ran through the hospital grounds parallel to Highway 359. It had taken them the best part of an hour searching both banks in the failing light to find the place where the driver had left the water and to determine that he had headed towards the highway. However, there the trail had gone cold. Lars figured the driver must have either flagged down a passing car or been picked up by an accomplice. He favored the latter explanation. Whatever had caused them to start shooting at each other, he was coming to suspect that the men in the van had had some training. If the driver had gone to ground their chances of finding him quickly were small.

He checked his watch. It was late and there wasn't much more he could do here tonight, so he decided to head home to get some sleep. He left Jed at the scene to assist the forensics team who had set up powerful arc lights and were continuing to search the van for evidence. Ten minutes later he rolled the cruiser into his driveway. As he walked into the kitchen Jake, their three-year-old Alsatian, stretched lazily on his blanket, ambling over to shove his muzzle into Lars' hand. Ellie had left a note on the kitchen table telling him that there were sandwiches in the fridge if he was hungry but not to feed them to the dog. Jake looked on expectantly as

Lars ate one of the sandwiches. In the end he broke the other one up and fed the dog the pieces. Then he sat in the dark, absent-mindedly scratching the Alsatian's ear, trying again to fit what he knew into a coherent explanation. But after ten minutes he realized he was getting nowhere. The man who was lying unconscious in the hospital might be his only chance of getting to the bottom of what had happened. His only hope was that, somehow, against the odds, he would recover sufficiently and be willing to talk.

6

IT WAS A Saturday night and the small restaurant was crowded, waiters weaving backwards and forwards between the tables, outstretched arms carrying steaming dishes or trays laden with drinks. The room was noisy, filled with the sounds of diners enjoying an evening out with friends or family on the last weekend before Christmas. Alison made her way to a small table at the back where she could see the dean already waiting.

She had come straight from the university, without bothering to change out of the jeans and t-shirt that were her normal lab attire. She would have preferred to meet on campus, but Rutherford was a busy man, and he seemed to prefer to meet in less formal surroundings. She rarely bothered with make-up and tonight was no exception. As she approached the table she absent-mindedly pulled the rubber band that she had used to tie back her long blond hair. The dean stood, leaning over to kiss her on the cheek.

'Working till now?'

She nodded.

'Always plenty to do.'

He pulled a bottle of Sauvignon Blanc from an ice bucket, holding it up to offer her a glass. Alison shook her head no but he poured anyway. She let it pass. As he replaced the bottle she noticed it was already almost empty. She checked her watch. She was almost an hour late.

He smiled, raising his glass.

'You really don't need to work so hard you know. I'm already impressed.'

In his late forties, with dark brown eyes and hair just beginning to grey at the temples Rutherford had something of a reputation in the faculty. A confirmed bachelor, he lived in a converted loft apartment in the prestigious Berkeley Marina, driving his vintage Porsche Speedster the mile and a half up University Avenue to the Faculty each morning. He had had a distinguished career, pioneering early developments in the field of transgenics, earning the Gruber prize for his contribution to recombinant DNA technology. At twenty-nine Alison was by far the youngest faculty member of the University of California's Department of Genetics, and at first she had been intrigued, and more than a little flattered, by the interest he had shown in her work. She had even dared to hope that with his help an early breakthrough might be possible. She was aware that the interest he had shown in her had not gone un-noticed among her colleagues. But her work was the most important thing to her; if Rutherford was prepared to offer assistance she would take it. And if he wanted to meet her in a restaurant on a Saturday night to discuss her research then so be it. The rest of the faculty could think what they wanted.

She took a sip from her glass of water. 'So how are things going with your pigs?'

The EcoPig was the trademark for a genetically modified line of Duroc pigs that Rutherford had been working on. The aim was to develop a transgenic pig with an enhanced digestive system capable of breaking down otherwise indigestible chemicals in pig feed, thus reducing the environmental damage caused by farming pigs on an industrial scale.

Before Rutherford could answer the waiter arrived to take their order. Alison had missed lunch and she chose the pasta bake and a side salad, asking the waiter if she could have the salad without tomatoes. The dean finished his wine, pouring himself another glass while she ordered. When it was his turn he chose the sea bass and another bottle of the Sauvignon. For a few minutes he talked while they waited for their food. In truth Alison had little interest in Rutherford's pigs. It seemed to her that the problem might just as easily have been solved by either altering their diets or alternatively changing the conditions in which they were reared. But agripharmaceuticals - pharming, as Rutherford liked to call it - was big business, and the department was always in need of funding.

Transgenics - using DNA from different sources to genetically engineer new organisms – *was* important to her, however. It might even hold the key to her own research. For years studies of Alzheimer's had been limited by the lack of a reliable animal model. The development of the amyloid precursor protein mouse in the 'nineties had helped researchers understand the pathology of the disease, but the mouse had not been the perfect model. In the last few years pigs containing genes thought to be responsible for Alzheimer's had been created at universities in Copenhagen and Århus and she had followed the work of the Danish scientists closely. Based on the growth rates and life expectancy of the animals, it was expected that the transgenetically cloned pigs would soon start to show symptoms of the disease. And because pigs were in many ways comparable to humans it was hoped that research into their behavior would yield better results than the mice had.

The technology was not new: DNA contained the genetic instructions for life, and scientists had been swapping those instructions between different organisms since the early 'seventies. The theory was relatively straightforward. Take a fragment responsible for a unique trait in one organism and splice that DNA into a different host, in the hope that the gene would perform in the same way as it had in the old organism. Restriction enzymes acted as the scissors to cut the DNA, attacking a specific sequence, splitting the base pairs apart, leaving single helix strands at the end of two double helixes. You were then free to add whatever genetic sequences you wished into the broken chain. Another enzyme, ligase, to repair the spliced strand, and suddenly you had a new creation, a species that would never have existed otherwise.

In practice the process was seldom that simple however. For a start, the DNA segment from a source organism was rarely capable of being spliced directly into the host DNA. It needed to be introduced biologically, through bacteria plasmid, or mechanically, using gene guns or micropipettes. Alison had studied these techniques as well, and knew them intimately. But even so, the process was complex and unpredictable. The same gene-splicing operation might need to be performed hundreds of times before a successful result, a 'viable', could be achieved, with often little clue as to why scores of earlier, seemingly identical, attempts had failed.

And then would begin the watching, the waiting. Inserted genes were prone to overexpression, becoming overactive. Or the spliced material might mutate, disrupting the functioning of other genes. Transgenic animals often underwent complex and unanticipated physical changes that caused painful diseases, accelerated ageing, death. What might initially appear to be a normal, healthy organism could have unexpected flaws in its internal make-up. Immuno-deficiencies, unusual growth patterns, debilitating diseases were all common, and might not appear for months or even years.

But the potential was huge. Once the relevant genome had been mapped in theory the technology was only limited by the imagination of the bio-engineer. Some of the projects that had already been completed were truly unbelievable. Rabbits and cats spliced with transgenes from jelly fish, making them appear fluorescent; pigs with a desaturase gene from spinach, inserted to convert saturated fats into unsaturated linoleic acid. Canadian scientists had even spliced spider DNA into a goat, and had extracted spider silk protein from the animal's milk. Once purified the protein could be spun into super strong fibers. Lightweight, more durable than Kevlar, stronger than steel and yet more elastic than nylon, the applications were endless.

But it was the combination of human and animal DNA that interested her most, for there lay the greatest potential to find cures for hundreds of diseases that afflicted mankind. Unfortunately experimenting with human genetic material was still regarded as controversial. Certainly, gene splicing with human DNA was more complex, the risks significant. But the objections to the technology typically weren't expressed rationally. Most were based on nothing more than what she thought of as the 'yuk' factor, a negative gut reaction to procedures that seemed 'unnatural'. She could understand it; she'd had trouble eating tomatoes ever since she had learned that a splice with a cockroach gene had been created in the hope of producing a subspecies with a harder skin to protect the fruit during transportation.

But nearly all of modern medicine required unnatural intervention. The first vaccines had been extracted from cow sores. And before scientists had found a way to harvest insulin from plasmid DNA spliced with a human gene it had had to be extracted from the pancreases of fresh corpses. Besides, it wasn't as if they were creating real hybrids; the goat-spider splice had contained only a single spider gene. Understanding of genetic modification remained low however, with most of the public seemingly happy to receive their science lessons from Hollywood.

'So have you thought any more about my offer?'

Rutherford's question brought her back. He had a small farmhouse in Napa and had been trying to persuade her to spend Christmas with him, suggesting that it might be a good time for them to work on her research. The offer had made her uncomfortable. She had hoped he had forgotten about it.

'Listen, Mark, I'm not sure it's a good idea. Besides, I already have plans to spend Christmas with my mother.'

He took another drink and reached across the table, placing his hand over hers.

'Well I'm sure your mother could spare for you for a few days, Alison. Especially if she realized how important I might be to your work. To your career.' He paused, letting the meaning sink in. 'Your research is so important, Alison. You don't want others to suffer like your father.'

Alison stared back across the table, for the moment unsure what to say. How could she have been so naive? She was aware that most of her colleagues at the faculty regarded her as driven, even obsessed. Few of them knew her well enough to understand the reason. She now regretted having confided in the dean.

She had grown up in Manchester, Maryland, a small suburban town in the north-eastern corner of Carroll County. An only child, her parents had doted on her and her early memories were as idyllic as the tidy picket-fenced houses and quaint downtown shops that epitomized the sleepy town. The Stone family's world was soon to be torn apart however. In her junior year of high school her father had been diagnosed with early onset Alzheimer's. He was forty-five.

The news had devastated the small family. Alison remembered sitting between her parents as a consultant had quietly explained what lay ahead. Her father could expect increasing forgetfulness and as the disease progressed, confusion. His personality would change. There were treatments, many of them experimental, that might delay the progress of the condition for a while, but there was no cure. In the end he would suffer from seizures and would have difficulty eating or swallowing. Death would most likely come from either infection or malnutrition. Her mother had started to sob quietly as the doctor had explained that they probably had no more than ten years.

Alison adored her father and hadn't been prepared to lose him, piece by piece, to this horrific disease. She had read everything she could lay her hands on, desperate for theories on how to manage the disease, for details of the cures that were being worked on. At school she had been a bright if somewhat relaxed student, but now she focused all her energy on obtaining a scholarship to Johns Hopkins where she could continue to study her father's illness. Baltimore was less than twenty-five miles from Manchester. Studying there would allow her to continue to live at home to help her parents.

At twenty she had graduated *magna cum laude* with a major in biomedical engineering. By then Pete Stone's illness had progressed beyond its early stages, and previously a placid man, he was increasingly subject to fits of agitation, followed by bouts of depression. She would often come home to find him standing by the curb outside their house, with no recollection of why he had come outside.

Realizing that her father might not have the time she needed to find a cure, she had enrolled in the university's medical school hoping that she might at least learn enough to ease his symptoms as he progressed through the disease's final stages. But the condition had proved unusually aggressive in Pete Stone and by the time she was in her third year he was completely bedridden, no longer recognizing either her or her mother. As the disease moved to his brain stem, shutting down the basic processes of digestion and respiration, it was no longer possible for him to remain at home. She would visit him every day in the hospital, but by then he had stopped eating and was sleeping most of the time. In the end, one spring morning barely seven years after he had first been diagnosed, her father had simply stopped breathing.

Alison had graduated medical school three months later. The faculty had pleaded with her to take up a place as an intern but the memories of her father had been too painful for her to remain there. Stem cell research provided the most promising field for a cure and so she had transferred to the graduate program in genetics at Harvard Medical School. Although her father was gone she was determined that others wouldn't have to experience a similar loss. Completing her doctorate at the age of twenty-seven, she had been offered a position as a post-doctoral fellow at the university. But when California had passed Proposition 71, with a single stroke making available funding that promised to change the landscape for stem cell research in the United States, she had decided to move west, and had accepted a teaching post at Berkeley.

She knew that the disease that she had chosen as an adversary, that in reality had selected her, was a formidable one. In reality they still knew so very little about how the human brain really worked. She had been certain however that with the facilities available to her at Berkeley she would be able to make significant steps towards finding a cure for the condition that had killed her father. It might take years, decades, but she would dedicate her life to finding a cure if she had to.

But now Rutherford was letting her know that if she chose to refuse his advances her position at the university was likely to become a lot more tenuous. He certainly had the power to make good on the threat. She didn't have tenure, and was unlikely to be eligible for consideration for several more years. And as dean of the faculty he would have a large say in that decision when the time came. The publicity that her article had generated a few months before certainly hadn't helped her case. Neither could she rely on a breakthrough in her research to guarantee her a position. Even with Rutherford's help, progress, if it came, was more likely to come in modest increments. And California was a popular choice for researchers. The university would have little trouble finding someone to replace her.

She saw the waiter arriving with her salad. As he placed it on the table she saw that he had forgotten about the tomatoes.

It didn't matter.

She had lost her appetite.

7

THE PERSISTENT CHIRPING dragged Lars from a deep slumber. He groped with one hand on the nightstand for the phone, carefully shifting the other from under Ellie's neck, hoping not to wake her. It was still dark outside, probably an hour yet till dawn. He flipped up the phone to silence the ringing, mumbling to the caller to hold on while he climbed out of bed. The young man who had been tied to the gurney in the back of the van was his only hope to get to the bottom of what had happened, and Lars had left his cell number with instructions to be contacted the moment anything changed with his condition. He was expecting to hear that the man had died. But instead the doctor on the other end of the line was telling him he was gone.

Lars collected his clothes from where he had left them only a few short hours before. His gun belt hung over the back of the chair that stood next to his side of the bed, and he picked it up, buckling the old leather around his waist, feeling its familiar weight settle on his hip. He knew Ellie hated having a gun in the bedroom but until Mineral County's tiny budget could stretch to getting him one of those fancy gun cabinets installed there was nowhere else in the small house that he felt safe leaving it. Jake looked up expectantly from his basket as he made his way out through the kitchen to where the cruiser sat parked by the side of the house.

He drove in silence back towards Hawthorne. The narrow strip of asphalt hugged the contours of Walker Lake, the twin beams from the cruiser's headlights occasionally illuminated the glassy still of the waters only yards to his left. But the road was familiar to him and Lars let his mind wander, trying in vain to piece together the pieces of the puzzle that lay before him.

Ten minutes later he pulled into the parking lot at Mount Grant, the sky to the east already slowly turning from indigo to bruised gold behind Mable Mountain. He picked up his hat from the passenger seat and climbed slowly out of the cruiser. Forensics had finished with the van and it sat, abandoned behind a thin cordon of police tape fluttering gently in the early morning breeze, the soft yellow light from the hospital's small entrance reflecting off its paneled black sides. A nurse at reception directed him towards ICU.

The security guard had been found strapped to the bed where the young man had been. He remembered nothing. Marks on his neck and a pounding headache suggested that his air supply had been cut off, causing him to pass out. His attacker had dragged him into the room so that he wouldn't be noticed, removing his trousers and shirt and using the restraining straps on the bed and the guard's own tie to bind and gag him. The blood pressure cuff had been wrapped around his arm and the pulse sensor replaced on his finger so that the monitor at the nurse's station wouldn't flatline, triggering an alarm. The guard thought he'd been struggling with the straps for about twenty minutes before a nurse had finally noticed the elevated blood pressure and pulse levels on her monitor and decided to investigate.

As he was taking a couple of final details Doug Whitley joined them, together with another man the administrator introduced as Lionel Keegan, the surgeon who had been about to operate on the now missing patient when he'd first been brought into the OR. Whitley had also left instructions to be contacted the moment there was any change in the man's condition.

He'd also been expecting a call informing him that the man had died and had been steeling himself for the criticism the hospital would no doubt face for transfusing a patient with the wrong blood.

Lars flipped his notebook closed, returning it to his shirt pocket.

'Well Doug, looks like this guy wasn't so sick after all.'

The surgeon responded before Whitley had a chance to say anything.

'Sheriff, that's nonsense. He must have had help. With his injuries and the complications from the transfusion he simply would have been in no condition to escape by himself. There must have been someone else.'

Lars paused for a moment before answering.

'Well, Doctor Keegan, I'm not so sure. There's no evidence that another person was present. The guard is missing his firearm, the keys to his Ford Taurus, his clothes, a watch and about two hundred dollars in cash. Now it's possible that if someone else was involved they'd have taken the guard's gun just to make sure he was disarmed, although they way he was tied to that bed they could have just left the gun in the room. They may even have taken the opportunity to rob him while they were at it, might even have taken a shine to the cheap digital watch he was wearing. But one thing I am pretty sure of is that anyone planning to bust an injured man out of here would have organized transport ahead of time, and not relied on stealing something we can put an APB out on.'

He looked at Whitley.

'No, Doug, I think our man's managed this by himself.'

The administrator turned to his surgeon.

'Lionel, I suggest you have a look again at his charts to see whether anything explains this guy's recovery. And get one of the nurses to retrieve whatever they can from the monitors. I forget how much of a patient's history they store but you may get blood pressure and heart rate for the last few hours if nothing else. I'll speak to Sue when she gets in and see if she found anything in his blood work. Lars, we'll let you know the moment we find anything.'

Lars had already put out an APB on the missing man on his way back in to the hospital. When he got back to his cruiser he updated it with details of the security guard's Ford, although he was sure that the car would soon be switched, if it hadn't been already.

This was getting out of hand. He now had two armed men on the loose, a body in the morgue and a conspiracy theory that threatened the very future of his town. He desperately needed something to break, some piece of information that would make everything else fit into place.

8

HE CHECKED INTO a small motel just off I-50. He had abandoned the security guard's Taurus in long-term parking at Carson City airport, switching the license plates with another Ford parked nearby. A taxi from the rank outside had dropped him two blocks away. He knew he hadn't covered his tracks well, but it was all that he could manage for now. He had paid for the room for four nights, using most of the cash he had stolen. Thankfully the clerk at reception had seemed more interested in the talk show on the small TV behind her desk, barely looking up as he had filled out the form.

He found the room easily. Once inside he closed the blinds, the small, tired accommodation appearing only marginally more inviting in the dim light. The clerk had told him that the maids wouldn't be cleaning until after Christmas but he hung the faded 'Do Not Disturb' sign on the door handle anyway. The effort of overpowering the guard and escaping from the hospital had exhausted him and he longed to collapse on the small, musty bed. But there was one more thing he needed to do first.

He removed the jacket he had stolen from the security guard, letting it fall to the floor. The dressing they had applied at the hospital was still in place but blood had seeped through the bandage, soaking the shirt. He had considered finding an all-night pharmacy but that would have been too dangerous; he had to hope that the room would have what he needed. He staggered into the small bathroom, grabbing a grey, threadbare towel from the rail, and tore it in two. Wrapping his fist in one half, he broke the mirror bolted to the wall above the sink, carefully picking up a large fragment of the glass from the basin. Then he headed back into the bedroom. A small tray with a kettle and provisions for coffee and tea. A mug with teaspoons, dirty but stainless steel, not plastic. Good. He grabbed a handful of sugar sachets and laid them with the teaspoon on the bed next to the broken shard of glass and the torn pieces of the towel. The minibar was stocked and he grabbed a handful of plastic miniatures. An ice bucket sat on top of the small fridge. Ice would help numb the wound. Should he try and find the motel's ice machine? Too risky to venture out again. Besides, in a place like this there was a good chance the machine wasn't even working.

He lay back on the bed, pulling up his shirt. The bandage was soaked, and he lifted it clear, examining the wound. The bullet had entered his right side. Low velocity round, handgun probably. The bleeding hadn't stopped, which meant he needed to get to the bullet. He probed around the opening with his fingers, ignoring the blood that was now flowing freely from the wound. There. A lump of metal, just below his ribcage.

He sat up, twisting the caps off two of the plastic miniatures of vodka, using one to disinfect the teaspoon. The other he used to rinse his fingers, hesitating only an instant before pouring the remainder into the wound. The alcohol burned like acid and he gritted his teeth against the pain, forcing himself to continue. He placed the broken shard of mirror beside the wound, angling it so that he could see. Then before he had time to change his mind he pushed the end of the spoon in, his other hand against his back, fingers working the bullet forward.

The pain was immense and his head swam, but he fought to remain conscious. Just a few more seconds. Blood was pouring from the wound, running down his side, but he ignored it, probing with the end of the spoon to trap the bullet. That was it. Slowly, millimeter by millimeter he worked it free until finally he could see it reflected in the mirror. The deformed slug emerged from the wound and dropped onto the bedspread, already dark with his blood. With what remained of his strength he twisted the cap off another bottle from the minibar and poured the burning liquid into the wound. He tore the corner off one of the sachets of sugar and emptied the contents in after it. The granules would stem the blood flow and promote clotting. When the first sachet was empty he tore the top off another, repeating the process.

He just managed to stuff one of the ripped pieces of towel into the wound before he passed out.

9

LARS WAS IN the parking lot supervising the removal of the van to the police pound in town when Doug Whitley found him.

The preliminary forensics report had come through earlier that morning but it hadn't told him much. The van had been remarkably clean. The license plates were fake and the engine and chassis serial numbers had been removed, making it virtually impossible to trace. Other than those belonging to the two hospital orderlies, forensics had only lifted a single partial print, taken from the handgun that had been recovered from the back of the van. It was assumed that it belonged to the man who had recently fled the hospital. A match was likely to be difficult, but it was nevertheless being run through the FBI's Integrated Automated Fingerprint Identification System. There were no prints from the driver, although the techs had found traces of powder on the steering wheel that indicated he might have been wearing latex gloves. The ballistics report confirmed what Lars had suspected – all shots had been fired from inside the van. The bullet that had wounded the man who had been strapped to the gurney had come from the front of the vehicle. The man in the back wearing the Nevada Highway Patrol uniform had been killed by a 9mm round fired from the handgun that had been found on the floor next to the bench seat, powder burns on his shirt indicating that the shot had been fired at close range. Lars was staring into the back of the van, trying once again to figure out what in hell might have caused the men in the back to start shooting at each other when Doug walked over.

'Sheriff, just got a call from Sue over in the lab, says she has something to show me. Care to tag along?'

A middle-aged woman in a white lab coat was bent over a microscope when they entered the lab. She stood up, ushering them over to a corner next to the window where a pot of coffee was bubbling over an old Bunsen burner. She offered them each a paper cup brimming with the thick, dark liquid. Lars suspected it wasn't Sue's first hit of the morning. She looked about as tired as he felt.

'So, Sue, what've you found?'

'Well Doug, I'm not really sure. I had no luck trying to find supplies of this guy's blood last night so I started to run tests on the samples we'd taken, to see whether anything else might show up that would help us. The first batch didn't show up anything other than trace amounts of methohexital. I checked with OR and they'd administered a combination of ketamine and benzodiazepine in anticipation of surgery to repair his kidney, but there was no record of methohexital having been given. I planned to check with the Sheriff here whether he found anything in the back of that van that might tell us how it got in his system.'

Lars dug his notebook out of the pocket of his shirt, flipping to the page where he had jotted down the contents of the custom cabinets in the back of the van. Sure enough, methohexital was on the list. He asked what it was used for.

'It's a fast acting sedative, Sheriff.'

That might indicate the man hadn't been in the back of the van voluntarily. He scribbled a note next to where he had written the name of the drug in his notebook, returning his attention to Sue Ellis.

'Well, anyway Doug, the last set of tests I ran last night involved checking the levels of HSCs in the man's blood.'

Lars interrupted again.

'HSCs?'

'Hematopoietic stem cells, Sheriff. They replace damaged blood cells.'

Lars flipped open his notebook again. After a moment's hesitation he wrote down the name. He was sure he'd made a pig's breakfast of the spelling. He'd get Connie to look it up on the internet later.

'The test takes an hour or so and I wasn't hopeful that it would show anything relevant so I planned to go home and check the results in the morning. As I was preparing to leave I realized I'd used the last of the blood samples. So I called the nurses' station. Janice was on last night and I explained that I needed a fresh sample. I'd already finished up here so I told her I'd walk over to collect it.'

'Well, I arrived at the station just as she was heading for the patient's room, so I decided to tag along. It took a little longer than usual to collect the sample, but low blood pressure's to be expected with an acute hemolytic response and I saw they already had him on a low-dose epinephrine drip to try and counteract it. Anyway, when the vial was full I dropped the sample back to the lab, and then I headed for the parking lot. But then when I get back in this morning and check the results I find this.' She handed a sheet of paper to the hospital administrator.

'Well that can't be right.'

'I know Doug, I thought the same thing.'

Whitley passed the sheet to Lars, who looked at it for a moment before handing it back.

'So these HSC cells shouldn't be there?'

'It's not the presence of the cells themselves that's unusual, Sheriff. With the gunshot wound and the damage that would have been caused to his blood as a result of the transfusion I would have been surprised if his body hadn't started producing them. It's the sheer concentration that I just can't get over. The sample of blood I tested last night was taken only minutes after the man was admitted. Lionel estimated he'd been shot less than an hour before he got to the OR. His body simply shouldn't have reacted that quickly to repair itself.'

She turned her attention back to Whitley.

'Well anyway, I was now convinced that somehow the blood samples had been mixed up. Sometimes these things happen.' She shot a look to the hospital administrator that Lars interpreted as *But not in my lab*.

'So I decided the best thing to do would be to re-run the same test on the sample that had been taken the night before. I was there when that was taken, and I'd brought it back to the lab myself. There was no way it could have been mislabeled or somehow become contaminated.'

'It was when I got these results back that I called you.'

She handed a second sheet to Whitley, explaining to Lars that instead of showing reduced levels of hematopoietic stem cells, the results from the second test showed concentrations that were literally off the charts. The administrator said nothing for a while.

'Sue, who can we talk to to get a better read on this?'

'Well, Doug, I attended a seminar up in Berkeley last year. So I called the Genetics Department and managed to get hold of a teaching assistant there. He said one of the faculty members would probably be interested. We've got to move with it though, least if we want them to look at it this side of the holidays. Term's ended and they're all likely to disappear over the next day or two.'

Lars volunteered to take what remained of the blood sample to Berkeley first thing the following morning, together with the results of the tests Sue had run, the patient's medical charts and the additional samples and medication that had been found in the van. As they were leaving the lab he asked Doug what he made of what Sue Ellis had told them.

'Well, to be honest with you Sheriff, stem cells aren't my specialty, but I know enough to realize that we shouldn't be seeing levels like that. If it had been any of the other technicians I would have told them to re-do the tests and stop wasting everyone's time. But Sue runs that lab, has for the last twelve years, and hematology is her area. She'll have been beating herself up over that transfusion. Not her fault of course. But if I know her she'll have checked and re-checked those results before she picked up that phone to call me this morning.'

'And there's something very strange about the way this guy seems to have just overpowered a security guard and walked right out of here only hours after we'd pretty much written him off for dead. I spoke with Lionel. The monitors showed his heart rate and blood pressure stabilizing in the hours before his escape, but he was unable to offer any explanation for the apparent improvement in the man's condition. Hell, Sheriff, right now I don't know what to make of it.'

Twenty minutes later Lars walked back into his office with a fresh cup of coffee in one hand and one of those Danish pastries from Starbucks that Ellie didn't allow him to eat in the other. On his way back into town he'd called Connie and asked her to gather up the remaining items he needed from the evidence locker at the station.

Connie wasn't at her desk but that wasn't unusual. The woman got through three packs of unfiltered Camels a day; she was probably in the parking lot on a smoke break. In any event he saw that the items he had requested from the back of the van were already bagged and on his desk. She'd left a note telling him that she hadn't been able to find the blood samples he'd mentioned, but that everything else was there.

He reached for the report the forensics team had prepared, flipping to the back page for the schedule of items recovered from the van. There was no mention of the three vials of blood there either. Picking up the phone he dialed the lab in Carson City and waited while the agent checked with the other members of the team. After a few minutes he came back on the line. No-one remembered seeing blood samples in the refrigerated container.

Now that was odd. Sue Ellis had confirmed that what remained of the sample she had taken should be enough for the guys over at Berkeley to analyze, but it troubled him that items of evidence might have been removed from his crime scene. While he was finishing his coffee Connie walked into his office.

'I got all the stuff you asked for, Sheriff, except them blood samples. Couldn't find 'em anywhere. Weren't no mention of them in the forensics report either.'

Lars nodded, holding up the report to show he had checked.

'Connie, will you talk to Jed and Larry when they get back? See if they know of anyone who might have got into the van before forensics showed up.'

She nodded.

'Sure Sheriff. Oh, and I checked with the base commander over at the Depot. All of his guys are accounted for. The air force base at Nellis are still checking but they don't think they're missing anyone either. However the Navy guys at Fallon have an instructor been missing since yesterday. Highway patrol up in Churchill found his bike in a ravine out by 50, just past Salt Wells. Pretty busted up. No sign of a body yet. We don't have a picture of the guy who did a runner from Mount Grant but I've asked Fallon to run a check

64

on their guy's blood type to see if it's a match and to send us a photo if they got one. They've promised to get back to me within the hour.'

Lars sat up in his chair. Could this be the break he'd been waiting for? Why hadn't he thought to check the other bases in Nevada? He'd been too focused on the implications for Hawthorne if the depot were shut down to think about anywhere else. Dammit, Fallon was less than seventy miles away - of course this guy could have been from there. Well, thankfully Connie had done some thinking of her own.

'Connie you are a wonder. Let me know soon as you hear back from Fallon.'

'Sure Sheriff. Want me to enter Gant as a missing person in NCIC? I checked with highway patrol up in Churchill and they haven't done anything about it yet. Figured if this guy's linked to your case might as well do it here.'

Lars thought about that for a moment. The National Crime Information Center database had been pioneered by the FBI in the late 'sixties, recognizing that law enforcement officers all over the country needed fast access to the growing pool of criminal data. When the database had first gone online its records had been limited to stolen cars, vehicle license plates, stolen or missing firearms and wanted persons, but a missing persons database had subsequently been added. The NCIC computer was housed in the Bureau's headquarters in Washington but connecting terminals were located in FBI field offices, police departments, sheriff's offices and other criminal justice agencies throughout the country. Lars was certified to use the terminal here in Hawthorne – he'd been on the required refresher course only that fall - but Connie knew he hated computers.

'Let's wait 'till I've spoken with the base commander at Fallon. No sense running point on a missing person that doesn't belong to us if it's not connected to what happened at Mount Grant.'

But twenty minutes later he was on the phone to Captain John James Fitzpatrick at Fallon, a scanned picture of Master Chief Carl Gant on the desk in front of him. The quality was poor but he was certain it was their man. Fallon had also confirmed Gant's blood group as *hh*. They even maintained stocks at the base in case he was injured.

Fitzpatrick had no idea however what his Master Chief had been doing strapped to a gurney in the back of a van that had crashed into Mount Grant the day before. He explained to the sheriff that he wasn't at liberty to disclose much about Gant's military background, other than to confirm that he was a highly experienced member of one of the Navy's most prestigious special forces units. When Lars raised the possibility that Gant might have been involved in a terrorist plot the commander laughed out loud.

'Listen Sheriff, I may not be able to tell you much about what Gant's done during his time with the Navy, but I have known him personally for almost ten years. He's no Oklahoma bomber. Only thing that's got me puzzled though is why he allowed himself to be bundled into the back of that van if he didn't want to be there. As I expect you've read from his jacket, Cody's job here at Fallon is to train Navy SEALs. I can't see him going anywhere against his will.'

'Cody?'

'Sorry Sheriff, that's what everyone here at the base calls Gant. Except for the CSAR candidates of course. To them he's just Master Chief. I haven't heard anyone call him Carl in years.'

Lars flipped back in his notebook to find where he had first written Gant's name and then scribbled *Cody* next to it in the margin. Then he explained to the base commander that traces of a fast acting sedative had also been found in Gant's blood, and at least one of the other men in the van had been ex-military. Fingerprints had been taken from the man in the morgue and a match had already been found. Vincent Keogh had served with the 10th Special Forces in the Gulf. He had left the army shortly afterwards, but the report showed nothing about his activities in the sixteen years since. Lars asked a few more questions, jotting the answers down in his notebook. He was about to end the call when it occurred to him to ask why Gant might have chosen to break out of the hospital and why he hadn't contacted his base.

'Well, Sheriff, I'm guessing he broke out of the hospital because he didn't feel safe there. I mean, if he could overpower your guard and leave without anyone noticing, in the state he was in, why then I suspect he'd also figured out it wouldn't be difficult for someone else to get to him. As to why he hasn't got in touch with anyone here, I honestly have no idea. However, we're just as keen as you are to find him, so just let us know what we can do to help.'

Lars replaced the receiver and leaned back in his chair. What Fitzpatrick had told him tied in with what he had already suspected. But if Gant wasn't a terrorist, what had he been doing in the back of that van?

10

ALISON WAS KNEELING on the floor sorting through a stack of periodicals when Lars walked in. She was wearing faded jeans and an old Harvard sweatshirt, a rubber band holding her hair back in a loose ponytail. The sheriff placed the cooler box he was carrying on one of the lab benches, removing his hat before holding out his hand.

'Much obliged you could find time to meet with me on such short notice, Doctor Stone.'

Alison got to her feet. In truth she had been a little annoyed when she had found out that her assistant had committed her to the meeting. She had a flight to catch that evening and there was still a lot she needed to do around the lab. And Rutherford had been on her mind. She had explained to him outside the restaurant that she was only interested in a professional relationship and he had been offended, claiming that she had misunderstood. She hadn't seen him since, which was unusual; in recent months he had been a frequent visitor to the lab. Had she over-reacted, reading something into what he had said? She didn't think so - she had replayed the conversation in her head a thousand times. Not that that would ultimately matter; if the dean decided to make life difficult for her she would have no way to prove he had suggested anything inappropriate. The man certainly had a reputation, but then she had been spending a lot of time with him since she had arrived. Her colleagues at the faculty might be just as likely to believe she had led him on. More than anything she just wanted to forget the whole incident. She had half hoped to finish up early, grab an earlier flight and surprise her mother; seeing her might take her mind off Rutherford for a few days. Well, she could forget about that idea now.

'So, Sheriff, what is it that brings you all the way out to California just before Christmas?'

'Well, Doctor Stone, I'm not sure how much you've been told, but we've had an interesting few days in Hawthorne. Far more excitement than we're accustomed to.'

She nodded towards one of the lab stools.

'Why don't you start at the beginning, and I'll see what I can do to help.'

Alison listened as the sheriff explained the events of the last few days, starting with a van that had crashed in his town, and ending with the sudden disappearance of a man named Gant from the local hospital.

'If you've been watching the news Doctor Stone you'll have seen that Hawthorne's getting a lot of press over this. There's a theory spreading that this was all part of some terrorist attack on the munitions depot just outside town, and now there's talk of shutting it down. There's a lot of folks in Hawthorne that depend on that depot for their livelihoods and they're all pretty worried right now. It's my job to get to the bottom of what actually happened, and if the truth is that the guys in the van were terrorists then that's what I'll report.'

'But as things stand right now I just don't see that being the case. Problem is for anyone to listen to me I've got to show what these guys were actually doing if they weren't planning to blow up the depot. Now we caught a bit of a break yesterday when we figured out this guy Gant's identity, but the truth is we're no closer to finding him or the driver. For what it's worth I don't think Gant planned to be in that van that day. But if he wasn't there by choice I need to understand what he *was* doing there. Now the van was set up with medical equipment and chemicals to test for a rare blood type that Gant has. The lab at Mount Grant have also found something in his blood that they can't explain. I'm hoping whatever you can tell me will throw some light on this whole mess.'

'Okay Sheriff, show me what you've got. I can't promise anything and I really have to be out of here in a few hours, but that should be enough time for an initial look. It'll take me a little while to prep the samples, so I'd suggest you head for the cafeteria and get yourself a coffee. Leave me your cell number and I'll call you when I'm done.'

An hour and two pieces of apple cobbler later Lars was back in the lab, bent over the eyepiece of a microscope staring at what looked like overlapping splotches of vivid blues and reds. Beside him Alison was describing what she had found. She seemed much more excited than she'd been when he'd first arrived.

'What you're seeing, Sheriff, are cells taken from Gant's first set of blood samples. Now as you probably know blood cells are responsible for the maintenance and protection of every cell type in the body. As a result they have the greatest powers of self-renewal of any adult tissue – your blood literally has to produce billions of new cells each day. This capacity to renew is down to a type of cell called a hematopoietic stem cell. HSCs are created in the bone marrow. You've probably heard of patients with blood disorders like leukemia getting bone marrow transplants, right?'

Lars nodded.

'Good, well HSCs have a couple of important characteristics. They can move out of bone marrow and into the bloodstream and once there they can differentiate, or change themselves, into any type of blood cell the body might need. In this regard they're very flexible. Knowledge about how HSCs work has been key to developing treatments for a number of diseases over the last fifty years.'

Alison paused. What she was about to explain was complicated and she needed him to understand.

'Okay, Sheriff, so in the sample you're looking at the bright blues are the nuclei, or centers, of the cells. You'll see that a number of the cells have a red corona, like a halo. Those are the HSCs in Gant's blood. I've used a marker – think of it as a dye – to show them up.'

'Now the first thing that's surprising is the number of HSCs we see in the sample. About one in every ten to fifteen thousand bone marrow cells is thought to be a stem cell. In the bloodstream the proportion falls to one in a hundred thousand blood cells. We simply shouldn't be seeing anything like the number of HSCs that seem to be in Gant's blood.'

Lars looked up from the microscope. That was consistent with what Sue Ellis had said.

'So would the high concentrations of these HSCs explain Gant's sudden recovery?'

'I don't think so, at least not completely. As powerful as HSCs are, they have a number of limitations. The most important is that they can only differentiate into blood cells. Even though some recent studies with animals have shown that HSCs might be able to form other cell types, like muscle, blood vessels or bone, in humans it's thought that this simply isn't possible. But there's something else.'

She removed the slide on the microscope, carefully replacing it with another.

'This is from the second sample taken from Gant.'

He bent over the microscope again. The blue splodges were still there, but now there were a lot more with red marking their edges. In addition, there were a significant number of green areas that hadn't been present before.

71

'The first thing you'll notice is that the number of HSCs has increased dramatically. The number was exceptional before, now it's frankly unbelievable. Secondly, you've probably noticed the green areas in the sample. This is as a result of a second marker, called Oct-4, that I introduced to the sample. Oct-4 is a master regulator of pluripotency that controls lineage commitment – it's the most recognized marker used for the identification of totipotent embryonic stem cells.'

Lars look told her that she had lost him.

Of course, slow down.

'Sorry, Sheriff, it's just that if this isn't some sort of elaborate hoax it is very exciting. Okay, you've probably heard of embryonic stem cells? Well, embryonic stem cells are a very special type of cell found in early stage embryos. They're important because they're what's known as *totipotent*, which just means that they are able to differentiate into every type of cell type in the body. They need to be able to do this in order for a fully-grown human, like you or me, to develop from a fertilized egg. Well, because embryonic stem cells are so flexible, and because of their unlimited capacity for self-renewal, they have been at the center of advances in regenerative medicine. It is hoped that research into this type of stem cell will ultimately allow us to replace tissues or organs damaged by injury or disease.'

'Sadly for humans these incredibly flexible stem cells are only found in the developing embryo. The stem cells found in adults are far less potent – even the most plastic, the most flexible, types of adult stem cells like HSCs are only capable of differentiating into specific types of cells. We still don't understand why this is. You've probably heard of certain types of animals – crabs, geckos, salamanders - that have the ability to regrow tissue following injury? Well, the current thinking is that complex molecular signals control the

72

behavior of stem cells in the bodies of those animals, switching them on and off, telling them when to change into another type of cell. If we could find some way to understand and ultimately control that signaling within humans then the potential for our bodies to repair themselves could be enormous. So you see, Sheriff, if Gant's body does actually possess the ability to generate large concentrations of the most powerful stem cell types when it needs them to repair injury, studying him may provide us with answers to some of the most important questions currently faced by medical science.'

The sheriff was staring at her. Alison realized that what she had described probably sounded far-fetched. She now regretted meeting him wearing jeans and a sweatshirt. She was used to skepticism from colleagues when they saw how young she was and she had seen that same look on the sheriff's face when they had met earlier. But she desperately needed to examine this guy Gant and to do that she would need the sheriff to find him for her. And if he thought she was some kid fresh out of grad school with a crazy theory she might never see him again. She had to make him believe her.

'Listen Sheriff, I know this might sound implausible. And I'll admit that so far all we've got to go on are some preliminary tests. There's a lot more work to be done to substantiate what we seem to be seeing here. To be perfectly honest we've been struggling since the 'sixties to even accurately identify stem cells. HSCs for instance look and behave in culture like ordinary white blood cells and so we have to rely on cell surface proteins - the markers I was talking about earlier - to identify them. Unfortunately the process is far from perfect. Some of the cells that have stained positive in the blood samples may not be true stem cells, they could be progenitors, or they may not even be stem cells at all. However, the concentrations we saw in both samples would suggest that even if a small percentage of what the markers have identified are actually HSCs or embryonic cells then Gant is very special. We need to find him.'

She looked across the lab bench at the sheriff, unsure of what else to say. He seemed to be making his mind up about what she had told him, but his face was unreadable. She was desperate to find something else to say that might convince him but she thought it best to give him a moment to reach his own conclusions on what he had just heard. She realized she was holding her breath.

'Doctor, I won't pretend to understand what you do here. I suspect you could explain it to me a hundred times and still I wouldn't get the whole picture. Now I don't know whether your theory about this guy having the ability to produce these super cells makes sense or not but I suspect you are right that there is something special about this guy and that it relates to his blood. The van was rigged to carry someone who might need medical attention, or at least someone who might need to be tested for something. The guys who grabbed him knew that Gant had a rare blood condition. The chemical necessary to test for it was found in the van and it looks like samples of his blood had already been taken. So the best I can come up with is that somebody was trying to abduct him, that it had something to do with his blood, and that something went badly wrong in the process. Looks like my best chance of getting to the bottom of this is still to try and find him, if I can.'

Lars paused for a moment. When he continued, it seemed to Alison that he was speaking to himself rather than to her.

'It worries me that he hasn't shown up at the base though. I get that he might not have felt safe in Mount Grant but Fallon's less than seventy miles up 95. It's got to be the safest place in the United States for him right now and he could have been there before we even knew he was gone.'

'Well, Sheriff, I can't help you with that. I have to leave for the airport shortly but I promise I will run more tests as soon as I get back to see what else I can find out from his blood. I'd be grateful if you could also let me know as soon as you find him. If Gant's blood behaves the way the tests seem to indicate I can't over-emphasize how important he could be.'

Lars thanked her again, leaving the files from the hospital together with copies of Gant's records from Fallon and details of where he could be contacted day or night.

After he had gone Alison checked her watch. She really had to be making her way to the airport, but for a moment she wished that she didn't have to go. The last of her colleagues had left that morning and the lab was quiet. She would dearly have loved to spend a couple of days alone running tests on Gant's blood. But her mother was expecting her; she would be disappointed if she cancelled now. She quickly tidied the lab, placing the files on Gant in the carry-on bag she had brought with her that morning. Then she called a cab to take her to Oakland City for her flight.

11

HE WOKE SLOWLY. The blinds in the small room were drawn but he could tell from the failing light that it was already late afternoon. After he had removed the bullet he had passed out, only coming to in the early hours of the following morning. Thirst had driven him into the small bathroom. When he had drunk as much as he could from the washbasin's tap he had removed the bloodstained clothes he had taken from the security guard and climbed back into bed, falling asleep again almost immediately. He had slept most of the day.

Now he sat up. The muscles in his abdomen were stiff and he winced at the pain in his side. He slowly lifted the strip of towel that was serving as a makeshift dressing. The skin around the area was bruised and tender, but the wound had stopped bleeding. Infection wouldn't be a concern. The alcohol probably hadn't been necessary, a product of his training.

He was annoyed with himself. He had no idea who they were, or why they had come for him. But they had had him under surveillance, and he hadn't even noticed. They were professionals, but the signs would have been there, if he had bothered to look in the right places. Perhaps in recent months he had spent too much time training candidates, too little operational, and had lost a fraction of his edge. Whatever the reason for the lapse, he couldn't afford to repeat it. He lay back on the bed, forcing himself to replay what he remembered of the abduction. Maybe there would be something there that might offer a clue as to the identity of his attackers.

The tall man. He had seen him the moment he had stepped from behind the sign, the raised hand, the dark blue uniform even from that distance marking him immediately as Nevada Highway Patrol. Or at least that was what they had wanted him to think. He should have been suspicious. Highway patrol rarely policed that stretch of road, particularly that close to Christmas. But instead he'd hit the brakes, the radially-mounted calipers biting instantly, the bike squirming underneath him as he'd fought to control the sudden deceleration. Then the cruiser, its roof lights flashing lazy blue and red as it pulled slowly out behind the patrolman, blocking the road.

He'd brought the bike to a halt on the side of the road where the tall traffic cop had indicated, the tires crunching on the loose gravel. Fitzpatrick made sure that the men at the base knew they weren't to cause trouble whenever they headed into town and as a result relations between the Navy and local law enforcement were generally good. He'd lifted off his helmet, resting it on the tank in front of him, and opened his jacket, still hoping to escape with a caution. But the man had ignored the olive drab t-shirt and dog tags, motioning to him to step off the bike, beckoning him over to the cruiser, his face impassive behind mirrored Ray-Bans. He'd been told to place his hands flat on the hood and to spread his legs.

Only then as he'd waited, hands resting on the wing of the cruiser, had he begun to realize something wasn't right. Two patrolmen, not one. Neither of them had asked to see his license or registration, neither had mentioned the traffic violation he had committed. And the second man, swarthy, stocky, now out of the cruiser, walking around to take up a position behind him. He'd recognized the posture and concise, efficient movements of someone who had served years in one or other of the military's special forces' communities. The man hadn't taken his hand from the taser in his belt since he'd stepped from the cruiser. His partner was concealing it better but both men had been tense, continuously taking in their surroundings. What did *they* have to be nervous about?

He'd turned his head to address them, still keeping his palms flat on the cruiser's hood. As he'd done so he'd caught sunlight glinting off something to his right, behind a shack at the side of the road. The wing mirror of a van, for an instant reflecting the low December sun. And earlier, sunlight reflecting off something else on the peak of Grimes Point. A spotting scope. The man with binoculars as he had left the base. The sudden realization that these men had known he had been coming, had been waiting for him.

He'd started to move then, turning to face them. But he'd been too late. Something sharp had jabbed the side of his neck and as he'd turned he'd seen a syringe in the tall man's hand. Both men looking at him, waiting for his reaction, the shorter man's hand still hovering over the taser in his holster. His head had swum, his vision reducing to a dark tunnel as he'd felt his knees buckle. He'd staggered backwards, reaching out with one hand to steady himself against the cruiser. Then he was slipping to the ground, and the two men in the Nevada Highway Patrol uniforms had stepped forward, placing strong hands under his arms to hold him up as he felt his legs give way. The last thing he remembered was the dog tags being pulled from his neck as he had succumbed to the darkness.

His hand flew there as he remembered. He didn't care about the tags but the St. Christopher medal was all he had from her. It couldn't be gone. But it was, and there was nothing he could do about it for now. He forced himself to return to the abduction. He would worry about recovering it later.

He didn't remember much of the van. He'd come to slowly, his head swimming. Movement. The sound of an engine. The drone of tires on asphalt. Voices. Two men laughing, discussing what they were going to do with the money somebody called *El Conde* was going to pay them.

He had opened his eyes a fraction. He was strapped to a gurney. The tall man was leaning forward to talk to the driver through a partition in the bulkhead, ignoring him for now. A tube snaking from a drip into his arm, presumably a sedative. It would explain why he had felt so light-headed, why the man in the back of the van with him seemed so relaxed. An automatic in a holster on his hip, within reach as he twisted forward on the bench seat to talk to his companion in the front.

He had managed to free a hand. But as he had reached for the handgun the tall man had noticed him. There had been a struggle and the gun had gone off. Then another gunshot, a searing pain in his abdomen. He thought he had managed to aim a single round at the driver of the van before he had passed out, no longer able to fight the effects of the sedative.

The next thing he remembered was waking up in hospital, a guard posted outside the door to his room. He had glanced at the medical charts that had been clipped to the base of his bed before he had fled. The bullet had taken out one of his kidneys and the transfusion had caused the other to fail. Well, at least one of his kidneys now seemed to be functioning again. He wondered whether the other one would heal. It didn't matter. He could survive with a single kidney.

He had no idea who *El Conde* was or why the men had been sent for him. Was it possible that they knew? But how could they have found out? He didn't think he had been careless, but he had been at Fallon a long time. Too long.

For now he needed to rest up, to give his body a few days to heal. Then he could think about what to do next.

12

AN HOUR AFTER she had left the lab Alison had cleared security and was waiting to board. She realized she hadn't been this excited in a long time. What she had witnessed in Gant's blood was truly amazing. Something was triggering his body to produce large quantities of stem cells, initially hematopoietic stem cells and later both HSCs and cells that showed similar characteristics to embryonic stem cells. The key would be to identify the signaling mechanisms in his blood, and assuming there was more than one factor, how they were working in concert to make his body respond to his injuries in the way it had. She had a two and a half hour flight to Denver, and then an hour layover before the three and a half hour flight to Baltimore, plenty of time to read through what the sheriff had given her and devise a set of tests that she could carry out on her return to the lab after Christmas. Hopefully by then Henrikssen would have caught up with Gant.

She boarded the plane and found her seat quickly, removing the thin file the sheriff had handed her before stowing her bag in the overhead bin. As soon as she was seated she grabbed a pad and a pen and started to jot some notes. If the sheriff's theory was correct, Gant had been abducted while riding his motorbike. She checked the medical report from Mount Grant. There was no record of injuries consistent with a bike accident. The report showed that he had been shot, but according to the sheriff that had occurred later, while he was in the van. He must have stopped the bike. That made sense. If the sheriff was right the men who had abducted him needed him for something, most likely his blood; they would certainly have figured out how to get him into the van uninjured. Hadn't the sheriff mentioned that the other men in the van had been wearing highway patrol uniforms? Gant might have been exhibiting symptoms of excitement or stress, but it was impossible to tell. He was after all a member of a special forces team and so he may not have reacted to being abducted in the way that a normal person might. She scribbled:

Prior to/at abduction – possible elevated heart rate/bp/adrenaline (??)

Gant had then been placed in the back of the van. At some point he had been sedated. She reached again for the medical records from Mount Grant. The blood report identified the sedative as methohexital. It was unclear when it had been administered but she guessed it would have been given to get him into the van. Methohexital was a fast acting barbiturate but its effects were short-lived. If Gant had been given a regular dose his liver would have started to remove it from his system within minutes. In the meantime however it would have suppressed his cardiovascular system, causing his breathing, heart rate and blood pressure to fall. Any adrenaline that had been in his system would quickly have been metabolized.

Underneath her first note, she continued:

Methohexital – heart rate/bp fall (briefly); adrenaline absorbed.

And then the van had ended up at Mount Grant hospital. Fallon was less than seventy miles from Hawthorne – perhaps just over an hour's drive. At some point during that hour Gant had been shot, and by the time the driver had driven to Mount Grant he had been unresponsive.

The cabin crew were going through their safety presentation, donning lifejackets and pointing out

82

emergency exits, but Alison barely noticed. She was so engrossed with Gant's file that she only realized they had taken off when the 'Fasten Seat Belts' sign went off and the man sitting next to her asked to get past her to go to the bathroom. She sat back in her seat, buckling the belt loosely around her waist.

Gant shouldn't have been unconscious when they admitted him. His gunshot wound would almost certainly have caused him to go into shock, but it would take some time for him to lose consciousness, particularly given his age, level of fitness and military training. She flicked through the report again. The lab technician at Mount Grant had also found ketamine and benzodiazepine in his blood but had noted that those were the anesthetics administered by the hospital. Referring back to his charts, she confirmed that was the case.

However, it was possible that one or both of those drugs had also been given to him by the other men in the van. He would have started to come around from the methohexital after only a few minutes. If they had planned to transport him any distance it would have been necessary to administer a longer lasting sedative, or an anesthetic. Because it suppressed breathing less than other drugs, ketamine was often a preferred anesthetic when reliable ventilation equipment wasn't available, such as when a patient needed to be transported by ambulance. Benzodiazepine was a common sedative, with longer lasting effect. Like methohexital, both drugs were readily available. As a third bullet point she wrote:

Patient further sedated once in van (??)

She was sure that the sheriff had mentioned a list that he had made of the drugs found in the back of the van, but it wasn't in the file he had given her. She added a note in the margin beside her third point:

Check with sheriff if ketamine/benzodiazepine found.

Then there was the gunshot wound. She flicked back to Sue Ellis's handwritten notes on the copy of his medical chart. The surgeon at Mount Grant had thought that he had been shot less than an hour before arriving at the OR. The drive from Salt Wells would have taken longer than that, which indicated that Gant had indeed been shot after he had got into the van. And the forensics report seemed to support the theory that he had been shot while he was strapped to the gurney. They had no way of knowing for sure whether this was before or after he had been sedated but she was prepared to bet that it was afterwards. If they had given him methohexital to get him into the van they would have needed to administer the second longer-lasting sedative fairly shortly thereafter.

The remainder of Gant's history was well documented. He had been admitted to Mount Grant just after four p.m., the blood work completed quickly. Too quickly as it turned out, but she couldn't blame Sue Ellis for that. There wouldn't have been time to type and cross his blood and the *hh* phenotype was so rare that the possibility of it being an issue would have been discounted even if anyone at the hospital had thought to consider it. Then the transfusion – 4 units of O negative - followed almost immediately by the first indications of an acute hemolytic response: the increase in heart rate, the rapid, weak pulse, the drop in blood pressure, the uncontrollable bleeding from the wound site. The other symptoms - fever, chills, facial flushing, severe lumbar pain - would most likely have been masked by the fact that he had been anaesthetized. She saw from his records that Gant had been placed on an epinephrine drip to counteract the hypotension. She simply scribbled a new note under the last:

Adrenaline administered.

Satisfied that she had considered the external factors available from the evidence she turned to the blood tests both she and the technician at Mount Grant had run. If they were to be believed the results were simply amazing. The number of hematopoietic stem cells in the first sample was incredible, but it was the results of the second test that really interested her.

Embryonic stem cells had started to appear in Gant's blood.

What were they doing there? Was it possible that his body had the ability to produce totipotent stem cells – an almost infinitely flexible type of cell – at will in order to repair damage to his body? And if so how was he doing it? Were these entirely new cells that his body was producing or were his existing cells de-differentiating, regressing to an earlier more plastic form? She warned herself again against getting carried away. She would of course need to verify every aspect of the process by which the samples had been obtained. Ideally she would take her own samples from Gant, assuming they were able to find him.

It suddenly occurred to her that she still didn't know what the man looked like. There had been no photos in his file from Mount Grant but the sheriff had also left her with a copy of his medical records from Fallon. There might be something there. She opened the folder. On the second page was a photograph of Master Chief Carl Gant.

She felt her heart skip a beat.

The picture had been photocopied but there was no mistaking the face. It was the man who had approached her a couple of months before, just after term had started. He had seemed vaguely familiar at the time, as though she had seen him somewhere before. She had assumed at first it was because she must have seen him somewhere on campus, but somehow she knew that wasn't it. And she hadn't seen him since - she had been looking out for him. The more she had thought about it the more she had become convinced that she recognized him from somewhere else, but for the life of her she hadn't been able to remember where she might have seen him. Now seeing the photocopy of his photo in the file made him seem even more familiar, as if for some strange reason he was more recognizable to her without those piercing green eyes.

She remembered now the subject he had wanted to discuss with her that day: enhanced regenerative capacity in humans. He had been trying to confide in her back then, and she had dismissed him. She was suddenly annoyed with herself. How often had she impressed upon her students the importance of keeping an open mind? Stem cell research was a new field with a short history, characterized by findings that a few short years before wouldn't have seemed possible. And yet she had sent this man away when he had come to her with perhaps the key to what might prove the most important medical discovery of their generation.

She tried to remember if there was anything else from their brief encounter, anything that might be relevant. When he had mentioned human regenerative capabilities she had asked him to be more specific. He had mentioned recuperation but also something else. What was it? Not just the ability to repair but also improvements in eyesight and hearing. She flicked through the rest of his navy medical chart. His eyesight was slightly better than 20/20 but that really wasn't unusual. She wondered what he had meant.

The pilot announced that the plane was coming into land at Denver and she replaced the files in her carry-on bag, fastening her seatbelt. Twenty minutes later she was in the terminal, with an hour before her next flight. Should she call the sheriff with what she remembered about Gant? It didn't seem particularly relevant to his investigation but then it might help to convince him that the man was important. She dug out the card he had given her with his contact details, checking her watch. He should be back in Hawthorne by now.

She dialed the number he had given her for the sheriff's office. A woman answered, polite but direct, her gravelly voice explaining that the sheriff was still on his way back. Did she want to leave her name and a number where he might reach her? As soon as Alison gave her name the woman told her to hold; the sheriff had left instructions to transfer any calls from her immediately. A moment later she heard him answer, a slight echo and the background hum of tires and engine confirming he was still at the wheel of his cruiser.

She quickly explained that she had met Gant before, that he had come to see her a few months ago to discuss a paper she had written on stem cell research, that he had been particularly interested in human regenerative capabilities, that she had only recognized him when she had looked through his naval records. As she was finishing it suddenly occurred to her that what she had told the sheriff sounded contrived. She had been worried that she had appeared over-excited about the possibilities that Gant presented when she had met the sheriff in the lab earlier. Would he now think she had made up this encounter to try and lend credibility to her claims?

The sheriff said nothing for a long moment.

'You're certain it was Gant that came to see you?'

She thought she detected a tone in his voice. Not disbelief exactly, but an edge, a skepticism. It was his job to probe for the truth. He would assume – correctly – that over the course of a few months literally hundreds of students would approach her with questions, topics for discussion. Even if he didn't suspect her of

87

fabricating the encounter he probably thought she was getting Gant confused with someone else.

'Yes.'

'Did he introduce himself as Carl Gant?'

'No. I never got his name.'

Silence again.

She heard her flight being called, and told the sheriff that she had to go.

'Of course. Well, thank you for the call Doctor Stone. You have a safe trip now.'

13

IT WAS AFTER seven when Lars made it back to Hawthorne. It had been a long day and he was keen to get home to Ellie but he had to stop by the office first. He didn't know what to make of Alison Stone's claim that she had met Gant. He was convinced that Gant's blood had something to do with his abduction however. He had called Connie from the car and asked her to search NCIC for anything connected with the *hh* blood type. Minutes after he arrived he was sitting behind his desk staring at three printouts she had left for him.

The first was for Shilpa Desai, a fifteen-year old high school student who had gone missing from Rockport, Massachusetts in 1965. There was little other than personal details and the fact that she possessed a rare blood group. The database indicated that she had never been found.

The second report was for Cindy Rowe, a primary school teacher from Pleasant Grove, Utah who had been reported missing a decade later. Her body had never been recovered but the entry had been amended to reflect the fact that a man named Joseph Brandt had been charged with and convicted of her murder.

The final printout was for Robin Taft. Taft had been reported missing in 1981, and, like Shilpa Desai, had never been found. There was something familiar about Taft, some half-remembered detail that made Lars think he knew the name. But after a few minutes it had not come to him and with a sigh he pushed the button on the computer that normally lay dormant on his desk, waiting while the hard drive went through a series of muted clicks and the screen on his desk came to life.

He started with Robin Taft, convinced that he should somehow recognize the name. An internet search revealed three articles.

The first was a brief report of a car accident Taft had been involved in on a stretch of I-79 just past Hurricane, Utah in the summer of 1975.

The other articles were longer.

The second was an appeal two days later from the man's uncle, Byron Sedgwick Taft, the governor of Utah, for donors to come forward for his nephew. The article explained that the young man had an exceptionally rare blood type and needed a transfusion from a compatible donor before he could undergo surgery necessary to save his life.

The third article, a week later, reported that after an emotional television appeal by the governor a schoolteacher had come forward and donated blood. Robin Taft had undergone surgery and was now expected to make a full recovery.

So that was it – that was where he must have heard of Robin Taft. Byron Taft had been an important man; he remembered the press coverage at the time. It really didn't help to explain why six years later the man had gone missing though. He typed Cindy Rowe's name into the search field and hit 'Enter'.

Again there were only three articles.

The first, a short piece in the *Daily Herald* about how a local schoolteacher had responded to an appeal from the governor of Utah for a donation of a rare blood type that his nephew desperately needed following his involvement in a car accident.

The second article was from the *Salt Lake Tribune*, ten days later. It described how a man had been arrested in connection with the disappearance of a young schoolteacher and mother of two from Pleasant Grove who had been missing for a week. Joseph Brandt, from Bluffdale, worked as a driver for a car service that Mrs. Rowe had used on the day of her disappearance and was believed to be the last person to have seen her alive. The police wouldn't comment further, although sources close to the investigation had revealed that traces of what was believed to be Mrs. Rowe's blood had been found on the back seat of the car he had been driving on the day she had gone missing.

The last article, also from the *Salt Lake Tribune*, was from 1976, almost a year later. It described Brandt's trial. Brandt had been charged with the abduction and murder of the schoolteacher, who had been missing for almost a year. Her body had never been recovered, but traces of her blood and fragments of her underwear had been found on the back seat of the car Brandt had used to collect her from the airport that day. The jury had found Brandt guilty on both counts and he had been given a term of not less than thirty years at the Utah State Penitentiary, the state's maximum security prison. Passing sentence the judge had referred to the fact that Brandt had failed to show even a trace of remorse for his actions, maintaining his innocence throughout in spite of the overwhelming forensic evidence, forcing Mrs. Rowe's husband and young family to endure a protracted public trial. Brandt had also refused to disclose the whereabouts of the young woman's body, denying her family even the possibility of a burial. The article concluded by reporting that the jury had been particularly moved by a statement read to the court by the governor of Utah, Byron Sedgwick Taft, in which he indicated that he felt responsible for her fate given that it had been his office that had arranged for the car service for which Brandt had worked to collect Mrs. Rowe after she had flown to St. George to donate blood in order to save the life of his nephew.

There was still nothing to connect the disappearance of Robin Taft with that of Cindy Rowe six years earlier but now Lars' curiosity was piqued. The only thing that seemed to link the two was their blood type.

Last he searched for anything that might have been written about the schoolgirl. This time he found only two articles, both from the *Gloucester Daily Times*. The first was dated 27th October 1965 and described how Shilpa Desai had been admitted to the Addison Gilbert Hospital in Gloucester following a road traffic accident. The girl had been given an emergency blood transfusion after which her condition had rapidly deteriorated, prompting the hospital to conduct further tests that resulted in her being diagnosed with a rare blood type.

The second article was dated three weeks later and described how a local schoolgirl had been reported missing from her parents' home in Rockport. The article contained a recent picture from her high school yearbook and urged anyone who might have seen her to contact the local sheriff's office with information.

Another person with the *hh* blood group who had gone missing shortly after her details had been published. Was it more than a coincidence? How did three missing persons, the most recent gone for almost thirty years, stack up against - what had Sue Ellis said about the *hh* blood group – maybe only a handful of people in the United States having it? He had no idea. But there was something about it that was bothering him.

And there was something else Sue had said: even amongst those few that were living with it most would be unaware of the fact.

Until they needed a transfusion.

An idea was starting to form. Could there be a connection between the disappearance of Shilpa Desai,

Cindy Rowe and Robin Taft after all? If you had this blood group, and you needed a transfusion, you'd be in trouble. The odds of finding a compatible donor, at least within the time frame that you'd be likely to have, would be slim.

But then if you knew you had the condition there would have to be things you could do to prepare. Fitzpatrick had mentioned that the base stored supplies of Gant's blood in case he was injured. Couldn't everyone who had this condition just do that? There was something here he wasn't getting. After a few moments he picked up the phone and dialed Mount Grant, asking to be put through to Sue Ellis in the lab, hoping that she would still be there.

The phone was answered on the second ring.

'Sue, Lars here over at the sheriff's office. Listen, we've found out that the guy we're looking for is actually Navy – he's been stationed up at Fallon for the last ten years. Now I've spoken with the base commander up there who says they keep supplies of his blood, in case he's ever injured. I assume most people who knew they had this blood type would do something similar, to make sure they never ran into problems like this.'

'Sure, Sheriff. Although in practice it's actually a lot more difficult to maintain stocks of your own blood than you'd think. Firstly there's a limit to the amount any person can safely donate over a given period – typically one unit, about a pint, every eight weeks or so. And while serum can be frozen and stored almost indefinitely, red blood cells only remain viable in storage for a matter of weeks. And that all assumes that there's nothing wrong with your own blood that's causing the need for the transfusion in the first place.'

Was there something here that had been missed? What did he have? Four people with an incredibly rare blood type, three of whom had disappeared, the fourth who had possibly been the target of an abduction. Byron Sedgwick Taft had publicly sought donors for his nephew and when Cindy Rowe had come forward that had also been reported in the press, so the fact that both of them had the *hh* blood type would have been publicly known. The schoolgirl from Massachusetts' blood group had also been reported. Given how rare it was and how difficult it was to detect not many people would be on record as sharing the blood type – Byron Sedgwick Taft had made a public appeal for donors and had found only one.

So if you were someone who had an illness that required a transfusion of that blood type then Robin Taft, Cindy Rowe and Shilpa Desai would have appeared on your radar pretty quickly. But then why wouldn't you just ask them to donate blood? Cindy Rowe had been happy enough to, and he assumed that most people would probably act in the way she had. Why would you need to go to the trouble of abducting them? And the Rowe woman and the Desai girl had disappeared immediately after their existence had become known yet Robin Taft had only gone missing six years after the appeal that had identified him as having the *hh* blood group.

'Sheriff, are you still there?'

'Sure Sue, sorry, I was just thinking about something. Listen, why else might someone with the *hh* blood type be valuable, I mean for medical purposes, other than as a potential blood donor?'

'Well that's easy Sheriff. Matching blood groups is vitally important for organ transplantation. Although it's probably more of a theoretical point for persons with that blood group. However slim the chances might be of finding a person with the *hh* type to donate blood, imagine how hard it would be to convince them to give you a kidney. And if you needed a liver, well unless you could time your liver failure to coincide with their death you'd be out of luck.'

Lars thanked her again and put the phone down. Had Shilpa Desai, Cindy Rowe and Robin Taft each been abducted for their organs? Was that why the men in the van had wanted Gant? Or was he getting carried away, looking for a link between three persons who had gone missing decades ago that didn't actually exist? All he had at the moment was supposition – a crazy theory with no evidence to back it up, no suspect, hell no way to even prove that any of the victims other than the Rowe woman hadn't just decided to up and start a new life somewhere else. He had to admit it was pretty thin. Cindy Rowe wasn't even technically a missing person. She was presumed dead and a man had been convicted of her murder. Although her body had never been recovered and Brandt had continued to protest his innocence even when changing his plea and disclosing where he had disposed of the body would almost certainly have shortened his sentence. If he were to justify his theory in relation to Cindy Rowe first he would need to show that Joseph Brandt had been framed for her murder.

He sat back in his chair, thinking for a moment.

Was that where he should start?

14

HE WAITED UNTIL the sun had set before venturing out.

The parking lot was deserted. He found a vending machine around the corner from his room and spent five dollars of what remained of his cash, returning to his room with an armful of candy bars and cola. He switched on the TV while he ate, flicking through the channels in search of any news of his escape from the hospital.

Thankfully there was very little. Most of the networks were leading with news of a storm that was dumping snow across the midsection of the United States, stranding Christmas travellers. CNN was reporting a passenger aboard a Delta Air Lines flight from Amsterdam had attempted to blow up the plane as it landed in Detroit. Only a local station, KHNV, seemed interested in Hawthorne. The report recapped the events of the last few days at Mount Grant hospital, repeating the theory that the three men who had been in the crashed van, two of whom were still at large, had been planning some sort of terrorist attack on the arms depot situated just outside the town. The report didn't reveal his identity or that of any of the other men. It concluded with a segment from a CNN interview, a senator from Alabama in a seersucker suit querying whether the base should be kept open.

Well, at least it didn't look as though he was a priority for the authorities. Whoever had tried to abduct him at Salt Wells was a different matter. He had to assume they would still be looking for him. He hadn't covered his tracks well. If they had found him before they could find him here, which meant he was still in danger. At least his side was healing well. Soon he would be able to think about moving on.

When he had escaped from the hospital he had considered taking the security guard's Taurus straight back to Fallon. But he had quickly dismissed the idea. The men who had tried to abduct him were professionals. They had known his movements, had identified the most opportune time to snatch him. Which meant the base had been under surveillance for some time. They would have expected him to try and return there.

Of course he could have contacted Fitzpatrick and arranged to be brought in. The commander would have sent a Black Hawk with a team of his own men to pick him up without batting an eyelid. They might be well-resourced, but his abductors were unlikely to have the means or the will to attempt to take him again under those circumstances. He had almost made the call.

But whoever had sent the men to Salt Wells had gone to significant lengths to plan his abduction; he had to assume that sooner or later they would try again. Unless he planned to remain within the confines of the base indefinitely he would at some stage need to venture out, at which point there was a good chance they'd be waiting. No, it was better that his abductors didn't know where he was.

Besides, returning to Fallon was likely to present its own set of problems, like how he would explain his recovery from the injuries he had sustained. He might have had some chance of playing the incident down if it were just Fitzpatrick, but the hospital would need an explanation. And the media were already involved, even if they didn't yet know what they were dealing with.

But now the time was approaching to decide where he would go he found himself delaying, reluctant to take the step that would begin the next stage of his life. He had been at Fallon for almost ten years. A good run, more than he could have expected. And he had been happy there. He had always known this day would come, however. He could read the looks on the faces of each new batch of candidates the first time they met him. It would only have been a matter of time before someone at the base had started to pay closer attention. But this time the decision was harder than usual, for he knew that he would need to leave the United States. The genetic tagging that all service personnel were now required to submit to meant that it would be too risky for him to attempt to find a new identity and re-enlist.

Even if the authorities weren't putting too much effort into finding him it was probably still too risky to chance an airport. Which meant north to Canada or south to Mexico. Choose a town on the border, try to slip over un-noticed. But first he needed to gather some things. What little cash he had in the bank couldn't be touched – he had to assume his account was being watched. But he had learned from experience that the opportunity to disappear could present itself unexpectedly, and the importance of being ready when the time came; he knew how hard it could be to make a fresh start without at least a small amount of money. A few years back he had buried an ammo can with a portion of his savings in a piece of scrubland just north of where White Pine County Road ran off the highway. Each time he had ridden out as far as Humboldt he had checked that the box hadn't been disturbed, adding to the stash. There should be enough to keep him going while he worked out a new identity and sorted out where he would start again.

And then he would disappear for good.

15

IT WAS AFTER nine when the plane touched down in Baltimore. Her mother had wanted to meet her at the airport but Alison had insisted she would take a cab. It was late, the weather was bad and the roads were likely to be busy with Christmas traffic. Thankfully the driver hadn't seemed in the mood to engage her in conversation. He had turned the car's heater up against the cold and she had sat back in the seat for the thirty-mile drive to Manchester, letting her thoughts wander. It had been a strange day. She had spent the three and a half hour flight from Denver trying to remember why Gant seemed strangely familiar to her but she was no closer to figuring it out. In the end she decided that if she just let her mind relax it might come to her.

Her mother was waiting at the front door as she paid the taxi driver and collected her small bag from the trunk. They went inside, closing the door against the cold. The house smelled of her mother's cooking. It was late and she wasn't particularly hungry but she knew it would cause disappointment if she didn't eat something and so she sat at the kitchen table while her mother transferred a healthy serving of lasagna to her plate. Alison had caused consternation when she had announced in high school that she was becoming a vegetarian and she suspected that her mother had for a long time nurtured the hope that one day she might simply grow out of it. After fifteen years that hope had probably died, but not Violet Stone's belief that she needed to compensate for the deficiencies in her daughter's diet by doubling the size of the portions she served whenever she came home.

When she had eaten as much as she could manage they moved into the small sitting room. For an hour or so they talked in front of the fire, her mother eager to hear every detail of her daughter's life in California, trying but ultimately failing to hide her disappointment when Alison informed her that no, she still hadn't found a nice young doctor to settle down with. The question made her think about Rutherford. She couldn't tell her mother about his proposal, or the implicit threat he had made. There was nothing she could do about it and it would only make her worry. In an attempt to divert her mother from one of her favorite topics she told her about the visit she had had from the sheriff from Hawthorne earlier that day, and how she had been trying all day to work out why the young soldier who had been abducted from the base at Fallon seemed familiar to her.

'Well do you have a photo of the man? Maybe I might recognize him.'

Alison had been about to respond that it was a waste of time. Gant was from Nevada - if she had seen him anywhere it was probably somewhere she had been since she moved out to California. But then she realized her mother was simply trying to help solve a problem she had brought to her; as fruitless as the exercise was likely to be there was nothing to be gained by pointing this out. Besides, the distraction might be sufficient to prevent the conversation from returning to the subject of her non-existent love life. She went back into the kitchen to retrieve the file containing the picture of Gant from her bag.

By the time she had returned her mother had found her reading glasses and was sitting forward in her chair, waiting for her daughter to produce the photo. Alison flipped through the pages in the file until she found the photocopied image and handed it over. She was apologizing for the quality of the picture and already had her hand out ready to take the sheet back when she saw her mother's eyes widen with surprise.

'Mom, what is it?'

Without saying a word her mother got up from the chair and walked over to the sideboard next to the small dining table at the far end of the room, the piece of paper still in her hand. There was a single picture frame on the top of the sideboard, which she was now bringing back. Alison knew it well – the frame contained the black and white photograph of her father standing next to the helicopter he had flown in Vietnam. She must have looked at that photo thousands of times growing up. It was how she liked to remember him, young and brave. In that photo the terrible disease that would in the end strip him of the very qualities that had made him her father did not yet exist; it was still part of some other man's future. But why was her mother bringing her *that* picture? Alison felt something stirring deep in her memory.

Her mother sat next to her on the small sofa. The fire had died down and she flicked on the small lamp that sat on the occasional table beside her. She gave the photocopied image back and then handed her the picture frame, her finger pointing to a man standing to the right of her father in the photo.

Alison had never really paid attention to it before but now she saw that there were three other men in the photograph. Sitting inside the open cargo bay of the helicopter, their legs hanging over the edge were two men in fatigues. Her father was to the right of the photograph, standing in front of the swept-back cargo door. To the left of the photo in front of the cockpit door was another man, taller than her father but wearing the same baggy flight suit, his dark hair cut short, his features immediately familiar. There was no mistaking it. The man her mother was pointing to was the same man in the photocopied image from the records the sheriff had given her that morning.

It was Gant.

She stared at the photo for several seconds, barely aware that her mother was still talking.

'The man in the photo with your father is Luke Jackson. Pete was Jackson's co-pilot for the first six months of his tour. Your father never talked much about what he'd done once he got back, but he wrote me regularly when he was out there. It was what kept me going that year. I read enough from those letters to know that your father worshipped this man. Wouldn't leave his side. I think your father would have followed him to the gates of hell if Jackson had asked it of him, and I suspect on more than one occasion he probably did.'

'So what happened to him? Did Dad stay in touch with him when his tour ended?'

'No. Jackson never made it back from Vietnam. Your father was with him when it happened. They'd flown somewhere – a lot of the time he wasn't allowed to say where they were flying, so don't ask me – to pick up some soldiers who'd got themselves into trouble. It had gotten pretty hairy I guess and well to cut a long story short their helicopter was shot down just as they'd got the men on board. Your father said he was sure at that moment it was all over. But anyway somehow Jackson and your father – Pete said it was Jackson but I suspect he had a hand in it as well – managed to get their helicopter on the ground. Anyway they got the men out and loaded them into another helicopter. They were all ready to take off when this young kid comes running out of the jungle. I guess he'd been left behind by his squad, or perhaps he was too frightened to run out into the open to get in one of the helicopters. Anyway, he ran right up to the helicopter your father and Jackson had gotten into - it was the last one left, all the others had loaded up and were on their way out – and tried to climb in. Well the helicopter was already full, it just wouldn't lift off with the weight of one more man aboard, but Jackson grabbed this kid and hauled him in anyway. They were taking fire from all sides but they couldn't go anywhere, and the enemy were coming out of the jungle towards them. Then all of a sudden Jackson just stepped off the helicopter and they took off.'

'Your father took it pretty bad. He used to write me every week, regular as clockwork. After Jackson died I didn't hear from him for almost a month. It was the longest month of my life, I can tell you. I was sure each day I would get a telegram telling me he'd died over there. It got so bad I wouldn't answer the door. Then finally a letter arrives from him, telling me what had happened.'

She paused, as if uncertain whether to go on. In the end she seemed to make up her mind.

'Your father said that Jackson had looked right at him the moment before he stepped off the helicopter and in that instant he had known what he was about to do. I believe Pete would have jumped off that helicopter in place of Jackson if he could have, but he was stuck behind one of the machine guns. Instead he drew his service pistol. He told me afterwards that he was ready to shoot the kid if Jackson hadn't jumped off before he had a chance.'

Alison looked up at her mother.

'Oh, you shouldn't think any less of your father for this Alison. I doubt anyone would have criticized him if he had gone ahead and done it. Hell, I suspect half the men in the back of that helicopter were thinking the same thing. If someone hadn't gotten off that helicopter they were all dead. I was so relieved when I got that letter and learned he was alive I couldn't have cared whether he'd been planning to shoot everyone in the damned helicopter. But I think a little part of me was also relieved that Jackson was gone. I never said it to your father of course but that man inspired him so much it scared me. I think to this day he would have signed up for another tour just to stay out there with him. But after that he was just counting the days 'till his tour ended, which suited me just fine.'

Her mother was silent for a while, the only sound from the dying fire as one of the embers shifted in the grate.

'So I guess that's where you recognize this Gant from. They must be related in some way I guess. Jackson had been in Vietnam since '65 and was a few years older than your father, even though from that photo you wouldn't think it. He'd be pushing seventy now if he were alive. This young man is probably his grandson.'

She examined the photocopied image of Gant a moment longer.

'The resemblance is uncanny however. Why they could be twins.'

With that she got up and squeezed her daughter's shoulder, telling her not to stay up late.

Alison sat on the sofa for a long while after her mother had gone to bed. The mystery of why Gant had seemed familiar to her had been solved, but what was the connection between Jackson and Gant? Gant didn't just bear a resemblance to Jackson, it was like her mother had said - they were identical. She guessed the sheriff would be able to look up both men's service records and determine whether they were related. She would call him the following morning. Maybe she would walk into town and find one of those print and copy shops and see if she could send him the photo. There was nothing more she could do tonight. She checked that the fire had died down sufficiently, placing the old metal guard in front of it just in case. Then she returned the picture frame containing the photograph of her father and Jackson to its place on the sideboard before heading upstairs to bed.

16

LARS SET OFF before sunrise, anxious to make good time. An hour later as he drove east towards Tonopah a bright yellow sun was rising in a clear blue sky. It was going to be a beautiful winter's day.

He'd lived in Nevada all his life and in those fifty-seven years Lars had never ceased to wonder at the beauty of his state. Normally he would have taken time to appreciate the spectacle, pulling his cruiser to the side of the road to enjoy a cup of coffee from the thermos Ellie had prepared for him that morning, taking time to stretch out his leg. But today he was troubled, and for once the splendor of the scenery did little to ease his mind. Besides, it was four hundred miles to Draper. If he wanted to make it there and back in a day he needed to keep moving.

He arrived at the Utah State Penitentiary just before two that afternoon. The facility was an imposing structure, set on over seven hundred acres twenty miles southwest of Salt Lake City. Its concrete walls housed over four thousand inmates as well as the state's only supermax facility and the execution chamber for those on death row. The maximum security unit had been designed in response to a spate of riots at similar institutions across the country, and procedures had been developed to minimize inmate-staff contact. Communal dining rooms and exercise yards had been dispensed with and instead prisoners spent twenty-three hours a day in concrete seven-by-eleven cells, one wall of which was made of perforated steel, allowing the inmates to squint out through the holes. Not that there was anything to see. The cells were arranged in lines radiating out like spokes from a central control hub, meaning that no prisoner could see another human being from their cell. Most of the inmates served their time in near-total isolation.

Lars had phoned ahead, explaining to the warden that he needed to speak with one of the prisoners in connection with an ongoing investigation. He had no authority in Utah; hell, strictly speaking his jurisdiction ended at the Mineral County line just after Garfield Flats Road out on US-95. But thankfully the warden hadn't called him on it. After reviewing Brandt's file in the governor's office he was shown to the visiting area, where he took a seat at a small booth. A thick perspex pane separated the visitors from the inmates, a telephone handset attached to the wall in each booth allowing communication. He waited while the guard brought Brandt from his cell.

Joseph Brandt looked older than the fifty-five years his file indicated. He shuffled into the visitors' area, his head down, hands and feet shackled, a chain connecting the 'cuffs around his wrists and ankles to a belt around his waist. At first he seemed uncertain of his surroundings and the guard who had brought him from his cell had to guide him to the booth where Lars was waiting. Brandt had been married at the time of his conviction but Lars had read from his file that he hadn't had a single visitor in the three decades he had been at the facility. The guard unhooked the telephone handset from the wall and placed it in the prisoner's hands, signaling that he could go ahead. Lars waited a moment for Brandt to get used to his new surroundings before he began.

'Mr. Brandt, I am Sheriff Lars Henrikssen from Mineral County.'

He held his badge to the perspex but Brandt barely looked up.

'I'm hoping you can help me. I'm investigating a crime that might be related to the disappearance of Robin Taft.'

Lars had hoped that the mention of Taft's name might trigger a reaction but Brandt continued to look down, cradling the handset to the side of his head with both hands.

'You may remember that Cindy Rowe had travelled to St. George to donate blood to Mr. Taft immediately before her disappearance.'

The mention of Cindy Rowe's name at last seemed to prompt a response. Brandt looked up briefly, staring blankly through the perspex pane, before looking down again. His lips were moving. The man was repeating something over and over but it was hard to make it out. Lars pressed his ear to the headset to hear what he was saying.

'No. Didn't do it. No. Didn't do it. No. *Didn't* do it.'

It was no use. Lars had read that the sensory deprivation in facilities like this frequently led otherwise healthy inmates to develop manifestations of psychosis – fits of rage, paranoia, catatonic depression, even hallucinations. After thirty years the man's mind had gone. He nodded to the guard that he was finished. It had been a wasted trip.

As he replaced the handset Brandt looked up, fixing him with a stare. The guard had placed his hand on Brandt's shoulders and was about to escort him away from the booth but something about the way the man was looking at him caused Lars to signal the guard to wait. He put the handset back to his ear, nodding at Brandt to go on.

'She made it back to her house. Somebody must have seen. Somebody must have seen. *Somebody must have seen.*'

There was nothing else. Brandt kept on repeating the sentence even as the guard lifted him out of the seat. He kept his eyes on Lars all the way to the door, his lips silently forming the words over and over. Then he was gone.

Lars signed himself out and returned to the car park. He sat in the cruiser for a long time. The one thing that Brandt's mind had held on to was that he was innocent. Was that normal? Could a person who was actually guilty convince themselves of their innocence to such an extent that that would be all that would remain after the rest of their faculties had gone? He had no idea.

Somebody must have seen.

Was that what Brandt had been tormenting himself with all these years? That somebody out there must know that Cindy Rowe had arrived back at her home safely? Even if it were true it didn't prove that Brandt hadn't subsequently abducted her. But if he had intended to kill her, why would he have driven her back to her home, why would he have allowed her to leave the car?

He checked his watch. It was just after three. Pleasant Grove was only a few miles away. He could make a few discreet inquiries; see whether any of Cindy Rowe's neighbors remembered seeing anything. After thirty years it was a long shot but there was something about his interview with Brandt that made him want to believe the man. He turned the key in the ignition, pulled out of the facility car park and headed north on I-15.

The house where Cindy Rowe had lived was at the end of a small cul de sac. The woman who answered the door had never heard of the Rowes. Lars was a little relieved. From the newspaper reports on Cindy Rowe's murder her husband had been at work on the day his wife had been abducted. There was nothing he could have seen that might help and the news that an investigation might still be ongoing was only likely to cause him distress. The woman told him that most of the current residents of the street had moved in over the last ten years. As far as she was aware only Mrs. Mortimer, a retired schoolteacher that lived directly opposite, had been around for longer. She liked to keep to herself but maybe she could help him.

Lars walked across the street and rang the doorbell. For a long time there was no answer. It was already dusk and there were no lights on in the house, but nevertheless he could have sworn he had seen one of the upstairs curtains twitch as he had made his way up the drive. He rang the doorbell again, longer this time. Finally a light came on in the hallway, followed a moment later by the porch light above his head. He heard the sound of latches being released and bolts being pulled back. The door opened a crack to reveal an elderly woman, tall and thin, her grey hair pulled back in a tight bun. She regarded him suspiciously over the top of a pair of tortoiseshell spectacles. The door was still on its chain. Lars held his badge up so that she could see, taking half a step backwards so that his face was directly under the porch light.

'Sheriff Lars Henrikssen, ma'am. I apologize for calling so late but I wonder if I might have a moment of your time to ask a few questions about the disappearance of Cindy Rowe.'

The old woman looked at the badge for a long moment, then at him, and then at the badge again. She made no move to unclip the chain from the door.

'It was a long time ago, that business with the Rowe woman. Why are you back here now?'

He explained what had happened in Hawthorne, and how Carl Gant shared the same rare blood group as Cindy Rowe and Robin Taft.

'Yes, yes, I remember the stories in the newspaper. The young man who was in the car accident. His uncle was the governor, organized some sort of appeal on the television. Mrs. Rowe flew up there to donate blood. They said it was the driver that was hired to pick her up from the airport that did it.'

'Yes.'

For the first time he thought that Mrs. Mortimer looked uncomfortable.

'Is...is he still in prison?'

'Yes he is. I visited with him not more than an hour ago at the penitentiary up in Draper.' He paused before adding 'He's not doing so well.'

Mrs. Mortimer looked down. Through the crack in the door he could see her wringing her hands.

'Mrs. Mortimer, is there anything you can tell me about Cindy Rowe's disappearance?'

The old woman looked up. She appeared undecided for a moment then finally she seemed to make up her mind, removing the chain from the door and indicating that he should follow her in. He sat at the kitchen table while she put the kettle on. Five minutes later she was sitting opposite him, stirring sugar into her tea.

'It was a Tuesday morning, the day Mrs. Rowe disappeared. I remember because Tuesdays used to be the day when I did my shopping. Anyway, the night before I hadn't slept well. Truth be told I've always been a light sleeper but that was the year my Harold passed on,' - she nodded to a picture on the kitchen window sill - 'and I guess I was still not used to him not being around. We were married twenty-nine years you know.'

She looked up, and Lars got the impression that after thirty years she still felt aggrieved to have been left alone.

'Anyway, as I said, I'd had trouble sleeping and by about five-thirty I figured this just wasn't going to be my night and there was no point in lollygagging around in bed anymore. So I got up, came down here and made myself a pot of tea. You know to this day I still make a pot, even though I'm by myself now. A cup would be plenty of course, but I just can't seem to break the habit. I keep meaning to, but then I find myself getting out the pot again.'

She trailed off, as if remembering something. Lars sat quietly, not wanting to rush her.

'Anyway, where were we? Yes, I had gotten up and made some tea, and then I brought it into the front room. I like sitting in there; you can see the street. Not that I'm in the habit of spying on people, mind you. But sometimes it's nice to sit and watch the world go by outside your window. Harold and I used to do that a lot after we both retired.'

She paused again.

'Well, not long after I'd sat down I saw Mr. Rowe heading off for work. He was store manager at the K-Mart up Orem way you know. He had to get up early most mornings to take deliveries. It was still dark and the street was quiet and I was just sitting there minding my own business when not five minutes after Mr. Rowe had left I saw this van pull up outside their house. It had some markings on the side but I couldn't make them out, least not at that point. Anyway the back door opens and two men climb out and head up the Rowe's driveway. Not rushing mind you, just as cool and calm as you like. Well at this point I think maybe it's a delivery or something, even though it's still early. But then they don't head for the front door, like you'd expect, they walk straight around the side and I lose sight of them. Well maybe half a minute later the van pulls off, turns at the end of the road here and then heads back out onto Victoria Street. I didn't see which way it went after that.'

Mrs. Mortimer stopped to take a sip of her tea.

'Anyway, later that morning I'm back in the front room having a rest after doing the shopping and I see a car pull up. This young man gets out of the driver's side and opens the back door and out gets Mrs. Rowe. She walks up her driveway and goes in her front door. A moment later the car pulls off, going down to the end of the street to turn, just like the van had that morning.'

'Do you remember what time that was?'

'Well, not exactly. But it would have been after I got back from my shopping but before I'd set about fixing myself some lunch. Probably eleven, or eleven-thirty, not much later.'

'And do you remember anything about the car?'

'Why yes, it was a grey Cadillac, a late model back then, if I'm not mistaken. I remember because Harold had bought Cadillacs for us all his life. He loved them. He'd been thinking of trading ours in for that very model and had come back from the dealer up in Provo with a stack of brochures, literally not a month before he died. I remember thinking that he would have liked the car that Mrs. Rowe had come back in. Just the color he would have chosen as well.'

She waited while Lars scribbled a few details in his notepad before indicating to her to continue.

'Well, I remember thinking that it was very unusual for Mrs. Rowe to be climbing out of a chauffeur-driven car. I didn't know it at the time but I read later in the *Tribune* – that's the *Salt Lake Tribune* by the way – that that was the car that the governor had booked to bring her back from the airfield out at Lehi. Anyway, I was just getting up to put something on for my lunch when I see the van from that morning pulling up in front of the Rowe's place again. But this time no-one gets out. So I watch it for a while. It's brighter now and I can read the writing on the side – it's the name of some television cable company. I remember thinking that Harold would have gotten a kick out of that. He'd been hoping for years that they were going to finally get around to installing cable in our street – he liked his TV programs you see. Anyway, a few minutes later two men come out the front door, carrying something between them, like a roll of carpet. They're dressed in overalls and they're wearing those baseball caps so don't ask me to describe what they looked like. They're not rushing, but not hanging around either if you know what I mean. As soon as they get to the back of the van the door opens and they push in whatever they're carrying and climb in after it. Then the doors close and the van pulls away again. And that was the last I saw of it.'

Lars had been taking notes as the old lady had talked. Now he put down the pen and looked across the table at her.

'Well, Sheriff, I expect you're wondering why I didn't call the police. I've asked myself the same question a lot these past thirty years, so I have an answer for you, of sorts. I should have been suspicious when I saw that van first thing that morning and those men going around the side of the Rowes' house. But it was dark, and I hadn't slept well, and as the morning wore on I began to doubt myself. I thought maybe my eyes had been playing tricks on me. Maybe the men hadn't gone around the side of the house after all. Maybe they had rung the front door bell first and I just hadn't seen it. Maybe they had come back out from the side of the house and climbed back into the van on the other side and I hadn't seen that either. Then the next day when I saw the piece in the *Tribune* about Mrs. Rowe helping

114

out that man, the nephew of the governor of Utah, well I just thought that maybe those men were there on his behalf. Like some sort of security detail, you know, checking out the place. I almost put the whole thing out of my mind. Then a few days later I hear that Mrs. Rowe has disappeared. Well that's when I should have come forward, I know that now. But truth be told I didn't want to get involved and I thought the police would just figure it out, with or without me putting in my two cents' worth. So I did nothing. And then a week or so later I read in the *Tribune* that they've picked up the driver of the car and they're charging him with Mrs. Rowe's murder on account of the blood they found on the back seat.'

'Only now I'm scared, you see. Because I know that the driver probably didn't do anything other than drive Mrs. Rowe home like he was supposed to. And those men that I saw going in to her house early that morning and then coming back out later on, well they almost certainly did have something to do with what happened to her. But if they can just walk into her house and … and do whatever they did to that poor woman and then just walk out, calm as you like, and drive off, and then later on make it look like it was all that driver's doing, well it made me wonder what they might do to me if I were to interfere. I have no-one Sheriff, not since my Harold died. They could come in here and kill me and it might be weeks before anyone would even think to notice I wasn't around.'

She paused to wipe her eyes with the back of her hand.

'Well, perhaps that might not be such a bad thing. I've told the children in my class year after year never to be afraid to do the right thing and here I am, the first real test I'm put to and I sit on my hands for thirty years while that poor man is locked up in jail.'

Lars reached across the table and put his hand on the old woman's.

'It'll be alright Mrs. Mortimer. The important thing is that you do the right thing now and come forward with what you know.'

He finished his tea. It was getting late and he had a long drive ahead of him if he were to make it back to Hawthorne that night. He stood up from the table, took a card from his wallet, flipped it over and scribbled his home telephone number on the back, handing it to her as they stood in the small hallway.

'There you go. The number of the sheriff's office is on the front and I've written my home number on the back, just in case. This is a matter for the FBI now, and I suspect you'll be hearing from them before too long. In the meantime though you feel free to call me any time of the day or night, even if you just want to talk.'

The old woman stood in her doorway watching him as he walked back across the street to where his cruiser was parked. By the time he had driven to the end of the street to turn around she had gone back inside.

17

ALISON WOKE TO the sound of her mother in the kitchen preparing breakfast, the smell of fresh coffee wafting up the stairs and into her room. She showered quickly, throwing on a pair of jeans and a t-shirt and headed downstairs. A stack of blueberry pancakes sat in the middle of the table beside an unopened jar of maple syrup and a glass of freshly squeezed orange juice. It had been her favorite growing up. Her mother smiled when she saw her, asking how she had slept.

She had slept surprisingly well. It had been a busy day, what with the excitement of the sheriff's visit and travelling back from the university, and she had been more tired than she had realized. The soft mattress and warm flannel sheets on the bed in her room had sent her to sleep as soon as her head had touched the pillow.

While her mother poured her a mug of coffee she mentioned that she planned to walk into Manchester to see whether she could find anywhere to fax a copy of the photograph of Jackson to the sheriff in Hawthorne.

'There's one of those new internet places just off Main Street, right next to the music shop.' To Violet Stone anything that had arrived in Manchester over the last ten years was by default new, especially if it had anything to do with technology. 'I suspect they might be able to help you.'

Alison went into the sitting room to get the picture frame from the sideboard, marveling again at the similarity between Jackson and Gant as she brought it back to the kitchen table. While she waited for her coffee to cool she turned the picture over. The frame had a wooden back that was held in place by simple swivel catches on the top and one of the side edges. A strip of brown masking tape had been placed all around the edge of the back section, over the catches, to hold it in place. She searched for the edge of the tape with her finger. Once she had found the edge and lifted it with a fingernail it came away easily, the adhesive long since dried out. The catches were a little stiff but using the knife her mother had left on the table for her pancakes she managed to turn each one sufficiently to allow the back of the frame to be lifted free. She lifted the photograph out, holding it by its edges between her fingers. She would never grow tired of looking at her father in this picture.

She turned it over to see whether there might be a date. Sure enough, in the top left hand corner in her father's neat handwriting were the words *January, 1971*. Beneath, in the center and slightly to the left of the photo her father had written *Garcia* and just to the right of that *Davids*. Holding the photo up to the light she could see that her father had written the names behind where the two men were seated in the cargo area of the Huey. To the far right of the reverse of the photograph, behind where Jackson was standing, her father had written *Cody*.

She called her mother.

'What is it dear?'

'Did Dad ever call Luke Jackson by another name?'

Her mother left the porridge she had been stirring on the stove, coming over to stand beside her.

'Why yes, yes I believe he did. Well you know in the air force a lot of the pilots had names they called each other. Sort of like nicknames. What did they call them? Call signs. That's it. Although I don't ever remember your father having one. Now let me see what was Jackson's? Cody. That was it.' She reached into her pocket for her reading glasses. 'Why see, it's written there on the back of that photo. Is that important?'

'I don't know.'

She stared at the photo again. It was as her mother said, it wasn't just that Jackson and Gant bore a resemblance to each other, they were identical. She sat at the table for a little while, lost in thought. After a few minutes she got up, her breakfast untouched. Grabbing her coat from the back of the chair, she carefully placed the photograph in the inside pocket. She told her mother she was going in to town and that she'd be back in an hour.

Main Street was busy with last minute Christmas shoppers and she threaded her way through the crowds. She found the internet café where her mother had said it would be, sandwiched between Hedley's Music Supplies and a small newsagent. The café had seen better days. The computers looked old, bulky beige CRT screens sitting on formica worktops that were chipped and stained from what looked like years of use. The place was empty. She guessed most people just didn't need to use places like this anymore. She went up to the counter, taking the photograph of Jackson with her father to the desk, and asked whether it could be scanned and sent to one of the machines. She could email it to the sheriff. A bored teenager gave her a password and directed her to a cubicle towards the back.

Alison logged on, the web browser bringing her to the Google homepage. As she waited for the scanned image of the photo to appear on the screen her mind wandered back to Gant and Jackson. There had to be some explanation why they looked so alike. The cursor blinked inside the search field, inviting her to enter something.

Her fingers hovered over the keyboard. She might as well occupy herself while she waited for the scanned photo to arrive.

A search for Carl Gant revealed nothing, but that wasn't surprising. It made sense that the Navy wouldn't want to have details of active members of one of its special forces units available on the internet.

Next she tried Jackson. There were several hits. According to the first article she read Chief Warrant Officer Luke Jackson was one of the longest serving pilots of the conflict, having been in Vietnam almost continuously from when the war had begun in '65 until his death six years later. He'd enlisted as 11B, infantry, later that year fighting with the massively outnumbered American forces at Ia Drang, the first major engagement between the US and the NVA in Vietnam. According to the article it was at Ia Drang that Jackson had witnessed first hand the role that helicopters were to play in armed conflict. Huey pilots had dropped his company at the base of Chu Pong mountain and had provided air support throughout the battle, re-supplying them with ammunition, evacuating the wounded, and finally, four days later lifting the survivors and the dead off the field. Jackson had applied to the Air Cav the week after. He had completed his infantry tour in April the following year, and had returned stateside to begin primary flight at Fort Wolters, Texas, four months later moving to Fort Rucker, Alabama to complete advanced flight and collect his silver wings. By Christmas of 1966 he had been back in Vietnam, where he had remained until his Huey had been shot down over Laos four years later. She checked each of the other links but there were no photos of Jackson.

Well, that hadn't got her very far. A file containing the scanned photo of Jackson with her father had appeared on the computer's desktop and she contemplated just sending it to the sheriff and logging off. But it occurred to her that there was one more search she should try.

She typed her search into the Google bar and hit 'Enter'. An instant later the screen filled with the first page of her search results, the search engine proudly indicating that it had found over thirty million results for the word *Cody* in only 0.26 seconds. She scrolled through the first ten results - a town in Park County, Wyoming, named after William Frederick Cody, aka Buffalo Bill; a recruitment firm in London, England; an airport serving the East Yellowstone region. There was nothing more relevant in the pages that followed.

She needed to narrow the search. What else did Gant and Jackson have in common? They were both in the military. She returned to the search box and typed *Cody Military OR Navy OR Air Force OR Army OR Marines*. Again it took only an instant for the search engine to return its results; this time it had found just over a million. She scrolled through the first page. Stats on someone who played college football for the Air Force Falcons; an Air Force recruitment center from that town in Wyoming. There were a number of hits on the second page for servicemen whose name was Cody – a Chief Master Sergeant James A. Cody stationed at Lackland Air Force Base in Texas, a Major General Richard N. Cody of the United States Air Force Defense Nuclear Agency in Washington, D.C. But it was immediately obvious from the pictures they had posted that neither had anything to do with Gant or Jackson. The next two pages returned nothing of relevance either, and she was about to give up. She decided to try one more page and then she would call it a day. She clicked the *Next* icon at the bottom of the page and the screen refreshed, the header telling her that she was viewing results 41-50. The first few results yielded nothing. Half way down the page was a link to a website that listed fighter aces of the Korean war, the summary section highlighting *Jason Mitchell*. She clicked on the link. It took a moment for the page to load and then she was looking at a table listing those F-86 pilots who had shot down five or more enemy aircraft. At the top of the table was Jason 'Cody' Mitchell, with thirteen confirmed kills. She clicked on his name and a second later the website directed her to a page dedicated just to him. At the top of the page was a black and white image of a pilot climbing into the cockpit of an old single-seater fighter jet, his helmet under one arm, the other holding the edge of the open canopy. His back was to the camera but he had turned his head around, as if to respond to whoever had taken the photo. His short dark hair was ruffled by the wind and there was a trace of a smile on his lips, as if he was sharing a joke with whoever was behind the camera.

She sat back in the plastic seat, staring at the screen, barely able to believe what she was seeing.

The man was identical to Gant and Jackson.

The website indicated that the photo was one of the few that were known to exist of Second Lieutenant Jason 'Cody' Mitchell. It had been taken in March 1953. Later that month Mitchell had been shot down over the Yalu River by the Russian fighter ace Colonel Yevgeny Grupolov. Mitchell's wingman had seen him eject but that far behind enemy lines there had been little hope of him evading capture, even if he had survived. He had been declared MIA – missing in action – and the air force had changed his status to KIA a few months later when he hadn't been among the prisoners of war returned as part of the armistice. His body had never been recovered.

Alison sent the link to her hotmail account and printed the page. A search of the name Jason Mitchell yielded a few sites referring to the exploits of the Korean fighter pilot, but none contained any information beyond that which she had found in the first site.

She sat back in her chair, staring at the screen. The resemblance Mitchell, Jackson and Gant bore to each other was incredible, more than could be explained by them sharing a common ancestor. Was it possible the military had been experimenting with reproductive cloning? The technology had existed for some time, although its use with human subjects was universally regarded as unethical and had been banned in most countries. She had to get this information to the sheriff to impress upon him the importance of finding this man.

She was about to compose an email when it occurred to her that she still didn't know why each of the men she had found called themselves Cody. The name had to mean something to them.

She started a new search, this time typing *Cody name origin OR meaning* into the field at the top of the page. Once again there were numerous results, but most just referred to the origins of the name: *Cuidighthigh* – an unpronounceable Gaelic surname from the thirteenth century meaning 'helpful person'. Which didn't help her at all.

But she had asked the wrong question, hadn't she? The meaning of the name wasn't what she needed to find out. It was the meaning of the name *to them*. A Google search was unlikely to provide her with that information. What could be so important about that name to these men?

It had to be some sort of unique identifier, something that tied each of the men together. But she had already searched the name – there were simply too many results to sift through and no guarantee there was even anything there to find. How else could she refine the search? What else did she know about them? When she had met Gant he had referred to enhanced human regenerative capacity. Each of them had spent their lives in the military. There was a good chance at least one of them had been injured at some point. It was just possible *that* had been noticed somewhere. She typed *Cody regen* OR recup* OR heal**, using the wild card to catch all derivatives of the root of each word. She was about to send the search and then it occurred to her: if Cody was indeed some form of identifier it might be short for something else. She moved the mouse, amended the first word so that the search now read *Cod* regen* OR recup* OR heal** and then hit Enter.

Again, thousands of results: North Atlantic fish supplies, computer gaming tips, pain medication. She scanned the summaries quickly, clicking to the second and then the third pages. Oh well, it had been a long shot – she hadn't really held much hope of finding anything. She was about to start composing her e-mail to Sheriff Henrikssen when she noticed an entry at the bottom of the page.

She recognized the website immediately. The Lancet was one of the world's oldest and most respected peer-reviewed medical journals – she had used its research on numerous occasions as a student. The result summary referred to an article, the engine highlighting only the searched words in the title: '…Regenerative Capacity…' and in a partial reference from the article to '…subject Codratus Doyle…'. She clicked the URL at the top of the search result, the link bringing her to the Past Issues section of the Lancet's website, to a volume from February 1942. The full title of the article was *Findings on the Regenerative Capacity of Human Spinal and Other Tissue* by a Doctor Jerome Bryant, M.D. Camb., F.R.C.S. of Lambeth Hospital, London. A .pdf of the article was available for download for subscribers or to anyone else on payment of a thirty-dollar fee. She was sure her department at Berkeley had a subscription but she didn't know the login ID or password. She reached into her purse for her credit card and typed in the details. A few moments later a grey box appeared in the middle of the screen, a green progress bar telling her the file was downloading. When it was done she clicked the button to open the document. Her eyes flicked down through the opening paragraphs, impatient to read whether the article had anything to do with Gant.

The article described how two men had been admitted to Lambeth Hospital on the night of 29th December, 1940. They had been found outside a burning building in the Brixton area of south London by an Air Raid Precautions warden who had come to investigate the blaze. Both had been in critical condition, suffering from severe head injuries, extensive burns and the effects of smoke inhalation. Attempts to revive the men, both by the ARP warden who had been first on the scene and by members of the Auxiliary Fire Service who had arrived subsequently, had failed. London had that night suffered the most devastating air raid of the war, incendiaries and high explosives dropped by the Luftwaffe causing a firestorm that had swept through the city, and it had taken some time for the emergency services to get the men to the hospital. By the time they had been admitted the older man had died from his injuries, never having regained consciousness. The younger man had been examined and was found to be alive, but only just. Given the extent of his injuries he hadn't been expected to survive the night. The article reported that he had been sent for X-rays but admitted that otherwise he hadn't been prioritized, most likely receiving little treatment that first night as the hospital struggled to cope with the scores of casualties that were being admitted each hour.

By morning the situation at the hospital had stabilized and attention had finally turned to the young man.

Bryant remarked that it was perhaps fortunate that the patient had still not regained consciousness - he had suffered second and third degree burns to most of his body and his lungs had been scorched from breathing the air in the building from which he had been pulled. But as serious as those injuries were, they were not what had concerned the doctor who examined him that morning. The X-rays taken during the night had shown that the man had suffered extreme trauma to his head and neck. His jaw had been broken and there was extensive damage to four of the seven cervical vertebrae. The delicate atlas and axis bones that connected the skull to the spinal column allowing movement of the head and neck had each been fractured in several places, Bryant describing particular damage to both pedicles of the C2, C3 and C4 vertebrae. The first intervertebral disk of the spinal column had been ruptured. The injuries, particularly to the C3 and C4 vertebrae, indicated that one or more of the cervical spinal nerves had almost certainly been compromised, the damage caused by the initial trauma almost certainly exacerbated by the manner of the patient's transport to the hospital. The initial prognosis had been grim. In the unlikely event that he were to recover from his burn injuries, which would in any event leave him horribly scarred, he would almost certainly no longer have the use of his arms or legs. Surgery was not an option. Even had the patient been in a condition to survive it, no techniques existed to repair the damage that he had sustained. The hospital records showed that the attending doctor had simply instructed the nurses to immobilize his head and neck to prevent further damage to the spine, to clean and dress the man's wounds and to make sure that, in the unlikely event he regained consciousness, he was made comfortable. Beyond that there was little that could be done for him.

Alison leaned backwards in the chair, stretching her shoulders, her lower back protesting against the rigid plastic. While the author was clearly familiar with the terse prose required for publication in such a distinguished medical journal she couldn't help but think that there was a hint of the theatrical in the way that Bryant described the man's condition. She had started by skimming the paragraphs but now she found herself leaning forward to read the words on the screen, transfixed by the plight of the young man almost seventy years before, keen to discover what had happened to him. She read on.

Doyle had not died. For the next week the nurses had tended to his wounds, dressing them with tulle gras or vaseline gauze. At this point Bryant noted that since the outbreak of the war it had been discovered that severe shock invariably accompanied an extensive burn, and its treatment was therefore an immediate priority. Nevertheless, in spite of the fact that the patient had suffered horrendous burns to almost two-thirds of his body, plasma had not been given, the author simply explaining that blood products had been in incredibly short supply and that the prognosis had been that the man wasn't expected to survive for very long.

Which was probably just as well, Alison thought. In 1940 the *hh* phenotype had still not been discovered. Assuming this man did indeed share a common physiology with Gant, he would have tested simply as having blood group O. If the hospital had given him what it would have assumed to be compatible blood or plasma while he had been in that state it would certainly have killed him.

After a week it had been noticed that there was a marked improvement in the man's burns. The charred, suppurating tissue that had covered much of his body when he had first been admitted had been replaced with

127

new skin, still fleshy pink and tender, but lacking any indication of either infection or the scarring that was to be expected following such extensive injuries. The attending doctor had asked for a fresh set of X-rays to be carried out to see whether there had been any similar improvement in the injuries he had sustained to his head and neck. The results had been no less amazing. The man's jaw and four damaged vertebrae were almost completely healed, the multiple fracture lines so evident on the earlier X-rays no longer visible, layers of compact bone already well formed around each of the break sites. The doctor had immediately brought the case to the attention of the author, the hospital's consultant orthopedic surgeon.

She could tell that Bryant was now moving into his area of expertise. The paragraphs that followed described in detail the physiological processes involved in the healing of fractures – the initial formation of hematoma and granulation tissue around the fracture site, the development of hyaline cartilage – gristle – and woven bone from the membrane of periosteal cells lining the outer surface of the bone and the eventual joining of these two new tissue types from both sides of the broken bone to form the fracture callus, an intermediate stage in the recovery process that restored some of the original strength to the fractured bone. The hyaline cartilage around the fracture itself would later become ossified and finally the outer layers of lamellar tissue would transform into compact bone, the denser, harder, stiffer substance that forms the outer shell of most bones, giving them their ultimate strength. Alison wasn't a specialist in orthopedic medicine but she had studied the process while at medical school and she scanned quickly through the next few paragraphs.

Bryant concluded his description of the healing of fractures by pointing out that the length of the process was dependent on a variety of factors including the extent of the injury, the angle of dislocation or fracture, the nature of the treatment received and obviously the general health of the patient. Under optimal conditions the author noted that a straightforward fracture of a cervical vertebra might be expected to heal in twelve weeks. And yet in this instance the patient had shown almost full recovery from a variety of extreme compound fractures, having received little treatment other than the cleaning and dressing of his burns, in little over a week.

The seemingly incredible powers of recuperation exhibited by the patient had prompted Bryant to re-examine the spinal cord injuries diagnosed when the man had originally been admitted. The article explained that it was of course possible for a person to break their neck and yet not sustain a spinal cord injury as long as only the vertebrae around the spinal cord, and not the cord itself, had been damaged. However the sheer extent of the injuries to the patient's cervical vertebrae, as evident from the initial X-rays, had led Bryant in this instance to agree with the initial diagnosis that quadriplegia – the loss of function in all four limbs – was inevitable. Only the fact that the patient hadn't experienced respiratory failure indicated that the spinal cord hadn't also been compromised above that level.

However, as the article now explained, an accurate assessment of damage to the spinal cord typically involved an examination of an alert, orientated patient with no distracting injury. As the man had yet to regain consciousness such an examination had thus far not been possible. Bryant had therefore prescribed a myelogram, an x-ray examination of the spinal canal using a contrast agent injected through a needle into the spinal column to allow the spinal cord, spinal canal, and nerve roots to show up.

Alison winced as the article described the contrast agent that had been used. She had read about this in medical school. Thorium dioxide had first been used in radiology as a contrast medium in the nineteen-thirties and had initially appeared ideal for the purpose of myelography. It wasn't until the 'sixties that it had been realized that the highly radioactive substance was an exceptionally effective neurotoxin. An unusually high incidence of malignancies involving the brain and spinal cord had been found among those who had been exposed to it.

The article reported that Bryant had performed the myelogram himself. The results had shown that, as expected, the patient's spinal cord had been completely severed at the C4 vertebra. Regardless of the exceptional recuperative powers the man had thus far shown, recovery from such a trauma was impossible. If he were ever to regain consciousness the surgeon had concluded that he would spend the remainder of his life without any motor or sensory function below the neck. The patient had been returned to a convalescent ward where he could be cared for while his wounds continued to heal.

A week or so after the myelogram the patient's bandages had been removed. His burns had healed completely, without any trace of scarring. Nevertheless the young man hadn't regained consciousness. For the next six months he had remained on the ward, fed through a tube, catheterized. A subsequent review of the nurses' reports indicated that other than the occasional bed bath he had required little care, seemingly unaffected by the typical problems – circulatory issues, bed sores – that afflicted those who remained immobile for protracted periods.

Then in July of 1941, with no apparent warning, the patient had woken up. The nurses' report indicated that he had been agitated and confused. Showing little sign of the muscle atrophication that would be typical following such a prolonged period of inactivity, let alone any evidence of the debilitating spinal injuries that he had suffered, he had resisted the efforts of a hospital orderly to restrain him and had promptly discharged himself. A report was subsequently filed with the Metropolitan Police, through which the author had finally learned the man's name. The article went on to describe a number of attempts Bryant had personally made to track the man down, but all to no avail. As at the date of publication of the article – she checked the first page of the article again: February 1942 – Codratus Doyle hadn't returned to the hospital.

The article concluded with the author offering some theories as to the subject's apparently exceptional recuperative abilities but most of what followed was conjecture. For whatever reason, possibly because it wasn't his specialty, Bryant hadn't really focused on Doyle's burn injuries. There had been no analysis of blood, no tissue samples taken. The speed with which his fractures had healed had engaged him for a while but even that had apparently not prompted him to explore further once the supposedly irreversible injuries to the spinal cord had been revealed by the myelogram. Doyle had spent six months in a corner of a hospital ward, largely forgotten about other than by the nurses who would have been tasked with bathing him and changing his bedding. All the time his body had been repairing itself, regenerating spinal tissue in a way that even now, seventy years later, was regarded by medical science as utterly impossible. By the time the true extent of his regenerative capacity had become clear it had been too late. Doyle had fled, the only evidence of his remarkable abilities his dramatic departure, the opportunity to study him lost.

Alison sat back in her chair, suddenly realizing that she was angry with Jerome Bryant. To think what could have been learned if he had just read the signs, if he had realized the potential that the man had presented before it was too late. With that knowledge, and another seventy years to develop it, who knows what could have been achieved for her father?

She forced herself to return to the problem at hand. She felt sure now that Codratus Doyle was in some way linked to Mitchell, Jackson and Gant. But she had no proof – the article hadn't contained a photograph of the man that she could compare. She noticed for the first time that it was turning dark outside. She checked her watch. It was already almost four o'clock. She had spent most of the afternoon in the internet café; she should really finish up and get back to her mother. She sent the article to her hotmail account. She was about to begin composing an email to the sheriff when she realized there was one more search she should perform. Returning to the search page she typed *Codratus Doyle* into the text field and hit Enter.

This time there were only nine results. The first two were for the article she had just read. The third referred to a Catholic saint who had been abandoned as a child and had some power over wild beasts, the next two hits variations of the same nonsense. She clicked on the sixth entry, which took her to a website *www.victoriacross.co.uk*. The site contained details of all recipients of the Victoria Cross, which the homepage explained was the highest military decoration awarded for valor in the face of the enemy to members of the British armed forces. She clicked the site index. Following a link to a list of all the holders of the medal, she scrolled down to the following entry:

DOYLE, Codratus (reg No. 584).

Trooper, 1 Special Air Service
Gazetted on 17th August, 1944
Born 10 March, 1920 at Stockwell,
South London
Enlisted 17 July 1941
Died 6th June 1944, Normandy
France.
Memorial not known
Digest of Citation reads:
On the night of 5th June 1944 SAS
Trooper Doyle with SAS Trooper
Graeme Lyons were parachuted behind
enemy lines in Normandy, France as
part of Operation Titanic, a mission to
divert the enemy's attention from the
Allied landings the following morning.
Having completed their mission both
men made their way to the site of the
landings where SAS Trooper Doyle
single-handedly attacked a German
machine gun position which was firing
on Allied forces attempting to establish
a beachhead, displaying the utmost
gallantry. He perished shortly
afterwards while attempting to cross a
mined area on the same beach. It was
through his heroism and resource that
the beach was secured and that Allied
casualties were not heavier.
Additional information: VC awarded
posthumously. No known next of kin.

Beneath the entry was a black and white photograph
showing two men, both in uniform, standing side by side
outside a wooden barracks. The text beneath the image
explained that the photograph had been taken while the

men were undergoing Commando training at Achnacarry Castle in the Western Highlands of Scotland in 1941. According to the photograph the man on the right was Graeme 'Jock' Lyons.

The man on the left was Gant.

Alison stared at the screen. She was still unsure what this meant, but she no longer harbored even the slightest doubt that the resemblance between the men was more than coincidental. Had Doyle provided the DNA for Mitchell, Jackson and Gant? His name pointed to him as the source, but with what she knew all she could do was hypothesize. The important thing now was to let the sheriff know what she had discovered.

She copied the link to the Victoria Cross website from the browser's address bar and opened her hotmail account to begin an email to the sheriff. She kept the mail short, simply copying the information she had found in chronological order, starting with the article from The Lancet. She would explain everything when she called him. When she was done she attached the file containing the scanned photo of her father with Jackson, pressing 'Send' before she had a chance to rethink what she was doing. She reached in her pocket for her cell phone, searching her recent calls for the number of the sheriff's office in Hawthorne.

The same woman she had spoken with from the airport the day before answered, and again she was put straight through. It occurred to her for an instant that if the sheriff had not believed her before when she had told him that she had met Gant, what she was about to tell him now would sound truly incredible. She put the thought from her mind. She had more than enough evidence to establish a connection between Gant, Mitchell, Jackson and Doyle. The line clicked open, the now familiar sound of Henrikssen's voice on the other end of the line.

'Sheriff, I believe I've found some more information about Carl Gant that you should have. Before I start to explain, can you check your inbox for an e-mail I've just sent you?'

She waited while Henrikssen logged on to his machine. After what seemed like an eternity the sheriff announced he had found her e-mail.

'Good. Okay. Now I realize what I'm about to tell you will sound far-fetched, but please bear with me. The e-mail I've sent contains the sources for everything I've found. All the information is available to anyone who cares to look for it. You can check it all out after the call.'

Alison hesitated for a moment. Where should she begin? With her father and the photograph that had sat on the sideboard at her parents' house for decades, or with the article from The Lancet? She took a deep breath.

'Sheriff, I believe there is something very unusual about Carl Gant. I don't know quite what this means yet but I've found a connection between Gant and three other men – Codratus Doyle, Jason Mitchell and Luke Jackson.'

Henrikssen said nothing, waiting for her to continue.

'The article I've attached to the e-mail is from a medical journal called the Lancet. The article was written by an orthopedic surgeon in a London hospital describing how in 1940 during a German air raid Doyle was admitted with horrific injuries – a broken neck, second and third degree burns to most of his body - injuries that even today he couldn't hope to recover from. Somehow Doyle managed to heal completely.'

Now Henrikssen spoke. Clearly he had been skimming the article while she had been speaking.

'Okay Doctor, so why do you think this guy's got anything to do with Gant? Other than the fact that Gant approached you about a similar topic what's to connect him to this Doyle? I don't see a picture of him in the article.'

'No Sheriff, there isn't one. However, if you click on the first link in the e-mail I've sent you there's a picture of a Codratus Doyle who enlisted in the British Army in July 1941. That's the same month that the Codratus Doyle from the Lancet article discharged himself from the hospital where he had been treated. The dates of birth match, and the name can't be that common.'

'This guy's certainly the image of Gant. They must be related.'

'That was what I thought at first, but I think it's more than that. Take a look at the next link.' She waited while Henrikssen opened the page describing Jason Mitchell's exploits as a fighter pilot in Korea, giving him time to examine the picture of Mitchell.

'This guy's name was Jason *Cody* Mitchell?'

'Yes. I think it's short for Codratus. It was a search for the name Cody that led me to what I've found. Why?'

'Well, the commander at Fallon said that Cody is what everyone calls Gant on the base. But that wasn't in any of the files I gave you. I know because I checked myself. How did you know to search for it?'

She asked the sheriff to open the scanned image of her father with Luke Jackson.

'So how'd you find this photo?'

'Well, that's the strange thing Sheriff. It's been sitting on a sideboard in my parents' house for as long as I can remember. The man in the photo who looks like Gant is Luke Jackson. He was also known as Cody. The man to the right of Jackson in the photo is – was – my father. He and Jackson served a tour together in Vietnam in 1971, although Jackson had been out there since 1965. It's actually this photograph that caused me to start digging into Gant's past. I knew Gant was familiar to me from somewhere, but couldn't quite put my finger on it. I showed my mother a picture of him last night when I got home and she recognized him immediately.'

There was a pause at the other end of the line before Henrikssen spoke.

'So your father was with Air Cav, huh?'

'He was. Were you out there as well?'

'Yes, in '70, the year before your father. I was just a grunt, though. Only nineteen at the time, counting the days 'till it would be over and I could get home. Turned out that was sooner than I was expecting. I took a bullet seven months into my tour, somewhere up in the highlands northwest of Khe Sanh. It's what gave me this bum leg. Air Cav lifted me out and three weeks later I was back in Nevada. So have you tried to find out whether Jackson might still be alive?'

Alison told the sheriff what had happened to Jackson and how it had affected her father.

'It doesn't surprise me. It was a strange time, over there. You could form a bond, a trust, with a group of men over the course of a few days that might take you half a lifetime to achieve otherwise.'

His voice trailed off, as if remembering.

'Anyway Doctor, it looks like we both have a reason to find this Gant. I've made an appointment to meet with the base commander at Fallon right after Christmas. I don't suppose you'd be interested in heading up there with me? I'll be honest and say I don't know what to make of what you've dug up here. But there certainly is something unusual about him, something that might make it worth the effort to try and have him kidnapped. And I reckon you'll have a better shot at working out what that reason is than me.'

Alison agreed to meet Henrikssen in Fallon the day after Christmas Day. After he hung up she went back online, cancelled her return flight and booked a one-way ticket to Carson City. Her mother would be disappointed that she was cutting her visit short, but she would make it up to her. Despite the sheriff's skepticism she was convinced of the connection between Gant and Codratus Doyle. And if Gant possessed similar regenerative powers to Doyle he would be the most important medical find of the century. No, of any century.

She only hoped that whoever had tried to abduct him once already hadn't figured out what she had.

18

LARS SAT ALONE in his office, staring at the three printouts from NCIC. The email from Alison he had printed off sat next to them on his desk. Connie had left for the evening and it was quiet.

A serial killer abducting people who possessed a rare blood type for their organs. A man overpowering a security guard and checking himself out of Mount Grant just hours after having been shot and written off for dead. And now everything he had learned from the young doctor from Berkeley. Just what in the hell was he mixed up in?

Well, first things first. He needed to do something about Joseph Brandt. What Emily Mortimer had seen should be enough to re-open the man's case. He picked up the phone and dialed the number for the FBI agent who had led both the Rowe and the Taft cases. Lars saw that Lawrence DeWitty had done well for himself - he was now the Special Agent in Charge of the FBI's operations in Salt Lake City. The phone was answered on the second ring.

'DeWitty.'

'Special Agent DeWitty, my name is Lars Henrikssen. I'm sheriff of the town of Hawthorne, Nevada.'

'How can I help you, Sheriff?'

DeWitty sounded distracted, his thoughts elsewhere.

For the next ten minutes Lars proceeded to outline the events that had taken place in Hawthorne over the previous week, his description punctuated by the sound of papers being shuffled, the clatter of keys as something was typed on a computer, an occasional murmur of acknowledgment to indicate that the FBI agent was still listening. But as he began to describe how Carl Gant's blood type had led him to Shilpa Desai, Cindy Rowe and Robin Taft, Lars noticed that DeWitty had stopped whatever he was doing on the other end of the phone. By the time he got to his interview with Joseph Brandt and what the old woman had told him about the things she had seen the day Cindy Rowe had gone missing, Lars was certain he had the man's full attention. When he was finished there was a long pause before the FBI agent said anything.

'Well Sheriff Henrikssen, looks like you've been busy. I guess the homicide at Mount Grant just wasn't enough to keep you occupied. Operating a little outside your patch though, wouldn't you say? Last time I checked the Utah State Penitentiary didn't fall within the jurisdiction of the Mineral County sheriff's office.'

DeWitty didn't wait for a response before continuing.

'So let me get this straight, Sheriff. You've got two armed terrorists on the loose, one of whom escaped from your custody. Another in the morgue. Your town's in danger of losing its livelihood. But instead of attending to these important matters you've busied yourself by looking into a forty-year old missing persons case from Massachusetts, by attempting to re-open a murder case that was actually *solved* thirty years ago, and by carrying out unauthorized interviews with a convicted murderer and a woman who claims to have withheld material evidence in a murder case for three decades. And have you got anything to show for all this? Are you even any closer to finding any of these people - the girl, the schoolteacher, Robin Taft? Sure doesn't look like it. But yet based on the confused ramblings of a – by your own account – mentally ill convicted murderer and an elderly woman who thirty years ago witnessed a cable repair van parked suspiciously opposite her house, you want me to do what? Re-open the case of a man who was convicted on the basis of sound forensic evidence and tell a retired United States congressman that his nephew has been abducted by an organ-collecting serial killer you believe has escaped the Bureau's attention for the last forty years? You don't think that maybe you're getting a bit carried away, Sheriff? Do you think it might be time to let the professionals handle this.'

Lars said nothing for a long moment.

'Perhaps you're right, Special Agent DeWitty, perhaps you're right. When you put it like that it does sound like I've been on a bit of a wild goose chase. Maybe I should just let you fellas take it from here.'

'I'm sure that'd be for the best, Sheriff. Why don't you just send me over the details of that old lady who claims she saw the Rowe woman being abducted and we'll handle it? Nothing more for you to worry about. Now what'd you say her name was again?'

Lars hesitated for a second.

'Radcliffe. Ethel Radcliffe.'

'And you say she lives opposite where the Rowe woman used to live?'

'No, no. Used to live there. Moved years ago. She's in an old folks' home up by Spanish Fork these days. I don't have the address to hand right now.'

'But you'll send it on to me?'

'Sure.'

Lars pretended to take DeWitty's e-mail address, then he put down the phone. He didn't know why he hadn't mentioned Emily Mortimer's name to the FBI agent when he had first told him what he had discovered, but now he was glad he hadn't.

An organ-collecting serial killer.

He'd only come up with that possibility two days ago.

And he hadn't mentioned it to anyone.

19

CAPTAIN JOHN JAMES Fitzpatrick sat behind his desk, his face impassive. He had listened without interruption as the sheriff had summarized the events of the last few days, beginning with the van that had crashed into Mount Grant and Gant's admission to and subsequent escape from the hospital, ending with his visit to the Utah State Penitentiary and the telephone call he had had with the FBI agent the day before.

On the drive up from Carson City that morning Lars had filled Alison in on the other persons with the *hh* blood type who had gone missing. Alison wasn't sure how this new piece of information fit with her theory about Gant. The last recorded disappearance of a person with the *hh* blood group had been almost thirty years before. It was possible that it was just a coincidence, although knowing what she did about how rare the blood group was it was hard to ignore four such individuals having gone missing, even over such a long period. She would need to think about it more. Was it possible that Gant had been targeted just because of his blood group, that his abductors knew nothing of the other extraordinary abilities she believed he possessed?

She had paid particular attention to the base commander as Henrikssen had described her theory about Gant's connection with Codratus Doyle, Jason Mitchell and Luke Jackson. They were likely to need Fitzpatrick's assistance if they wanted to locate Gant and it was imperative that he understand how important Gant was. But the man had been impossible to read. She hadn't realized that the sheriff would forward her email and now she wished she had taken the time to compose a more compelling argument for the connection between the men. Otherwise though she had to admit that the sheriff had provided an accurate synopsis of what she had uncovered, showing neither support for her conclusions nor the skepticism she knew he felt. She forced herself to remain silent while he finished speaking.

Fitzpatrick looked at both of them for some time. When he finally spoke it was Alison he addressed.

'So, Doctor Stone, your father was in the Air Force?'

'Yes. He served a single tour in Vietnam in 1971.'

Fitzpatrick was quiet again for a moment.

'I've served with the Navy for almost thirty years, most of my career as a naval aviator like your father. Last operational experience was flying Combat Search and Rescue in the early days of the first Iraq war. After that they promoted me and gave me a desk job with the Office of the Secretary of Defense at the Pentagon. Spent nine months there – more than long enough to realize that I had no interest in being a career naval officer if that was what it meant. When I threatened to resign they sent me here.'

He paused before continuing.

'I hated every minute of my time in Washington, but if there was one good thing to come out of it, it was that it made me extraordinarily good at identifying when someone was bullshitting me. So, Doctor Stone, I guess you realize how incredible this theory of yours sounds?'

Alison started to say something to try and convince him, but he held his hand up to stop her.

'Just let me finish, Doctor. I must admit I was more than a little skeptical at first, like I see the sheriff here still is. But your email prompted me to do a little checking myself. Anyway, before I tell you what I've learned I'm going to ask both of you to promise me you'll exercise some discretion in dealing with Cody if you find him. Now, Sheriff you needn't look so worried. I'm aware people have been killed and I'm not asking you to compromise any part of your investigation in so far as it relates to any of that. If Cody's guilty of something in this whole sorry mess then so be it, you do what you need to to bring him to justice. I'd be prepared to bet dollars to donuts that he just got dragged into what happened at Mount Grant and I suspect that's the conclusion you're coming to as well, if you're not there already. But now he's in trouble, and it looks like you people are ahead of the game in trying to sort this out, so I'll help you if I can. All I'm asking is that if you do find him you listen to why he's decided he doesn't want to be found, and if he decides he wants it to remain that way, well then you respect that. Do we have an agreement?'

They both nodded.

'Good.'

Fitzpatrick opened a drawer and took out a thin file, sliding it across the desk. As Alison leaned forward to examine the file's contents he continued.

'Since the early 'nineties the military has contracted out the maintenance of its personnel records to the private sector, to a corporation called DataCore. The DataCore system holds complete records for all currently serving members of the armed forces, as well as archive files for most retired servicemen back to the First World War. That file you have in front of you contains the Army records for Jason Mitchell. There's a photo of him on the second page.'

Alison had already flipped to the photo of Mitchell. She looked puzzled.

'But that's not Doyle. Are you sure this is the same Jason Mitchell? It must be a fairly common name. There had to have been more than one serving at the time.'

'Yes, there were several. I checked them all. None looked anything like Cody. Now bear with me Doctor, this *is* the man we're looking for. Born Grinnell, Iowa 1925, youngest of three brothers. Parents died while the boys were still in school. Raised by the local orphanage. All three brothers enlisted the week after Pearl Harbor and all three were shipped to England to prepare for the Normandy landings. Jason Mitchell took part in the amphibious assault on D-Day; he would have been among the first men on the beach that morning. Neither of his brothers even made it as far as the shore. The landing craft Jason Mitchell was in was also hit and most of the men drowned. I checked the records for the others in his platoon. Of the few that managed to get ashore only Mitchell survived; the rest were cut down by machine gun fire before they'd even got out of the water. Mitchell made it onto the beach only to step on a land mine. He was evacuated to a hospital ship. I pulled his medical records. There's not a lot of detail; I guess the surgeons had better things to do that day than to write up case notes. But his file shows that Mitchell was unconscious when he was brought in and had to be ID'd from dog tags they found laced into his boots. His injuries were such that he wasn't expected to survive.'

Alison was busy flicking through the information she had printed out in the internet cafe in Manchester. When she found what she had been looking for she stopped, looking up at Fitzpatrick.

'Doyle was on that beach that morning. According to the citation for his Victoria Cross it was where he was killed.'

'Yes he was. At first I thought that was probably just a coincidence. Tens of thousands of troops were landed on only a handful of beaches that day. But then I read a little more of Mitchell's file. Turns out he recovered fully from his injuries. He was shipped back to the States and stayed with the Army until he was demobilized in 1946. Then in 1950 war broke out in Korea and he re-enlisted, this time as a candidate aviator. A copy of his air force records are in the file. The service numbers show it's the same Jason Mitchell from Iowa that landed in Normandy in 1944 but take a look at the photograph.'

'It's Doyle.'

'Yes. My guess is that Doyle came across Mitchell on Omaha that morning and for some reason assumed his identity.'

Alison felt an idea beginning to form. The British Army had thought Doyle had died in 1944, but they had been mistaken. And neither Mitchell nor Luke Jackson had ever been confirmed killed.

The dates.

Gant had come to her about regenerative capacity.

But if she was right it would mean...

It was preposterous, wasn't it?

When she had met him she had thought Gant was one of her students, a freshman, nineteen, maybe twenty years old at most. How old was he actually? She realized she didn't know. The answer would be in his Navy medical records. She could just ask Fitzpatrick but for now the idea was still too absurd to voice aloud. Instead she pulled the copy of the file Henrikssen had given her from her bag and began flicking through it. There it was, at the top of the second page:

Carl Austin Gant – D.O.B. 8/7/1978

That made him thirty-six. She hadn't focused on that until now, she had been pre-occupied with his recuperative abilities. She supposed it was possible he just looked very young for his age. There were thirty-year-olds who could pass for twenty, certainly, at least from a distance, or in a photograph. But she had met Gant, had seen him close up. He wouldn't just *pass* for someone who was twenty. He looked like he couldn't have been much older. Except...except hadn't she thought that there was something about him that *had* seemed older?

Was it possible no-one had noticed? Gant had been stationed at Fallon for almost a decade. People often didn't notice small changes in others, the almost imperceptible signs of ageing, when they saw them day after day. Would they be any more likely to notice the absence of those signs? Probably not after only a few years. Given long enough, certainly. No forty-year old could pass for someone twenty years younger close up, regardless of the care they had taken of themselves or how lucky they had been with their genetic make-up. If a person really wasn't ageing and they didn't want others to know about it, sooner or later they'd need to move on, to start afresh somewhere new.

Was *that* why Gant hadn't returned to the base as soon as he had escaped from the hospital?

Jesus. Could it really be that Doyle, Mitchell, Jackson and Gant were the same person? Doyle had assumed Mitchell's identity in 1944 and had maintained in until 1953. Had the same man resurfaced as Luke Jackson in Vietnam twelve years later, and as Carl Gant twenty-six years after that?

If it was true it was incredible. Gant would be almost a hundred years old. What could it be about his genetic makeup that prevented him from ageing, at least not in the conventional sense? He must have been younger at some point. Either he was continually ageing, just very slowly, or he had stopped getting older when he had reached his current age.

She was quiet for a while. If she was correct there might be some record of what he had been doing in the twenty-three years between stepping off that helicopter in Laos and when his records with the Navy as Carl Gant had begun again in 1997. Something that might help prove her theory.

'Did you search for other examples of men like Gant?'

'I did consider that. Given the number of personnel who have served in the armed forces over that period there was just no way to check their photos. I thought his blood type might be connected to it somehow. I went back to '95, when tests for *hh* first began, but there was no-one that resembled Cody.'

Alison paused, considering how to frame her next question.

'Captain, do you remember anything unusual about Cody during his time at Fallon? Anything that at the time seemed out of place, hard to explain?'

The commander stared hard at her for a long moment.

'Just where are you going with this Doctor Stone?'

She hesitated, afraid that if she simply blurted out her idea it would seem ridiculous. In the end it was Lars who answered for her.

'Doctor Stone here thinks Gant *is* Doyle, Mitchell and Jackson, don't you Doctor?'

Alison looked over at the sheriff, surprised that he had reached the same conclusion as her so quickly.

'Well if you buy into all this other stuff about Gant it's not as crazy as it first seems. If we're prepared to accept that he has all these super cells that allow him to heal like he seems able to, is it that much more of a stretch to suppose that he might also not age like the rest of us?'

Alison was unsure what else to say. She couldn't have thought of a better way to express it than the sheriff just had. Fitzpatrick looked from her to Lars and back again, as if they had both taken leave of their senses. When neither showed any signs of recanting he finally returned to the question.

'Well, there is one thing that's always bothered me. Cody's an instructor with the Combat Search and Rescue program the SEALs run here. Because of his experience he's often operational. A few years back he was part of a unit that was sent in to rescue a recon team that'd found itself in trouble. Anyway, things didn't go well and by the time Cody's team gets to the extraction point the place is crawling with hostiles. The helicopter that's supposed to be dropping the SEALs gets shot up pretty bad and both pilots were hit, one of them killed. Anyway the SEALs manage to get most of the recon boys on board in one piece and then Cody flies the helicopter back. He told me afterwards that the other pilot, the one who hadn't been killed, had just told him what to do. But I knew that wasn't the case. The pilot was unconscious when they brought him in.'

'Jackson was a helicopter pilot. Would that explain it?'

'Well it might, Doctor Stone, but I doubt it. I saw the helicopter they flew back in. I have over three thousand hours in Hueys and I wouldn't have attempted to fly one of *those* back shot to shit the way she was, let alone a bird like the 'Hawk. I talked to a couple of other pilots afterwards and they said the same thing. No way someone without a lot of time in that particular helicopter would have even tried to bring her home.'

'So can you search Datacore for pilots who might have had that experience?'

Fitzpatrick turned to face the computer on his desk, shaking the mouse to banish the screensaver. He moved the cursor, clicking the button to launch the Datacore application, pulling his chair closer to the keyboard to type in his password. After a moment the search page filled the monitor's screen. Fitzpatrick had clearly never learned to touch type, and his gaze flitted from keyboard to screen as his index and middle fingers hesitantly worked the keys. Alison felt like reaching across the desk and wrestling the keyboard from him, but she forced herself to be patient.

'Well, now, the Pave Hawk they were flying that day was a modified version of the Black Hawk, so I'll look for someone with time in either of those helicopters. The 'Hawk was introduced in the late 'seventies, so I'll set the search to start then.'

Alison realized she was leaning forward in her seat.

'You can also narrow the search by blood type. The *hh* group would have shown up as O negative before it was tested for specifically.'

Fitzpatrick added her suggestion, punching the 'Enter' key when he had finished typing. It took a few seconds for the program to compile the results and then the screen filled with the names, ranks and units of scores of pilots. He moved the mouse and clicked a box near the top of the display to show photographs of each, angling the monitor so that Alison and Lars could see. It took a couple of minutes to scroll through the twenty or so pages of results. Not one of the men resembled Gant.

Fitzpatrick stared at the screen.

'Well, Doctor, that's everyone who flew a variant of that helicopter for the Navy over the last thirty years. No sign of Cody among them.'

Alison's heart sank. She had been sure they would find him. She thought the commander also seemed disappointed not to have found what they were looking for.

'Why just Navy? Your man certainly likes the military, but he doesn't seem to care to limit himself to any one branch of it. Doyle was British Army, Mitchell was Air Force and Jackson was U.S. Army.'

Alison turned to look at the sheriff. Of course he was right. Fitzpatrick was already amending his search; as soon as he was done he tapped 'Enter' again. It seemed to take longer this time for the program to produce results. Alison realized she was holding her breath. Once again the screen filled with lists of names, ranks, units, many more this time. Fitzpatrick clicked the mouse to bring up thumbnails of service photos and immediately began scrolling through them. This time Alison noticed that the sheriff was also leaning forward to examine the screen on the commander's desk.

It was Alison who saw him first, her finger flying to the screen.

'There!'

Fitzpatrick leaned back in his chair, staring at the monitor.

'Well I'll be damned.'

Fitzpatrick moved the mouse, clicking on the thumbnail. The image enlarged to fill the top left corner of the screen. There could be no mistake. It was Gant. Fitzpatrick was reading aloud from details of the man's service record that now filled the remainder of the screen.

'Chief Warrant Officer Paul Kyle. Served with the Nightstalkers. That's the Army's Special Operations Aviation Regiment. Joined in '83, shortly after the unit was formed. With them for ten years until he was shot down over Mogadishu. They found Kyle's tags in the wreckage of the helicopter but his body was never recovered.'

Fitzpatrick sat back in his chair, still looking at the screen. There was silence in the office. It was Henrikssen who spoke first.

'Do you have any thoughts on how we might find your man, commander? I think we have to assume by now that he's not coming back to the base and unfortunately it seems like he's had quite a bit of practice making himself disappear.'

This time it was Alison who spoke.

'I think I might have an idea.'

20

HE WAS GLAD to finally leave the motel. His side still hurt a little but the wound was almost healed and he was well enough to travel. He kept the jacket he had taken from the security guard buttoned up as he walked into town. He had washed the shirt he had taken from the man in the small washbasin but the bloodstains, though faded, were still evident.

He found the Carson City Bus Depot, a drab, squat building opposite a low-rise mall, and paid forty dollars for a ticket to Ely. It was almost three hundred miles and the trip would take most of the day. He had an hour to kill before the bus departed and he crossed the street, going into an internet café. Choosing a booth near the back he logged on, first checking to see whether any of the news services were still running the story. Thankfully there was little coverage. Only KHNV were still carrying it, but even they seemed to have relegated its importance. Only a few short paragraphs had been dedicated and they focused mainly on the implications for the town's arms depot following the incident at Mount Grant, mentioning only in passing that two men were still being sought by the authorities. He checked the watch he had taken from the security guard at the hospital. Still twenty-five minutes before his bus left.

He had decided in the motel room not to check the base website for news of his disappearance. There was little point. He could never return and any messages from the people who had known him at Fallon were only likely to make the next step that much harder. It was always difficult to walk away, to leave behind the men he had served with, that he had fought alongside, knowing that if by some random chance he were ever to meet them again he would need to ignore them, to turn away, if challenged to deny any knowledge of their existence. Sometimes the urge to check up on people, on lives he had left behind, was almost too much to bear. A number of years back he had almost succumbed, riding his bike across country to an air force base in Alabama. He had read that Rudy would be there and had wanted to see the man, if only from a distance. It had been the last time he had allowed himself to entertain such thoughts. There was only pain when you looked back.

But now that he was sitting in front of the screen, the keyboard beneath his fingertips, he found the urge to check on his old life one last time almost irresistible. After hesitating a moment longer he typed in the address for CNIC – the Navy's Installations Command website, navigating to the 'Region Southwest' section of the site and selecting 'NAS Fallon' and then the 'Newsroom' tab. Under 'Recent News' there was a single entry, from two days before, under the heading 'Master Chief Carl Gant'. The entry was from the base commander, Captain John James Fitzpatrick, asking all service personnel at Fallon to pray for the safe return of the CSAR instructor who had been missing from the base since before Christmas. His eyes were drawn to the final sentence of the short paragraph:

Our thoughts are with the Master Chief and his partner, Alison Berkeley, at this difficult time.

What did that mean? He went over to the commander's quarters most Sundays for dinner and each week without fail Carla quizzed him about his personal life. Fitzpatrick knew that he wasn't seeing anyone, let alone someone called Alison Berkeley. Fitzpatrick must have hoped that he would check the website and was trying to send him a message. He read the paragraph again, in case there was another clue he had missed, but there wasn't. The only thing that stood out was the reference to this woman.

Alison Berkeley. He didn't know an Alison Berkeley. Could Fitzpatrick have been mistaken? Had he inadvertently sent him the wrong message? It was unlikely. He had left only this single piece of information – he would have chosen it carefully. The commander would know that he had been in the back of the van that had crashed into Mount Grant hospital. Hopefully he wouldn't believe he had any involvement in whatever the other men in the van had been up to, that he had been there against his will. If Fitzpatrick had figured that much out he would have realized that the base was probably under surveillance. The message was deliberately cryptic.

Alison Berkeley. The only Alison he had met recently had been that doctor at University of California. At Berkeley. That had to be what Fitzpatrick meant. But how did he know about her? He had told no one on the base that he had been to see her.

He checked his watch. The bus was leaving in five minutes. He logged off, paid the woman behind the counter for the use of the computer with the few dollars he had left, and walked back across the street to where his bus was now waiting. He climbed aboard, showing his ticket to the driver. The bus was almost empty, and he headed towards the back. As he settled into his seat he heard the soft hiss as the door closed. The bus pulled slowly away from the depot.

He stared out the window as they left Carson City, heading towards Dayton and Silver Springs beyond. Fitzpatrick must have meant Alison Stone. It was the only conclusion that even came close to making sense. He decided to put aside for now how that had come about; it was unlikely he was going to figure it out by himself. The question was whether he should attempt to get in touch with her. He trusted Fitzpatrick not to knowingly place him in danger, but there could well be factors that the commander hadn't considered. He had to assume that the base was still being watched, which would certainly include the website. The message was already two days old and it would be at least another day before he could get to Berkeley, assuming he chose to go at all. He had only met Alison Stone that one time, three months earlier, and had told her nothing about himself that should have allowed her to connect him with Fallon.

But clearly somehow that connection had been made, and now it seemed that Fitzpatrick was in contact with her. Was it possible that whoever was looking for him would figure out his cryptic instruction as well? It didn't seem likely but he clearly didn't have enough information to be sure. Perhaps it would be better if he just picked up his money and left it all behind.

He shifted in his seat, trying to take the pressure off his side. Well, he had some time to make up his mind. It would be five hours before the bus reached Ely and there wasn't much he could do until then.

21

AXL FRIEDRICHS LEFT Las Vegas before dawn, driving west through Red Rock Canyon. Twenty minutes later as the highway curved north he slowed. It had been several years since he had last been out here and the turnoff was easy to miss in the half-light. When he was certain he had found it he pulled on to the hard shoulder. With the growth in commuter traffic from Pahrump Route 160 had become busy. It was unlikely that anyone would follow him, but his training made him cautious, and this morning he did not wish to be seen. He sat for ten minutes, smoking a cigarette in the darkness, checking the Defender's large mirrors for traffic. When he was satisfied that the road was empty in both directions he switched off the headlights and turned off the highway, the Land Rover's large tires bouncing over the uneven surface as they followed the rutted dirt track south.

After two miles he stopped and climbed down from the cabin. A tree that had no business among the junipers, Joshua trees and creosote scrub of the Mojave lay on its side, blocking the track. He had placed it there years before. The trunk was a couple of feet in diameter for most of its length. It would take two strong men to drag it out of the way, more than enough to discourage whoever might have made it this far to turn back. The Land Rover had a winch mounted to the front bumper but he ignored it. Instead he bent down, linked the fingers of two huge hands underneath one end of the tree and lifted, the muscles in his forearms and thighs bunching with the effort.

When the trunk had been dragged off the track he climbed back up into the Defender. The Land Rover's cabin was generous but nevertheless he had to duck his head to fit his six foot seven inch frame. The diesel engine clattered into life and he drove forward twenty yards, stopping again to reposition the tree across the track. From this point on the terrain became more difficult and he selected low range from the gearbox, sliding the stubby second lever to lock the center differential, helping the vehicle to maintain traction as its tires scrabbled over the loose surface.

Gant's abduction had been a disaster. He had seen to it that Ramirez and Flood had shared Keogh's fate, but not before he had extracted the truth from Ramirez about what had happened in the back of the van. And then there had been nothing to do but wait. Gant would most likely die. If by some miracle he survived they would wait a few months until things had calmed down and then pick him up again. In the meantime they would move on to the next person on the list.

But then things had started to happen that he still did not fully understand. Thankfully he had sent a team back to recover the blood samples Keogh had taken from Gant before the forensics team had a chance to log them. When the samples had been analyzed *Der Eckzahn* had become very agitated, demanding that they bring the SEAL in immediately. Friedrichs had been trained by the KommandoSpezialkräfte, an elite military unit of the German army, and he would not admit to being afraid of any man. But Old Dogtooth was different. And he had never seen him this worked up about anything.

He would have to tread carefully. DeWitty had tipped them off about the sheriff from Hawthorne. They had been lucky there. He had flown a team in from Minnesota to keep Henrikssen under surveillance, and that had already paid dividends. But now *Der Eckzahn* was blaming him for not knowing about the woman. Old Dogtooth was right of course. If Gant had been seeing someone it was more likely that they'd find him through her. But neither team had made any mention of this woman in the weeks that they had had him under surveillance before Christmas. And almost three days had gone by before anyone had noticed the announcement on the website. That had not made *Der Eckzahn* happy either.

The woman who had visited the base with Henrikssen was also a mystery. He had finally obtained the visitor logs for the base but they hadn't proved helpful. The log for the 26th had shown only Henrikssen being admitted to meet with the base commander; there was no record of anyone else. It was possible that there had been an oversight but he thought not. The commander, or the sheriff, possibly the woman herself, had realized that someone was watching the base and steps had been taken to protect her identity. Which meant she had to be important. Was she Gant's girlfriend, the woman Fitzpatrick had referred to in his message? But that made no sense. Why would the base commander go to the trouble of removing the woman's name from the visitor log only to reveal it hours later to the world on the base's website? Well, whoever she was, Henrikssen had to be communicating with her. He needed access to the sheriff's telephone records. He would find her there.

But first he had to prepare for the Honduran's arrival. The sun was already creeping over the mountain ridges to the east as he approached his destination. The facility was in the middle of nowhere, served only by a track that was impassable to all but the most capable of off-road vehicles. If anyone did happen to make it out this far all they would find was a high chain-link fence with a rusty chained and padlocked gate, surrounding a shabby single story construction, its windows boarded up, once-white walls brown from the desert dust, the paint on the remaining shutters faded and flaking.

He climbed down from the Land Rover and walked up to the perimeter. The site might look derelict but despite their appearance the gates and fence were well maintained and the locks oiled and sturdy. He took a key from his pocket and inserted it into the padlock. It turned easily, the lock clicked open. The gate was heavy but was mounted on rollers and Friedrichs barely noticed its weight as he slid it out of the way. He drove the Land Rover in, parking it out of sight in one of the outbuildings towards the rear of the compound. He walked back to close and lock the gate behind him.

It had been several years since his last visit and he took a moment to survey the compound. The main building comprised three levels, two of them underground. It housed a fully equipped surgical theatre and an intensive care unit capable of keeping up to half a dozen potential donors alive indefinitely while their blood and remaining organs could be harvested. There were three small outbuildings at the rear of the structure. The first, where he had parked the Land Rover, contained a large garage where vehicles could be stored out of sight. Two electricity generators capable of powering a small city block occupied the second.

The third housed a furnace for disposing of human remains.

22

ALISON SAT AT one of the lab benches, a stack of periodicals in front of her. It was early evening, already dark outside. She had been here since before seven that morning, as she had for each of the last three days.

The lab was empty and she had told herself it would be a perfect time to catch up on the reading she hadn't found time for during the term. But she was finding it difficult to concentrate, unable to force her mind to focus on anything other than Gant. It had been four days since their meeting with Fitzpatrick at Fallon and still there had been no contact. After the second day she had begun to doubt her idea. Had the message been too vague, too cryptic? Surely Gant would recognize her name, would remember their meeting the previous October? But what if whoever else was looking for him found him first? They had already managed it once. Or perhaps he was already gone. If so it could be years before he resurfaced, assuming he ever did. What if he re-entered another branch of the military and ended up getting killed while on duty before she could find him?

Her head sank into her hands as she considered the prospect. How could she continue with her research, up until now her very life's work, knowing that he was out there, almost certainly holding the key to all of the answers she had dedicated her life to finding. Without him the rest of her work suddenly seemed trivial, pointless. And to think *he* had originally approached *her*, had sought her out to discuss the incredible gift he had. And she had dismissed him. All of this could have been avoided if she had just kept an open mind.

She checked her watch. It was after six and she realized that she was hungry. She hadn't gone out for lunch, afraid that he might choose that very moment to call. She would give him ten more minutes and then she would go home.

Half an hour later she was walking through the car park, deserted other than for her silver Honda Civic, sitting by itself under one of the tall metal lights in the far corner where she had left it that morning. She had just placed her bag on the hood and was starting to rummage around inside for the keys when something made her look up.

Standing on the other side of the car, just outside the pool of light cast by the lamp, was a young man. He had approached without a sound and was looking at her. For a split second his eyes shone, flashing luminescence in the darkness, but then he took a step closer into the light and it was gone. She let out a cry. Her bag slipped off the hood, spilling its contents on to the ground in the process.

The young man raised his hands slowly, but remained on the far side of the car.

'I'm sorry Doctor Stone – I didn't mean to startle you.'

It was the same accent she remembered from their first meeting - neutral, but with a slight twang. And now that he was in the light and she could see him properly she noticed again his eyes. All the photographs she had seen of him over the last few weeks had been black and white; she had almost forgotten how startlingly green they were. She found herself staring, momentarily unable to speak.

'Can I help you with that?'

He nodded towards the contents of her bag, a few photocopied articles, a purse, the car keys she had been looking for, some lipstick – she wondered how long that had been hiding in there – now scattered on the ground, but made no attempt to come closer.

The initial shock over, Alison suddenly realized how relieved she was to see him. She walked around the car, ignoring the contents of her bag, and threw her arms around him.

'Thank God. Thank God you came.'

A moment later she released him, starting to blush as she saw the confused look on his face. What was wrong with her? She had been waiting for him to show up for days and when he did she had screamed at him and then – despite the fact that she hardly knew him – embraced him.

'Oh look, I'm sorry, it's just that I'm so happy you've shown up. I've just been sitting by myself all day in an empty lab waiting for you to show. I suspect I've gone a little stir crazy.'

'Yes, I know.'

She gave him a quizzical look. Had he really just called her crazy?

'I mean I know you've been waiting. Not about the crazy bit.' He smiled. 'Sorry, I had to be sure you weren't being watched.'

He helped her gather her things from the ground, waiting while she shoved the last of the photocopies back into the bag before turning to him, tucking the stray strands of hair that had fallen in front of her face back behind her ears.

'So Cody we need to talk – I have so many questions to ask you. Do you want to go back into the lab?' She pointed in the direction she had come, adding 'It's that way' immediately realizing that of course he already knew that. He had just told her that he had been watching her sitting by herself for three days.

He hesitated. He was pretty sure that she wasn't under surveillance yet but it was the first place anyone who had worked out Fitzpatrick's message would look. And to make matters worse it was a really bad location; the lab building had limited exits and the campus was deserted. They'd have no chance against a team like the one that had picked him up at Salt Wells.

'Are you hungry?'

Alison nodded enthusiastically. In all the excitement she had forgotten just how hungry she was.

'Good, I'm starving. It's hard keeping watch on someone who never goes for lunch.' He smiled again. 'How about we grab some food? Do you like Thai? I passed a place on my way up here, looked like it might be okay.'

Ten minutes later they had parked her car and were sitting at the back of the restaurant. He had excused himself for a moment when they first sat down and had headed off in the direction of the restrooms, feigning embarrassment when he had walked into the kitchens by mistake. She wondered if he had been checking the exits. She hadn't noticed it when they had been seated but now she saw that he had chosen the booth carefully. He had let her sit first but had guided her towards the side closest the door so that when he sat opposite he had an unrestricted view of the room.

The restaurant was quiet and the owner, a plump Asian woman in her sixties, took their order. She returned a few moments later with a couple of Singhas before retreating into the kitchen.

Alison took a sip of the cold beer. She could contain herself no longer. She had thought a lot over the last few days about how she might get him to open up about his past, deciding that the best approach was to tell him what she already knew about him. And so she started talking, explaining quickly how she had been approached by the sheriff before Christmas when the lab technician at Mount Grant had found anomalies in the blood samples they had taken from him, how she had then started to piece together information about his background. When she told him how her mother had identified him from a photograph that had been taken with her father in Vietnam he interrupted her.

'Wait, you're Pete Stone's daughter?'

She nodded, suddenly realizing that in all the excitement of finally meeting him she had forgotten that this man had known her father. She had so many questions to ask him about that as well.

'How's he doing?'

At that moment their food arrived, the owner filling their table with a variety of steaming dishes. The old woman smiled again as she refilled their glasses before taking the empty tray away.

'My father died six years ago.'

He listened as Alison told him how, still only in his forties, her father had been diagnosed with Alzheimer's, how the disease had taken its toll on him, until in the end he hadn't recognized either her or her mother. She explained how finding a cure for the disease – initially simply to try and save her father, but later so that no other family should have to suffer its horrors – had led her first to Johns Hopkins, then to Harvard and finally to Berkeley.

'It's why I needed to find you Cody. You may well hold the key to curing countless diseases like the one that killed him. I need to learn as much as I can. I know that you've spent your life trying to keep people from finding out about you. I know that you were planning to disappear again after what happened at Mount Grant. And I can see why you would want to do that, believe me I can. But you may have the potential to end suffering for thousands, even millions of people. For people like my father. There has to be a way that I can convince you to stay around and help me.'

She had spent the last four days alone in the lab rehearsing what she might say if he showed up, how she might prevent him from leaving again. She had intended to build up to her request slowly, but the shift in the conversation to her father had meant that she before she had fully realized it she was making her plea, and now it sounded to her like she was rushing him, asking too much from this man she had only just met.

He sat back, silent for a moment.

'How long would you need me to stay?'

She had anticipated the question, but now she hesitated. Should she tell him something just to keep him here, at least for a while? Perhaps everything else would get resolved and then she might be able to convince him to stay longer.

'I honestly can't say. We could have a quick breakthrough but from my experience most of the progress tends to come in incremental steps, and takes time. I'll stop lecturing, devote myself fully to research, work as hard as it takes, nights, weekends, whatever.' She paused, realizing he needed a more precise answer. 'Months. Maybe longer.'

'It's not safe for me here until I know more about the people who tried to kidnap me. Which means it also wouldn't be safe for anyone around me. I need to think a little more about what I'm going to do next. For now why don't you ask me what you need to know and I'll try and answer your questions as fully as I can.'

Well at least he hadn't refused. She knew she couldn't push him any further and so she would just have to hope that he would reach the right decision if she left him to think about it. She only hoped she had said enough to convince him.

For the next few hours she quizzed him about his life and about the capabilities he seemed to possess. The facts she had pieced together from the internet and from speaking with Fitzpatrick were largely correct, but there were significant gaps in what she knew. He told her about how he had been found abandoned on the steps of an orphanage, how he had been taken in by a kitchen hand and named for a Catholic saint, Codratus, whose feast day it had been when he had been found. He had grown up in London between the wars, working at the docks after he left the orphanage, later enlisting with the British Army. He told her how he had found Jason Mitchell in the middle of a minefield on Omaha on the first morning of the D-Day landings, how he had been injured when Mitchell had stepped on a mine, and how their records must have become mixed up. He had been shipped back to the States, later to re-enlist, and had learned to fly jets. After he was shot down over North Korea he had made his way to the Philippines. He had spent several years there before returning to the United States as Luke Jackson. He told her about his time in Vietnam, and about his capture and the years he had spent moving between prisoner-of-war camps in Laos, about escaping to Thailand and returning once again to the United States, this time as Paul Kyle. He told her about joining the 160th SOAR and what had happened in Mogadishu, and how his time with that unit had prompted him to return to the States to enlist with the Navy and complete the SEAL CSAR training.

Mainly she let him talk, content to scribble an occasional note in a pad she had dug from her bag. When he spoke about his time in Vietnam she found it difficult to resist steering the conversation towards her father. As he told her about the last day he had flown with him she listened with rapt attention, eager for any detail he could give her that she hadn't already heard.

The story of his life was fascinating to her, and she had to force herself to focus on those aspects that were relevant to her research. As she had suspected he had aged as normal up to about the age of nineteen or twenty, and then it seemed to have stopped. It had taken him a long time to notice, and so he couldn't be certain when exactly he had stopped growing older, but most people thought he seemed about that age.

He told her about the abilities he had recognized, and when he had first realized he might have them. He had always been coordinated; learning new physical skills had always come easily. It required little effort to maintain physical fitness or stamina. He had what he thought was almost perfect recall, but his memory had only developed in this way after he had started school. He remembered as a child the first few weeks of lessons being particularly stressful. Other faculties had developed later as well. His distance vision had improved dramatically shortly after he had been sent to Korea. He had learned to fake eye tests to conceal the extent of his ability to see objects at extreme distances, explaining why his service records showed it as only slightly better than average. He thought his night vision had always been good but he had noticed a significant improvement during his first few months in Vietnam. He could now see perfectly well in the dark without the equipment the military supplied, but to avoid drawing attention to himself he typically used it, at least in training, notwithstanding the limits he found it placed on his distance and peripheral vision. While in Thailand he had learned to control many of his basic bodily functions – heart rate, respiration, even body temperature – through meditation, although he suspected this was something that most people could achieve, at least to a degree. For a while he had wondered whether he might be able to improve any of his faculties simply by willing it to happen or by focusing his mind, but after experimenting for years without any success he had given up. It seemed his body sensed when it needed to improve itself and just went ahead by itself and did it.

He knew much less about his ability to recuperate. He had been unaware of the Lancet article that Bryant had written. He didn't elaborate on how he had come to be injured, and Alison had seen something in his eyes that made her think that there was more than he was telling her, but she didn't press him on it. He had no memory of the months he had spent in hospital, only of waking up in a strange place, not knowing what had happened to him. He remembered a little more about the injuries he had sustained on Omaha on D-day, but not much. Again it seemed that his body had healed itself without any conscious direction, or even awareness, on his part. Apart from those episodes, and the gunshot wound he had sustained in the back of the van on the way to Mount Grant, he had suffered remarkably little in the way of physical injury. Cuts and bruises were commonplace given the career he had chosen, but they always healed quickly and without scarring. He had never been ill, not even during his time in the camps in Laos.

When she finally checked her watch it was after eleven and the restaurant owner was looking over at them, clearly hoping that they would finish so that she could close up. Reluctantly Alison suggested that they get the bill and call it a night. She would have loved to hear more about his life, to continue asking questions, but she would have to wait until the morning. He left money on the table for the meal, thanking the woman again for the food, which seemed to go some way to restoring them to her good graces. Then they were back at her car. As she fumbled in her bag for keys she asked him where he was staying. He gave her the name of a motel. When she offered to drive him there he seemed reluctant but it was a mile or so away and she insisted, finally convincing him to get in. On the way she asked him whether he would stop by the lab the following morning. He would only agree to think about it and they drove for a short while in awkward silence. She was desperate to find something to say that might convince him, anything that might extract a promise from him to continue to help her with her research. But then they were at the motel and he was climbing out, and all she could do was give him her cell phone number. He made no attempt to write it down, promising that he would remember. She sat and watched, the engine running, as he walked away. She waited for a few minutes after he had disappeared around the corner. Finally she turned the little Honda around and headed back to her apartment.

When she arrived home it was after midnight and the apartment was dark and cold. She turned on the lights. She had been up since early morning but she knew she wouldn't sleep. She hadn't felt this exhilarated, this apprehensive, since she could remember. She had just left him but already she was desperate for their next meeting, excited at the prospect of seeing him again, of what she might learn. But also frightened that he might simply choose to disappear and that she would never see him again. She dug out her notes, skimming through what she had written. His capacity to develop was fascinating, as were his powers of recuperation. To think he had been shot only a week before.

It suddenly occurred to her that she hadn't even asked whether the wound was healing, whether there was anything he might need. Instead she had run over and hugged him, and then proceeded to spend the evening quizzing him. He hadn't seemed to be in any discomfort, and it was clear he had some medical training, probably far more practical experience of emergency medicine than she did for that matter. But what kind of doctor must he think she was? She grabbed a telephone book, feeling the need to explain her behavior to him immediately. She remembered the name of the motel he had been staying in – the Shangri-La. She dialed the number. The reception clerk picked up after a few rings. She didn't know what name he was using – she knew it wouldn't be one that she would recognize - but she gave the clerk his description, adding that he had checked in during the last week. There had only been a handful of cars in the parking lot when she had dropped him off. At this time of year they couldn't be busy.

But the clerk was adamant that there was no-one staying with them that fitted the description she had given. Most of the motel had been closed for refurbishment since before Christmas and they had only a couple of guests, none of whom resembled the man she had described.

Alison slowly replaced the receiver.

So that was why he had seemed reluctant to have her drive him to the motel. He never had any intention of letting her know where he was staying. He must have waited until she had left before making his way back to wherever he had actually been staying. What did that mean? He had avoided agreeing to meet her at the lab the following morning, saying only that he would think about it. Her heart sank with the realization that he had probably never intended to show.

She had lost him.

23

HE LAY ON the bed in the darkness. The motel where he was staying had been in the opposite direction from the one where Alison had dropped him, and it had taken him half an hour to walk back, but it was important for her sake as well as for his that she didn't know where he was. He had asked her not to mention to either Fitzpatrick or the sheriff that he had contacted her. Since Fitzpatrick's message she remained the most likely target for whoever was looking for him, but the commander and Henrikssen were also in danger. It would be better for everyone if he just left.

He checked his watch. Twelve-thirty. It would take him less than a minute to stuff the few clothes he had bought in a duffel bag and be gone. There was a ticket in his pocket for a Greyhound leaving San Francisco at one-thirty that morning. By the morning after he had intended to be in Denver, fourteen hundred miles to the east. From there he could figure out where to go next. He had considered leaving the country immediately, but had decided against it. Attempting a border crossing would be too risky until he had established a new identity for himself.

Alison had said she might need months, possibly longer. From what he had seen of the men that had picked him up at Salt Wells he had to assume he had hours, a day or two at the outside. It would be suicide to wait around for them to find him.

But it had felt good, after so very long, to finally be able to talk to someone about his life. It had been a strange experience, having this woman expose the details of his past, secrets he had spent most of his life trying to protect. The various identities he had used had often been crudely assumed, the covers he had constructed far from perfect. He had always known that spending so long in each place, with the same unit, the same people, even returning again and again to a branch of the military, were all mistakes that some day would catch him out. He had even imagined how he might eventually be exposed. The military had for some time tested for his blood type, and more recently genetic dog-tagging had been applied to all service personnel, both of which made it unlikely that his identity could remain a secret much longer. It was why he had decided to leave the States. But he had never imagined that when the time came it would be like this. It had been almost surreal; sitting in a restaurant as a young woman he hardly knew laid out the history of his life as if she were describing the plot of a movie they had just seen together.

The mention of Pete Stone's name had made it seem real again however. They had only served together for six months and Pete hadn't been much of a talker. But they had been close, as close perhaps as he had been with Dylan or Jock. For a moment he had wondered whether he might at last have the opportunity to meet one of the friends he had been forced to leave behind. Then he had seen the look on her face as he had asked about her father. He had known at that moment that he could trust her. Her determination to find a cure for the disease that had taken him away from her was clear.

And with time she might even be able to help him learn more about why he was the way he was, how he might have come to be. For a long time he had tried to convince himself that it did not matter, but now he realized how badly he needed that information. Understanding the reasons behind the choices he has made with his life wasn't the same thing. He kept returning to the military because it was the closest thing to a family that he could hope for. Simply being a soldier was not what appealed to him. He had become good at it, but the occasional need to take a life was an unwanted by-product of that choice. He had loved flying jets, even the combat. But not the kill – that ultimate thrill that other fighter pilots seemed to experience so keenly had always eluded him. He had been happier flying slicks in Vietnam, his job simply to deliver men safely from the battlefield, a similar role to the one that he had performed with the Nightstalkers. Despite the regiment's fearsome name their task had been no different. CSAR had been the final distillation of that role. No longer merely ferrying soldiers off the battlefield but personally intervening to rescue those of his extended family who found themselves in trouble in a combat zone.

But how many lives had he really saved? Through CSAR not that many, at least not directly. Several dozen at most. More if you included the men he had over the years delivered from the battlefield in either a Huey or a 'Hawk. But now this woman was telling him that within him lay the potential to cure diseases that afflicted thousands, maybe even millions of people. People like Pete Stone.

He had simply never thought of his abilities in that way. He had attempted to study them as best he could, particularly in recent years, reading whatever research he could get his hands on. Nevertheless to him the fact that he didn't age, that his body seemed to have particular abilities to heal itself, had always been something peculiar to him, not transferable. Something to be concealed from others, not shared with them. Now that he thought of it that way the choices that he had made, the things that he had done, it all seemed limited, even futile, by comparison.

But it would be crazy to simply stay here at the university, waiting for whoever was looking for him to find them. He looked over at the duffel bag sitting by the door, and then at his watch.

Twelve forty-five.

He could still make the bus.

24

FRIEDRICHS SAT IN the back of the Lynx with the other men, his face impassive. They had just flown over the Bay Bridge, the water grey and choppy beneath the huge twin spans, the red towers of Golden Gate Bridge to their left and then briefly behind them as the pilot banked the helicopter sharply, turning inland. The Lynx was one of the fastest helicopters commercially available but it had still taken them over two hours. For most of the flight they had maintained formation, the second Lynx to their right and slightly behind. It had only finally turned away a few minutes before, heading for the woman's apartment.

It had taken longer than he had expected but he had finally managed to access the phone records from the sheriff's office in Hawthorne, together with details of the calls made to or from Lars Henrikssen's home and cell phone numbers. He'd had a team working on the records through the night. They had cross-referenced each number listed for every Alison Berkeley in the United States, but no matches had been found among the sheriff's calls. Every so often one of the screens would flicker as it refreshed itself, another annotation appearing beside one of the telephone numbers to identify the caller as his men painstakingly worked through the list of numbers. She had to be in there somewhere. It would only be a matter of time before they located her. But hours later, as the sun had been rising on the final day of the year, the last of the telephone numbers identified, they had failed to find any record of an Alison Berkeley having spoken with Henrikssen in the last month.

Friedrichs knew it wasn't possible. They had to have communicated. Something must have been missed.

Four of the calls had been with women whose first name was Alison and he had ordered background checks on each of them, prioritizing the women that lived closest to Fallon. The first three had yielded nothing, each just residents of Hawthorne who for whatever reason had had business with the sheriff's office. The fourth woman hadn't even been from Nevada but he had ordered her to be checked as well, although he hadn't been expecting anything there. He had already begun contemplating his next move. If Alison Berkeley couldn't be found he would disperse the teams to the surrounding states and hope that Gant would show at a train station or a bus depot. The man was still wanted by the authorities and so was unlikely to risk either an airport or a border, at least until he had managed to establish a new identity for himself. He had a little time – not much, but some. He would use that time to bring in both Henrikssen and Fitzpatrick. They might be able to tell him something. Two helicopters had been fuelled and were ready for take off, simply waiting for his instruction.

He'd had Henrikssen under surveillance for the last week; a team at Fallon for far longer. Nevertheless the snatch teams would have little time to prepare and even with proper planning it was a risky strategy. Kidnapping a Nevada sheriff and the commander of the Navy's premier aerial combat training facility was certain to draw more attention than he would ever have wished for. But what else could he do? If he didn't act quickly Gant would disappear and *Der Eckzahn* had told him that could not be allowed to happen.

He had been so engrossed in his thoughts that for a few moments he hadn't noticed the results of the final background check appear on his screen. When he looked up again Alison's picture was staring down at him from the center screen. He recognized her immediately from the photos his men had taken outside Fallon - it was the young blond woman who had been with Henrikssen when he had met with the base commander the day after Christmas. The brief report accompanying the photograph identified her as Doctor Alison Stone, lecturer and faculty member at the Department of Genetics, University of California, Berkeley. Alison Stone from Berkeley. Alison, Berkeley. His fingers had hit the comms link connecting him to the pilots of the two Lynxes even before he had finished reading.

Now through his headphones he heard the pilot announce that they were a minute out. He could already see the buildings of the campus ahead of them. From this height the place seemed deserted, a small silver hatchback pulling into the empty parking lot the only car visible. Good. With luck they could be in and out without running into anyone.

He looked around at the five men sitting in the back of the helicopter, all dressed in civilian clothes, weapons concealed inside their jackets. Two of the men he had recruited personally. The other three he knew less well, a team that had recently been called back from Minnesota. Each of them had been promised a million dollars for bringing the woman in alive, another two if they brought Gant in with her. He would receive a further five million if either team were successful. *Der Eckzahn* had insisted on two teams per helicopter, which was excessive; a single team would be more than enough for a woman and an injured man. Gant may well have some training - he wasn't about to make the mistake of underestimating his quarry - but so did his men. But what did he care if Old Dogtooth wanted to piss his money away? He wasn't about to take it personally as long as he got paid.

25

ALISON PULLED INTO the car park, choosing her usual space.

Heavy, grey clouds hung low in the winter sky. She had held out a tiny hope that she might see him waiting for her there, as he had been the night before. But the place was deserted, her Honda the only car in the large lot. A single fat drop of rain spattered on the windscreen, then another. She left the engine running, for a moment contemplating simply turning around and driving home. What was the point? He wasn't coming and she was exhausted. Her mind balked at the prospect of another day spent by herself in the lab. She hadn't slept much, watching as the small clock on her bedside table had slowly counted out the minutes and hours. She had been dreading getting up. The campus would be deserted and she would spend the day waiting in vain for him. If he didn't show – and she was now certain that he wouldn't – she would have confirmation that he didn't plan to help her. It was too late for her to try and make it back to Manchester and she was resigned to spending New Year's Eve alone in her apartment. What did it matter? Without him the year was already ruined. She should just go back to her apartment, climb under the covers and try and get some sleep, try and forget about him.

She switched off the engine. It was no use. As tired as she was she knew if she went home sleep would not come. She got out of the car, grabbing her bag from the front seat and the coffee she had picked up at Starbucks from its holder. As she was making her way towards the entrance to the lab building her cell phone rang. Her heart leapt as she recognized the voice.

'Alison? It's Cody. Listen, I've decided to stay for a little while but it's too dangerous for us to use your lab. Is there anywhere else we could use, somewhere you don't normally go?'

She thought of a place immediately. The university had ten campuses throughout California. Davis was only fifty-five miles to the northeast. She had worked there when the protesters had forced her from her lab that summer. The biomedical engineering faculty had all the lab facilities she would need - in many respects it was probably better equipped than her own lab for the tests she needed to run. And she still had access. She gave him the address, telling him that she would ring ahead and arrange a pass for him with campus security.

'No. I can find my own way in. And don't tell anyone where you're going either. Right after this call I want you to switch off your phone and remove the battery. We have to assume that by now they know your number, which means they can use it to trace you.'

'Okay. Okay. I just need to grab a few things from the lab, and then I'll go straight there.'

He hung up.

Alison stood in the car park, a smile spreading across her face. He hadn't left! She started walking towards the lobby, already thinking of the things she would need to bring with her to Davis. She looked at her phone. She thought he was being a little paranoid, but she would do whatever he wanted if it kept him around. She flipped the phone over, slid the back off the plastic case and dumped both phone and battery in her bag.

It wouldn't take her long to prepare. Twenty minutes at most. And then she could be on her way.

26

FRIEDRICHS WATCHED AS the pilot brought the helicopter over the campus, pointing down to a building where the woman was expected to be. They would set down on the sports field several blocks to the south and the pilot would take off again, maintaining a high orbit of the campus. Once Friedrichs radioed in that they had what they had come for the pilot would land the Lynx in the car park next to the lab and pick them up. If all went well the operation would be over in minutes.

The helicopter dropped almost vertically right in the center of a large oval running track. The high bleachers on both sides would shield them from prying eyes for the few moments it took his men to exit. He hadn't noticed anyone during the approach. Most of the students wouldn't return until the New Year and the rain that had started to fall would keep those few that might be on campus indoors.

The large sliding crew doors on each side were open before the Lynx had touched down. The last of his men jumped clear even as the pilot twisted the throttle, the twin Rolls Royce Gem turboshaft engines whining as the helicopter lifted back into the air, the downdraft from the four rotors tugging at their clothes as the men split into two teams and calmly walked off in opposite directions.

Each man had memorized a map of the campus on the flight in and now the two teams made their separate ways to the building where they expected to find Alison

Stone and hopefully Gant. There was supposed to be a single security guard at the entrance to the lab building. They would deal with him if they had to but it would be better if they could complete the mission without being seen. The schematics they had received in-flight showed a fire exit to the rear of the building. Friedrichs didn't expect difficulty with the alarm system, and once that had been disabled they could enter without being detected. From there a back staircase took them up three flights to the rear entrance to the lab.

It took less than half a minute to bypass the sensors on the fire door and then his men were running silently up the stairs, the rubber soles of their boots padding softly on the concrete steps as they took them two at a time. They gathered briefly outside the door to the lab, drawing tasers. Neither the woman nor Gant were to be harmed, at least for now. He paused for an instant to check the men. They were ready, each breathing slowly and regularly in spite of the rapid ascent. Satisfied, he moved forward, turned the door handle smoothly and stepped through. The other men followed immediately behind him, fanning out to secure the lab.

There was no-one there.

A single cup of coffee sat cooling beside a stack of journals on the woman's desk. He indicated to his men to stand ready. It was possible that she would be back any moment.

But after half an hour she hadn't returned and Friedrichs radioed the pilot to pick them up. The team in the second helicopter had found nothing at her apartment and were already on their way back to Las Vegas.

Scheiße.

She had been here. They had just missed her.

27

ALISON SPENT THE afternoon setting up.

In the end it had taken her less than ten minutes to grab what she needed from her lab and she had run back out to the car park, her coffee untouched, forgotten on the desk. She had headed north on the Eastshore Freeway, driving as fast as she dared in the rain, anxious to get to Davis as quickly as possible so that she could start preparing for his arrival. As she had left the campus in her little Honda she had failed to notice the sleek grey helicopter lifting out of the athletics stadium behind her, banking sharply, passing briefly overhead as it climbed, commencing its orbit of the campus.

Cody hadn't shown up until that evening. They could have waited until the morning but all traces of her earlier tiredness were gone and she had asked whether he minded if they began right away. She was still a little worried that something might cause him to change his mind and he would once again disappear.

She had decided to start with a superficial physiological examination. She wanted to confirm that his wound was healing satisfactorily. She also hoped to verify some of the things he had told her about how his senses had developed.

When he had lifted his shirt to let her examine his abdomen she had found only the slightest trace that he had even been injured. The wound certainly looked like it would heal without even a scar. An ultrasound revealed that his right kidney had re-formed and appeared to be functioning normally. It was incredible to think that a little over a week ago a bullet had removed much of the organ on that side.

Satisfied that he was in good health she started with a simple eye test. While she had waited for him to arrive she had printed a Snellen chart and had taped it to the wall, measuring out twenty feet. Now she asked him to read down through the rows of letters as they decreased in size, first using only his right eye, then the left. He read down to the eleventh row without difficulty, indicating his vision was better than 20/20. She had anticipated this and had printed smaller charts, rearranging the letters in each successive chart to prevent him simply memorizing the order in which the letters had appeared on the first. By the time he had read to the bottom of the second chart she realized that her last chart may not be sufficient to test the limits of his vision, at least at the standard distance of twenty feet. She marked off another twenty feet, almost the length of the lab, and asked him to read the final, smallest, chart. From that distance he had been able to read most of the chart, only finally beginning to struggle as he approached the second last line.

Alison hadn't intended to perform much more than a basic eye test as part of her initial examination but now her interest was piqued. Davis had an ophthalmology department but she wasn't sure whether the pass she had been given would grant her access. She left the lab, telling him to stay where he was. A few minutes later she returned with an ophthalmoscope. She turned off the lights, directing him to one of the lab stools so that she could examine the internal structure of his eyes. As she turned the scope on she noticed once again how his pupils were strangely luminescent in the dark, the same effect that had startled her the evening before in the car park. His pupils had dilated once the light was turned off, perhaps a little more than she would have expected, but not much. No doubt that contributed to the night vision he claimed to possess, although she wasn't sure that by itself it could explain it.

She had asked him to focus on the far corner of the room, switching on the ophthalmoscope and clicking between the lenses to show a magnified view of the back of his eye. She knew that the retina contained the photosensitive rod and cone cells with their associated neurons and blood vessels, and that the density of these photoreceptors was critical in determining a person's visual acuity. Towards the center of the retina would be the fovea, the part of the back of the eye with the greatest density of receptors, the area providing the sharpest, clearest vision. She located the optic nerve, a bundle of nerve fibers responsible for relaying messages from the eye to the relevant parts of the brain. There was a small blind spot without photoreceptors at the optic disc, under which the optic nerve and blood vessels joined the eye. But there were two additional structures she didn't recognize. The first was a comb-like collection of blood vessels projecting from the retina from the point where the optic nerve entered the eyeball. The second was an additional layer of tissue in the back of the eye that seemed to be reflecting light back through the retina. She made a note of what she had found. She would look it up later.

Next she examined his hearing. That afternoon she had downloaded software to her laptop that produced a series of tones at specific frequencies and volumes that were relayed through a set of headphones to each ear independently. She asked him to click the mouse pad to indicate whether the various tones could be heard. The software then plotted a graph showing the frequency of audible sounds on one axis and their loudness on the other. Alison knew that in humans the audible range of frequencies was usually between 20Hz and 20,000Hz, although a gradual decline with age at higher frequencies was considered normal. Most people over the age of twenty-five struggled to hear sounds above 15,000Hz. Prolonged and repeated exposure to high sound levels, such as he would have experienced from years flying jets and helicopters, was also likely to have caused permanent damage to the nerve endings on the basilar membrane, which should have further compromised his hearing.

It had taken him fifteen minutes to complete the test, the results showing that his range of hearing was in the range 2Hz to almost 60,000Hz, his ability to hear higher frequency sounds well beyond that of an average human. The software was specifically designed to be hard to fool, reducing the level of the tone until the subject indicated it was inaudible and then lowering it further, then raising it until the tone could just be heard once again, the process repeated until a number of consistent levels had been indicated. Alison had tested it on herself while she had been waiting for him to arrive. He couldn't have been faking it.

Finally she performed a simple memory test, showing him random pages from a medical textbook before taking the book away and asking him to read them back to her. He seemed to have no difficulty memorizing pages of information after being shown them for only a few seconds.

By the time she had finished her initial tests it had been getting late and he left her in the lab to write up her notes while he went in search of food. He returned half an hour later with half a dozen cartons of Chinese takeout and a cheap bottle of white wine. They ate sitting at one of the lab benches, Alison occasionally putting her food down to add to her notes as a new thought occurred to her. When they had finished eating he leaned forward to see what she had written.

'So, what did you find?'

She suddenly realized that she hadn't discussed the results of any of her tests with him. All evening he had patiently complied with each of her instructions and she hadn't once thought to share what she had found. Embarrassed, she immediately started to explain the purpose of each of the tests, and his results, starting with the eye exam. He let her continue for a few minutes before gently interrupting.

'Alison, I'm pretty used to eye tests. I've been getting them regularly, at least when I've been flying, since about 1950. I've been faking them for almost as long. Most times that just involved remembering not to read too far down the chart. The docs I've come across generally wouldn't bother with an internal exam unless they thought something was wrong, and so as long as you could read from the chart they'd leave the scope' - he nodded up at the ophthalmoscope she had left on one of the benches - 'in the desk drawer. Every once in a while one would however, and then they'd be curious about those additional blood vessels, or that reflective tissue that seems to be embedded in my retina. So then I'd have to convince them that I could see just fine, and generally they'd forget all about it and just pass me to keep flying. Seems like the military's always short of men to fly their planes, particularly in wartime, and no-one's really interested in grounding an otherwise healthy pilot just because they've found something they don't recognize.'

'But even though I would play it down it bothered me. Especially the reflective thing. It makes me easier to spot at night, and that's not always a good thing in my line of work. Besides it can freak people out a bit, like it did with you when we first met, and again last night in the car park. Anyway, I spent a lot of time trying to work out what it was, and where it came from. I haven't always had it, I'm pretty sure of that. I first noticed it in '65, a few months into my first tour in Vietnam. I was an 11B, a grunt, back then. I'd known for some time that I wasn't ageing, and I was starting to notice a few other things as well. Like the fact that I could see much better at night than the other guys in the platoon. Now I think it was those first few months in the jungle, night after night spent peering into the darkness, straining to spot whatever might have been out there trying to kill me, that triggered the improvements in my night vision.'

'But then that led me to think, well, if that was true and my body was capable of developing itself, why would it also decide to give me that reflective thing, something that might make it easier for me to get spotted, something that would increase the chance that I might get killed? That puzzled me for a long time. I didn't make the connection until years later. I was in Somalia at the time with the Nightstalkers and the CSAR guys who were stationed with us were showing us how to deal with bullet wounds. They'd head out at night in one of the Humvees with a flashlight and round up stray animals, goats mostly, and bring them back to the base. Then they'd shoot them and get us to practice fixing them up. And that's when it occurred to me - a lot of animals have exactly the same thing. So I did some reading, and the answer was right there. The eye shine is caused by something called the *tapetum lucidum*, a layer of tissue that lies immediately behind the retina and reflects light back into the eye, increasing the light available to the photoreceptors. You see it when you shine a torch at an animal at night, or when you take a picture of your cat or your dog with the flash on.'

'So that got me to thinking that maybe I had been looking in the wrong place all along, that maybe looking at the capabilities certain animals had might provide a better explanation for some of the other things that

190

seemed unusual about me. I did a lot of reading after that, particularly about how certain animals had developed characteristics that allowed them to perform better in their environment. That collection of blood vessels you found at the back of my eye, for instance. In humans and most other mammals the blood vessels in the eye lie in front of the retina, which partially obscures the image the brain is trying to interpret. But birds' eyes often have a structure called a *pecten* that lifts the blood vessels away from the retina, which solves the problem. It's part of what gives birds such as hawks their extremely sharp eyesight.'

Alison remained silent while he talked. She hadn't thought to simply ask him for an explanation of the things she had found. He had been aware of his abilities for decades, had been trying to hide most of them for just as long. Of course he would have tried to understand them, would have theories on where they had come from.

'I'm sorry, I've been stupid. It's just that I'm used to solving problems by myself. Most of my research involves examining tissue, cells, things that don't have well-formed opinions on why they're behaving the way they do. So what else can you tell me?'

He smiled again.

'Well I have never found a way to prove any of this but I suspect that a higher density of photoreceptors also contributes to my vision, maybe also a better ratio of nerve ganglia to receptors. Again, most species of bird have many times the number of rods and cones per square millimeter that humans have.'

She nodded. His assumption made sense, but she would need to devise a method to test his theory. She scribbled a note to remind herself.

'Anything else?'

He paused, as if for a moment unsure whether he should continue.

'Yes, although some of it may sound strange until you understand what is possible when you look outside human anatomy.'

'For instance?'

'Well, I don't like fluorescent lights.' He nodded at the rows of strip lighting on the ceiling of the lab. 'Or computer monitors.' She gave him a quizzical look.

'I know. This one puzzled me for a long time as well. Then I read that humans can't distinguish movement at a rate greater than 50 Hertz – 50 cycles a second. Anything faster than that appears as continuous movement, which means that you can't tell that a fluorescent light bulb oscillating at 60Hz is actually continuously flashing. It's the same with computer screens. Sometimes you can see the effect when you see a computer being filmed on TV. But birds have flicker thresholds that are much higher, almost twice as high as humans in many cases. It helps them to pursue small agile prey through difficult terrain, something that to most humans would simply appear as a blur.'

'But not to you.'

He shook his head.

'When did you first notice that?'

He paused again, considering for a moment. He remembered playing games as a child, and how he would see, perfectly clearly, the ball leaving a friend's hand, for an instant seemingly suspended in the air as it travelled the short space between them. His reflexes had always been good, but he suspected that at least part of his ability to react so quickly was due to the fact that he had been able to see what was happening around him with much greater clarity.

'I think that's one I've always had.'

'So what else?'

'Look at this.'

He reached behind her to pick up the ultrasound transducer she had used to examine his kidney, pulling up his t-shirt and pressing it to his stomach. He moved it around, watching the screen until he found what he was looking for.

'Humans have an adaptive immune system, allowing our bodies to deal with a continual stream of new threats.'

Alison nodded. He was now in her area.

'Yes. Antibodies, T-cells, Major Histocompatability Complexes, RAGs. A complex system of proteins that recognizes and marks foreign bodies for destruction.'

'Right; but this system isn't unique to humans. In fact we don't even have the best version of it. There.'

He pointed to the screen. Alison leaned closer, puzzled. The resolution from the ultrasound was poor but she could just make out a pair of elongated structures located beneath each kidney. She hadn't noticed them when she had examined him earlier.

'Sharks were the earliest creatures to develop a multi-stage immunological response. It's remarkably similar to that found in humans, only much older. They have each of the features you mentioned, as well as a spleen and thymus glands. In humans and most other vertebrates it's bone marrow that's responsible for producing red blood cells. But in sharks the skeleton is made of cartilage, not bone, which means no marrow. Instead the job of manufacturing red blood cells is performed by the spleen and two organs called the epigonal organ and the Leydig's organ. The Leydig's organ is found near the esophagus. I don't think I have one. But the epigonal…'

'…is found underneath each kidney.'

Alison had read about this. The two organs he had mentioned were entirely unique to sharks. No one was sure what, exactly, the Leydig's organ did. But recent studies indicated that the epigonal organ was the site of T-cell differentiation, which meant that it played an important role in the animal's immune system. As sharks were known to be remarkably resistant to cancers as well as a wide variety of other diseases, researchers had for some time been optimistic about the possibilities for applying what could be learned from studying their immune system to human medicine.

Alison also knew that the way their antibodies functioned was very different. In humans, the genes coding for various structural regions on a given antibody were separated by relatively large gaps of non-coding genes. Making a human antibody required that RAG proteins 'cut and paste' together antibody-coding genes, eliminating the intervening DNA. This process was responsible for the tremendous diversity of antibodies capable of being produced by the human immune system. But in sharks, the genes coding for the various functional regions of a given antibody were clustered, lying much closer together than in humans. As a result, some of these genes were fused to begin with, not requiring any cutting or pasting. The end result of all this genetic shuffling and non-shuffling was that sharks enjoyed the best of both immunologic worlds: they could cut and paste genes to enhance antibody diversity, but they also had 'ready to wear' antibody genes, allowing a much faster response to certain pathogens.

He pulled his t-shirt down, replacing the transducer.

'For a while I even considered getting a vet to examine me. But then there was always the danger that I wouldn't be able to keep a lid on whatever they might find. Besides, who wants to admit, even to themselves, that their physiology might be more suited to veterinary care?'

He smiled again, but this time the smile didn't reach his eyes and Alison could tell the humor masked an issue about which he was sensitive. What must it be like to be so different and yet not understand why you were that way, or how you had come to be? He had clearly tried to study his genetic make-up, had tried to understand what mixture of genes might have made him possible. And in the process he would no doubt have come across each of the arguments why someone like him shouldn't even have been allowed to come into existence. The erosion of the moral boundary between human and animal. The violation of some unspecified human right. There were plenty of good reasons why research in this area needed to be controlled, but she had always regarded arguments based on morality or some inherent, undefined quality of humanity as weak. The mixing of animal and human genetic material did not redefine the notion of human dignity. If the concept had meaning, it was only because humans might occasionally behave in a way that conferred that dignity, that their actions might from time to time command that respect. From what little she knew of the life he had led, from what her mother had told her about what her father had thought of him, it seemed that if there was a standard he had probably met it.

While she scribbled notes he talked about other abilities. Some he had always possessed, almost taken for granted, assuming that they were shared by others. And then a chance remark would make him realize that not everyone experienced the world as he did. Others he knew he had developed only later in his life, a response to a need his body must have recognized, although he admitted he was no closer to understanding the process by which this occurred than he ever had been. He told her things he had never considered sharing with another person, of abilities he himself was unsure he possessed, let alone understood. How he thought he could detect the slow orbit of the sun, the almost imperceptible movement of the constellations through the night sky.

He explained how sometimes he thought he could see colors outside the spectrum of light normally visible to humans, and how at times when flying he thought he had even been able to detect the earth's magnetic field.

He explained how in a quiet room he could hear the beating of another person's heart.

28

IT WAS THE car Lars noticed first. Almost hidden behind the Chevron gas station that sat opposite the squat building that housed Mineral County's Chamber of Commerce. Almost, but not quite.

Nevertheless he'd almost missed it. Too many things on his mind. He hadn't heard from Doctor Stone in a couple of days. He was beginning to regret letting her talk him into meeting Gant alone. And his call with DeWitty. What in the hell to do about that, or about Joseph Brandt or Emily Mortimer? Then on top of it all that morning the Mayor had summoned him to a meeting, demanding an update on the shooting at Mount Grant. The Chamber of Commerce was all the way across town, and he'd decided the walk would do him good, give him time to think. As he'd made his way up Veterans' Memorial Highway he'd barely noticed the decorations going up, the lights being hung, the small town preparing to celebrate the last day of the year.

But a late model Cadillac sedan. Black, V8. There weren't many cars like that in Hawthorne. You'd have to go all the way up to Carson City, maybe even Reno, to find a dealer who'd sell you one, and even then it'd run you more than he made in a year as sheriff. Considerably more. It was the second time he'd seen the car, he was sure of it. He'd spotted it the day before yesterday, parked up the street from the sheriff's office.

He continued walking, past the Chevron, still heading towards the Chamber of Commerce although his meeting with the Mayor was for the moment forgotten. When he was certain he could no longer be seen from the gas station he cut across the highway and doubled back, keeping the forecourt between him and the Cadillac until it was no more than twenty yards away.

Late afternoon. New Year's Eve, plenty of people around. *His* town. Nevertheless something made him flip the clasp that held his old .357 in its holster as he approached the car. For the first time he got a good look at the two men sitting in front.

Both wore sunglasses and sported crew cuts. Their eyes were hidden and they covered their reactions well but he knew they had both seen him the moment he broke cover. Now they were trying their best to ignore him.

He walked around to the driver's side of the car and knocked on the glass. After a moment the window slid down with a soft hum.

'How can we help you Sheriff?'

The driver smiled. Behind the mirrored Ray-Bans it was hard to see whether the smile made it as far as the man's eyes, but Lars would have bet against it. The accent wasn't local. Midwest somewhere. Wisconsin. Maybe Minnesota. His companion in the passenger seat said nothing, continuing to stare straight ahead.

'License and registration please.'

'Were we doing something wrong, Sheriff?'

'Just show me the documents.'

The man reached carefully into the pocket of his suit jacket, producing an Arizona license and the car's registration documents. The driver's license said John Langley. The car was registered in his name. The addresses on the vehicle registration document and the license matched. Lars called the license tags in to Connie anyway.

'You boys in town long?'

'Just passing through, Sheriff, just passing through.'

A burst of static. Connie confirmed that the vehicle was clean.

Lars examined the license a moment longer and then handed the documents back through the window. As the driver was about to take them from him, Lars let them fall into the footwell. As the man leaned forward to retrieve them his jacket shifted, offering a glimpse of what was concealed inside.

Lars hand dropped to the butt of his gun, drawing it.

'Hands on the wheel. Now.' He nodded towards the man in the passenger seat. 'You too. Palms flat on the dash. Keep them where I can see them.'

After only the briefest hesitation both men complied.

Lars reached in through the window, carefully withdrawing a compact submachine gun from a holster underneath the man's shoulder.

Heckler & Koch MP5K. He recognized the stubby barrel, the shortened cocking handle, the vertical foregrip. Two similar weapons had been found strapped to the side of the van that had crashed into Mount Grant. He had looked it up when the forensics report had come back. Weighing only a few pounds the small, powerful submachine gun cost almost twenty thousand dollars. The high rate of fire combined with the weapon's accuracy meant that the MP5K was favored by special forces around the world.

Lars nodded in the direction of the man in the passenger seat.

'You carrying one of these too?'

After a moment the man nodded, continuing to stare out of the windscreen.

'We have permits Sheriff, if you'll just let me show you.'

'Keep your hands where I can see them, Mr. Langley. You want to tell me where I might find these permits?'

'Inside jacket pocket.'

Lars reached into the man's jacket, pulling out a concealed-carry weapons permit in the name of John Langley. The address matched the address on the driver's license and registration documents.

'Your friend got one of these as well?'

'Yes.'

'Arizona too?'

'Yes.' The driver's smiled never wavered.

'Alright boys, well you'll need to hand these weapons over. Arizona permits are no good here in Nevada.'

For the first time the man in the passenger seat turned to look at him. He was wearing the same mirrored Ray Bans as his companion, but Lars didn't need to see the man's eyes to tell he wasn't smiling.

'This is bullshit. You don't need a permit to carry a gun in Nevada.'

Lars nodded. Much to his regret, for over fifteen years it had been legal for Nevada residents to carry a concealed weapon on their person, and there was nothing he could do about that. As long as he remained sheriff there wouldn't be a gun store within the town's boundaries however. He may not be able to stop folks wandering the streets of Hawthorne tooled up like Yosemite Sam, but he could make sure they had to travel all the way up to Carson City or Reno to buy their hardware.

'Well that'd be true for open carry, but seeing as I found these squirrelled away on your person that's a different matter. Concealed weapons require a permit unless you're residents of Nevada, which you boys aren't.'

The man in the passenger seat opened his mouth to argue but the driver cut across him.

'Now Billy, I'm sure the sheriff here knows the law in his own state. Let's not argue with him. Sheriff, isn't it true that Nevada is a "shall issue" state for concealed weapons?' The man turned to his companion. 'That means the sheriff here has no discretion in the matter – he has to issue a permit as long as the applicant demonstrates he's qualified. Maybe we can swing by tomorrow and get ourselves sorted out.'

'Sure Mr. Langley. You and Billy call by the sheriff's office and fill out your applications. We'll take your fingerprints and get you all checked out. Make sure you are who you say you are. Once we're happy on that score the law gives me a hundred and twenty days to deal with your applications. We're kinda busy here right now, what with everything that's been going on up Mount Grant, so might be a while before I get 'round to it. I'm sure I'll do my best. We wouldn't want you boys running off to the Supreme Court complaining your Second Amendment rights had been violated, now would we?'

The smile flickered on the driver's lips for the briefest of instants before returning. Lars collected the second machinegun from the man in the passenger seat and then they drove off, leaving him standing in the forecourt of the Chevron.

Lars couldn't remember the last time he'd had to draw his gun on duty. But that wasn't what really troubled him. These men were professionals. The fact that he'd been able to spot them, that they hadn't had time to sort out permits for their weapons, it all indicated things were happening quickly. And if they had him under surveillance they would also have teams covering the Doctor and probably Fitzpatrick. He wasn't worried about the commander. As long as he stayed on the base he was well protected and could take care of himself. Alison Stone was a different matter however. He'd give her another call as soon as he got back to the office.

He ejected the magazines from each weapon and checked the chambers for rounds, making sure the safeties were on. Satisfied, he started walking back in the direction of the sheriff's office, forty thousand dollars worth of military grade hardware that he knew would never be collected slung over his shoulder. In a year they'd hand them over to the Bureau of Alcohol, Tobacco and Firearms. If ATF auctioned the weapons then perhaps Mineral County might get some of the proceeds and maybe he'd get himself a gun cabinet for the house.

Well, at least that would make Ellie happy.

29

ALISON LOOKED OUT of the small window, checking her Honda was still where she had left it, parked next to the dumpster in the darkness of the motel's empty parking lot. She pulled the faded curtains closed, returning to the bed in the center of the small motel room where she had left her notes. She picked up the thin sheaf of papers, flicking through them as her hair dried, still not daring to believe what she thought she had found. She could hear the sound of water running as he took a shower in the adjoining room. They had learned that morning that the motel's plumbing wasn't up to the challenge of providing them with hot showers simultaneously, and she had squealed through the thin wall that separated their rooms as her shower had suddenly run cold when he had turned his on. This evening they had agreed to synchronize, and she had gone first.

The motel had certainly seen better days. Both of their rooms were musty, badly in need of decoration. It wasn't even that convenient for Davis. She had suggested that they might find somewhere a little better to stay but he had insisted that the place was perfect. Far enough away from the campus to make it unlikely that anyone would look for them there, at least for a while. And more importantly they had been able to pay in cash, without having to provide a credit card as a deposit.

Not that Alison cared. She would stay there indefinitely if she needed to. It had been a long day but she wasn't even remotely tired, and hadn't needed the shower to revive her. She flicked back through the pages of her notes, still incredulous. Was it even possible?

The first evening she had concentrated on his physiological abilities, looking for external clues as to how he might be different. She would readily admit that despite the years she had spent at medical school it wasn't her forte, and after she had performed a number of basic examinations she had been happy to let him simply explain to her what he had discovered about himself over the years. The things he had told her had been fascinating, but she had been eager to dig deeper, to start examining the structure of his blood, his cells, his genetic make-up, to start unraveling the mystery of why he didn't age, of how his body seemed to retain the ability to renew and even develop itself. It was her area of expertise, but she hadn't expected quick or easy answers. She knew that the process would be slow and painstaking.

She had begun that morning by taking some of his blood, repeating the tests she had run on the sample that the sheriff had given to her at their first meeting. She had explained to him as he had bent over the microscope the importance of hematopoietic stem cells, their incredible powers of self-renewal, and how to identify them in the slide he was looking at from the red marker she had added. As she had found with the first sample she had tested, his blood contained exceptional numbers of these cells, far in excess of the concentrations she would expect to find. When they had first met Henrikssen had asked her whether these cells might be capable of explaining his sudden recovery at Mount Grant and she had told him she didn't think that was possible, but she had scribbled a note to herself to look into this again. There were studies that showed that animal hematopoietic stem cells were indeed capable of forming other cell types - muscle, blood vessels or even bone.

Given what he had told her the night before she may have been too quick to dismiss that idea.

But the first blood sample she had taken hadn't shown what she had really been looking for – the cells she had seen when she had tested the second sample of his blood that the sheriff had brought her – the ones that had marked as embryonic stem cells. The test she had run had told her that increased levels of HSCs seemed to be normal for him but now she needed to identify the signaling mechanisms in his blood, the factors that triggered his body to produce even greater concentrations of HSCs and even more importantly to see whether she could recreate the conditions that had led to him producing what appeared to be embryonic stem cells.

The blood samples she had analyzed previously had both been taken at Mount Grant, the first shortly after he had been admitted, the second later that night. She remembered that she had made some notes on the flight back to Maryland the day the sheriff had come to see her – thoughts on external factors that might have been relevant based on what she had read from his medical records and what Henrikssen had told her. She had found the notes in her bag, re-reading them quickly.

> *~Prior to/at abduction – possible*
> *elevated heart rate/bp/adrenaline (??)*
> *~Methohexital – heart rate/bp fall*
> *(briefly); adrenaline absorbed*
> *~Patient further sedated once in van (??)*
> *~Check with sheriff if*
> *ketamine/benzodiazepine found*
> *~GSW right kidney*
> *~Adrenaline administered*

There hadn't been much to go on. Cody had been unable to provide much further detail as to what had happened to him after he had been abducted, other than that they had given him something to sedate him.

The most obvious starting point was adrenaline. It was likely that any amounts of the chemical in his system immediately prior to the abduction would have been metabolized shortly afterwards. He hadn't regained consciousness before the first sample had been taken and she had no reason to think it had been administered in the van by his abductors. But for an hour before the second sample had been taken he had been on an epinephrine drip to combat the hypotension caused by the transfusion. She'd checked the dosage from the hospital medical records while she explained to him what she was looking for, and then asked whether he minded if she tested his response to adrenaline. He'd shrugged, offering his arm. She'd quickly prepared an IV bag, reducing the dosage he had received at Mount Grant.

Half an hour later she had disconnected the IV and had taken another sample of his blood. It had taken her another twenty minutes to prepare a slide for the microscope, staining the sample with Oct-4, the marker that would identify whether his blood contained embryonic stem cells. When she was finished she had leaned over the microscope again, holding her breath. The blue splodges had been present as before, but this time there were a lot more with red marking their edges, showing that the number of hematopoietic stem cells had increased dramatically. But what had immediately caught her attention was the significant number of green areas that hadn't been present in the first sample, the Oct-4 highlighting the embryonic cells that hadn't been there before.

She had stepped back from the microscope, considering what she was seeing. She still didn't understand how the cells were being formed - were they being created somewhere within his body or were other cells, possibly the HSCs, de-differentiating, regressing back to a simpler, more flexible, form? But had she identified the trigger? Was it as simple as increased levels of adrenaline? Logically it made sense. Adrenaline was released into the bloodstream as part of the body's 'fight or flight' response to a perceived threat. What better way to kick-start preparations for repair and regeneration?

Before she got too carried away she had to demonstrate that it was in fact these embryonic stem cells that were responsible for his body's ability to heal. Although totipotent stem cells were invaluable in studying the pathology of diseases, Alison knew that the only stem cell studies that had ever shown success in the treatment of any human disease had involved adult rather than embryonic cells.

The Biological Sciences Department at UC Irvine had developed a neuronal cell culture model of Alzheimer's that she had used in her research and she had brought samples with her. What if she were to introduce a small sample of his blood to the Alzheimer's culture? Excited by what she had already discovered that morning she had been instantly drawn to the idea. It had taken only minutes for her to prepare the sample. She had shown him the culture model through the microscope, explaining both the nature of the disease and what she was hoping to see. Alzheimer's was caused by the destruction of the brain's circuits as a result of the formation of plaques – fragments of protein - outside and around neurons as well as by the build up of neurofibrillary tangles – insoluble twisted fibers - inside the nerve cells themselves. The degradation of the cells that this caused, together with a dramatic shrinkage of neural tissue, gave rise to the problems experienced by those suffering from the disease. Any effective treatment would need to reverse the formation of the plaques and tangles, while also regenerating lost neuronal connections. She was looking for any improvement, however slight, in those symptoms.

She'd had no idea how long she would need to leave the culture before she might expect to see results. Cody had suggested that they get some lunch while they waited and they had left the lab, finding an Italian restaurant just off campus that was open. But while they had waited for their food to arrive she had started to have doubts.

The more she had thought about it, the more she had begun to think she had become carried away by her discovery. It was true that scientists had had some success transplanting stem cells from a patient's own blood and bone marrow, subsequently stimulating those cells to differentiate into neural cells in order to treat the disease. But even if adrenaline was indeed the trigger for the production of embryonic stem cells in his blood, what she had done was incredibly crude. There were any number of reasons why it might not work.

They had finished their food and returned to the campus. By the time they were back in the lab she had already convinced herself that the experiment with the cell culture had been a waste of time, and had begun a more detailed examination of the hematopoietic and embryonic stem cells in his blood, trying to identify the features of his cells that allowed adrenaline to trigger the reaction she had witnessed.

Cody had decided to take a walk while she worked. It had been turning dark when he had returned an hour later. Alison had been engrossed in her work and he had wandered over to where she had set up the cell cultures that morning, leaning over the microscope to see whether he could spot any changes. After a few moments he had called her over, moving out of the way so that she could look for herself.

For a moment she had peered into the microscope, silent, barely able to believe what she was seeing. There were far more neurons than there had been before, each plumper, less fibrous, the protein deposits nestling between them much less pronounced. In a matter of hours the damage to the neurons caused by the disease had largely been reversed and it even seemed that new neural pathways were forming. When she had finally managed to drag herself away and look up she had realized there were tears running down her face. She didn't understand how yet, but somehow, somewhere within his blood lay the cure for the disease that had taken her father from her.

Now she sat on the bed in the small motel room, her mind still grappling with the implications of what she had found, the enormity of the discovery threatening to overwhelm her. She had so much to do, and there was no time to waste. Hundreds of people died every day from Alzheimer's in the United States alone. And even for those not yet in the final stages, the progression of the disease was relentless. Even though Cody's blood seemed capable of curing the physical aspects of the disease she knew that it could not cure the psychological. Computerized x-ray tomography and fMRI scanning had shown that memories, the cornerstone of human personality, were initially encoded in the hippocampus, before eventually being transferred to the more complex frontal lobe, its widely distributed neural network more adept at long-term storage and retrieval. But once the substrate in which memories were stored was destroyed those memories were lost forever.

Alzheimer's attacked the hippocampus first and most severely, later progressing to other regions of the cortex, causing those tissues to shrivel and atrophy. Every day that she now delayed converting what she had discovered into a workable cure those suffering from the disease would lose a little more of themselves to the disease, a portion of their personality gone forever.

There were so many problems she would need to overcome. Would a single dose of his blood be sufficient to permanently cure the disease, or would constant transfusions be necessary? And how would they even deliver the cells from his blood into the system of an Alzheimer's patient? The vascular system that fed the brain was the most obvious choice – no cell in the central nervous system was more than forty microns away from a capillary. But whatever was causing the healing would still need to pass through the blood-brain barrier, assuming it was small enough to fit through. And then there was the danger of auto-immune rejection – the risk that a patient's body might react badly to his blood. Although as Cody's blood type was *hh*, making him a superuniversal donor, that issue was likely to be manageable with a minimum of immunosuppressant medication.

Alison forced herself to remain calm. The important thing was that there was a cure. She would work harder, as hard as was necessary. Once she revealed her findings funding would no longer be a problem; she would have whatever resources she needed. Whatever the issues that needed to be worked out, she knew that solutions would ultimately be found. The disease that had killed her father, that she had dedicated most of her life to fighting, would inevitably be conquered. She hadn't even begun to consider what other diseases his cells might be capable of curing, or how those cells might also be responsible for the fact that he didn't age, or for the other extraordinary abilities he possessed.

On the way back to the motel he had raised the possibility that adrenaline might also account for how his body seemed to be able to develop itself. Each time there had been an improvement in his faculties it seemed to have been preceded by an extended period of stress. He had first realized he was able to memorize large amounts of information shortly after he had started school; he remembered as a small boy being afraid of the punishment he would suffer at the hands of the teachers at the orphanage if he couldn't complete his schoolwork. His distance vision had improved dramatically shortly after he had started flying in Korea. He could recall the apprehension he had felt on those first missions when someone in the flight had called out the MiGs and he hadn't been able to see them. He was certain his night vision and his hearing had both improved after the first weeks he had spent in the jungles of Vietnam, every nerve on edge as he had strained to see or hear any sign of the enemy in the darkness. If you accepted that adrenaline was the trigger for his recuperative abilities it certainly seemed logical. Something else for her, or others, to explore. There was enough work to keep an army of scientists busy for months, years.

What an incredible day.

Alison checked her watch. It was getting late. She should call her mother to let her know she was okay, that she would be out of contact for a few days and not to worry. She dug in her bag, looking for her cell phone, remembering at the last minute that Cody had warned her not to use it. She considered putting the battery back in – it would only take a minute to make the call – but then decided against it. There was a payphone outside in the parking lot. She emptied her purse onto the bed and grabbed some change.

Outside the air felt heavy, the smell of approaching rain. She walked across the empty lot to the phone. She unhooked the handset from its cradle, fed a couple of quarters into the slot, listening as they rattled down, dialing the number from memory. The phone rang once and then a man with a foreign accent answered. She was about to apologize for having called the wrong number when he used her name.

'Doctor Stone?'

What was a stranger doing in her mother's house? Why had her mother not picked up the phone?

'Yes. Who are you? Where is my mother?'

The man ignored the question.

'Listen very carefully Doctor Stone. Your mother is with us. For now she is unharmed. If you want her to remain that way you will do exactly as I say.'

30

THE PUNGENT SMELL of ammonia brought Alison around suddenly, the vapors from the capsule that had been broken under her nose burning the membranes of her nasal passages. She inhaled sharply, pulling her head back, away from the smell, her eyes already tearing.

She blinked several times, her eyes adjusting to the dim light, still groggy. Where was she? She heard a movement behind her and tried to turn around, but she was restrained, thick velcro straps binding her forearms and calves to the sturdy metal chair in which she was sitting. She felt cold, noticing for the first time she was only wearing her underwear. A small, white-walled room, no windows. A desk pushed against the wall in front of her, on top of which sat a monitor and what looked like a portable defibrillator, one of those machines that delivered electric shocks to restart the heart after a person had suffered a heart attack. She shook her head. What had happened? Was she in hospital?

All of a sudden a cold panic shot through her, flushing the final remnants of the drugs from her system as the memories came flooding back. The telephone call. They had her mother. She had led them to the motel where she and Cody had been staying. They had given her something and then she had blacked out. She tried again to look around, straining her neck to see who was behind her, but the straps were too tight.

'Doctor Stone, I see you've come around.'

A man's voice, but soft, high pitched. He spoke English well but the accent was foreign, maybe Central or South American.

'Who are you? What am I doing here?'

She tried her best to sound indignant, outraged, but it was hard to keep the fear from her voice.

The man walked around to stand in front of her. He was older than his voice suggested, maybe sixty, perhaps a few years older, and short, several inches shorter than she. He wore a pristine white lab coat over a shirt and tie. His skin was olive and he had a small moustache, neatly trimmed, but otherwise he was almost completely bald, only a few thin strands of hair carefully slicked back above his ears. He wasn't fat, but full cheeks and jowls and a paunch pushing against the belt of his trousers suggested he lived well. He didn't speak for a while, his dark eyes examining her carefully underneath half closed eyelids.

'You are here because you have certain information that my employer wishes to know. All that you need to know about me is that I have some experience in extracting information from people who may not wish to disclose it.'

Alison didn't know what to say. She felt her pulse race, her heart pounding in her ears. Had she heard him correctly? Was he really threatening to torture her? It was the sort of thing that only happened on TV, in the movies. It didn't happen to people in the real world, to people like her. She realized suddenly how naïve she had been. She knew what Cody represented, what he was worth, and that others were after him, had already tried to kidnap him once. How stupid had she been not to appreciate the danger they were in? He had realized it. She should have just let him go. Instead she had convinced him to stay, to help her. And now because of her they had him again, and her mother as well.

The man turned to the bench behind him and removed the pads from the defibrillator, carefully unwinding the cables that connected them to the machine. When he was done he removed the protective plastic covers from each pad and then turned to face her, bending over to place one pad against her stomach, kneeling to press the other to her ankle. The pads felt sticky and cold against her skin.

Her mind was racing. She felt herself starting to sweat in spite of the cold. What was he doing? She tried to tell herself it would be okay. Defibrillators had failsafes – inbuilt sensors that monitored the heart's activity to prevent a shock being delivered where one was not needed. She had seen ambulance crews attaching the pads to themselves, pressing the button to prove nothing could happen if one were used on a healthy person. Besides, he had placed the pads in the wrong position. The machine simply couldn't work. She forced herself to remain calm, staring at him with all the composure she could muster.

'Look, I don't know what you're trying to do, but...'

He cut her off.

'Doctor, it would save time if you listened. You will have recognized the machine to which you are now attached as an automated external defibrillator. It is also possible because of your medical training that you believe the machine will not activate when connected to a person who is not showing abnormal heart activity. That would be a mistake. I have removed the safeguards from this machine. It is capable of delivering between 200 and 1700 volts for whatever duration I choose to select. You will note that I have placed the pads so that the current should not pass directly through your heart, and so while it will be deeply unpleasant, the shock should not be life threatening. However, if I do manage to cause your heart to stop I can of course reposition the pads and restart it.'

He turned back to the table, appearing to adjust the settings on the small device to which she was now attached.

Alison was speechless, still not believing this could be happening to her. The man hadn't even asked her any questions. What was the point if he hadn't even given her an opportunity to talk? He had to be bluffing, simply trying to frighten her into telling him what she knew.

'Now listen, this makes no sense. You can't...'

Before she had a chance to finish the sentence he turned back to face her, at the same time pushing the large red button on the top of the machine. She felt an unbelievable pain, as if her entire body was suddenly on fire. Every muscle convulsed, her back arching against the chair, her legs and arms straining against the straps holding her to the chair. The shock caused her jaw to clench tightly and she found she couldn't even scream. The pain continued for what seemed like an eternity until finally, mercifully, she passed out.

When he was certain that it was safe, the man leaned over to check her. Her pulse was racing but the defibrillator told him that her heart hadn't been affected. She had bitten her cheek when the current had hit and blood was flowing steadily from her mouth. When he had first started to use the machine he had given his victims something to bite down on to protect against such injuries. But he had found that people broke more quickly if they had something tangible to remind them of the pain between the shocks. The slick, coppery taste of blood in the mouth worked well. He checked that she really was unconscious, then pulled on a pair of disposable latex gloves to check the cut. Her head was forward, and the bleeding was unlikely to obstruct her airway, but he couldn't risk the woman's death, at least not until she had told him everything she knew. He knew little about his current employer, but he was being paid an exceptional amount of money, and the type of people who needed his services were typically not forgiving. He would need to be careful.

He would have liked more time to study the woman's background. He had read her file carefully and he believed he knew where best to apply pressure to get her to talk quickly. With someone like her it would have been better to proceed more cautiously, but whoever was paying him was impatient for results. The woman was educated, but unlike most intellectuals he was certain that the simple application of pain would not be the most efficient way to break her resolve. Even a cursory inspection of her file revealed that her life had been characterized by sacrifice, first for her father and then when she hadn't been able to save him, for others like him. Everyone had physical limits of course, everyone broke in the end. But this woman valued the goals that defined her life more than her own wellbeing, which meant it would take time.

It was a pity, normally he would have relished the task. But whoever was employing him refused to wait and so he would simply apply pressure to those things she cared most about. Divulging the information he needed would cause her to jeopardize the very thing she had dedicated her life to, but now that they had her mother he was certain that he had the leverage to overcome that concern. And he had another plan if for some reason that didn't work.

After a few minutes he decided that she had been out long enough. It was just after three in the morning, but the room had no clocks, no windows that might let her know it was even night. Most people naturally reached their lowest ebb in the early hours, and after being knocked out twice she should be sufficiently disoriented.

The mind made emotional decisions when it was tired, he knew that well. It would make it easier for him. He reached into his pocket for another capsule of ammonium carbonate and broke it under her nose.

A few seconds later Alison came around. She spat the blood from her mouth, staring at him from the chair. She was frightened, he could see that, but there was something he hadn't seen before, a hint of defiance. He smiled. He had been right about her. He could always tell when they decided they were going to resist.

'Alison'.

He had purposely dispensed with 'Doctor Stone'. It was important that she realize the transition of power, that it was he who was now in charge.

'The shock that you experienced was relatively mild, towards the lower end of what this machine is capable of delivering. If I were to increase the voltage, or to make your skin more conductive, for instance by wetting it, the effects would be significantly more unpleasant.'

He turned around again to the bench and she flinched, bracing herself against the shock, expecting the current to flow through her again at any moment. But he simply turned on the monitor, stepping back so that she could see the image clearly.

It was her mother. She was tied to a chair, men wearing ski masks on either side of her. It looked like they were in her house, upstairs in one of the bedrooms.

'It was necessary for you to experience the effects of electrocution to appreciate in some small way what your mother will experience if you do not co-operate fully. The men who are holding her have electric batons that are far less sophisticated than the defibrillator whose effects you have experienced. Those batons can however deliver a much higher current, sufficient to severely burn or even rupture the skin. And these men, while no doubt skilled at administering pain, are unfortunately unlikely to be as careful as I might be in avoiding those areas, such as the heart or the head, that might cause death or permanent incapacitation.'

Alison stared at the monitor, her mind screaming. She knew now that she was already dead. They'd want to silence her just for what she knew about Cody. The man hadn't even bothered to hide his face. But she might be able to save her mother. The men who were holding her were wearing masks. Why would they bother to do that if they were going to kill her anyway? Cody had the potential to be the most important discovery in medical history and it was her fault he was being held by these people, but she couldn't change that now. All she could do was try and save her mother. She dropped her head, nodding that she would co-operate.

The man walked back around behind her. He pushed a button on the wall and spoke into an intercom.

'She is ready to talk.'

A camera mounted high in the wall in front of her blinked into life, an almost inaudible whirring as the lens focused on the woman strapped to the chair.

She began, explaining how Cody had first visited her the previous October, how she had heard nothing further until almost three months later she had been contacted by Lars Henrikssen, the sheriff from Hawthorne investigating the events at Mount Grant, and how she had subsequently uncovered various details about his past from the internet which suggested he had been born in Britain almost a century before. She was careful not to mention how she had first connected him to Luke Jackson through the picture of her father in her parents' house. If her mother was to survive this Alison had to convince her captors that she knew nothing about the man. She limited what she said to information she had found on the internet, facts that were therefore available to anybody who was looking for them. It wasn't much, but there was a good chance that these people had already found out what she had – maybe she wouldn't be telling them anything they didn't already know. She mentioned nothing about what she had found out in the lab the day before, that the most likely trigger for Cody's regenerative capabilities was adrenaline. She had destroyed her notes before they had arrived at the motel. She had to hope that it would still take them some time to make that discovery.

When she had finished the man left the room and closed the door behind him. Alison sat alone, waiting. She hoped she had done enough to save her mother. They wouldn't harm Cody, at least not immediately. He was too valuable to them. It would take them a long time to unlock his body's secrets. He was well trained and resourceful. Maybe he would find some way to get free. There would be no escape for her, she was sure of that now. Once they were certain she had told them everything she knew they would kill her.

After what seemed like an eternity the door opened. She looked up as the man with the white lab coat and the moustache entered the room, walking over to stand in front of her. He was alone. She had expected others, the men who would take her to where she would be killed. Then she noticed that he was filling a syringe from a vial he had taken from the bench. So that was it. He would do it here.

Alison was suddenly angry. She knew she was going to die, there was nothing she could do to prevent it, but what right did this little fuck have to take her life? She would at least show him that she was not afraid. She stared at him, nodding at the syringe.

'What have you got there?'

He ignored the question. He set the first syringe on the bench and filled another from the same vial.

'Alison, I have a problem. You have not told me everything that you know.'

She felt her heart race, her anger suddenly evaporating. She forced herself to keep a straight face. They mustn't find out how much her mother knew.

'What do you mean? I've told you everything.'

The man sighed.

'Alison, I have been doing this for a very long time. You have to believe me when I tell you that I know when people are withholding information from me. I do believe that you want more than anything to save your mother, and therefore I can only assume that you think that the information you are holding back is likely to endanger her. You might even be willing to allow her to suffer a certain amount of pain in order to preserve her life. Whatever the reason, my employer is not a patient man.'

'Thankfully I have developed a *poción*, how do you say in English, a concoction. What you would call a truth serum. It has taken me more than twenty years to perfect its composition. Once it takes effect you will find it almost impossible not to answer any questions I put to you with complete honesty.'

Alison shook her head. She knew more than most people how the brain worked. The truth drugs that were administered in films were a myth, a fiction created by Hollywood. Certain drugs were effective at suppressing higher cognitive functions, which could certainly make a person more talkative, even more co-operative, but there was little evidence that a sufficiently strong-willed person might not still be able to lie.

The man was watching her closely.

'I see you are skeptical. I forget, you have some experience in these matters. I would actually be interested in your professional opinion. I unfortunately do not know the precise composition of the serum I use.

It contains barbiturates of course – sodium thiopental, sodium amytal, scopolamine – all those that you might expect to find in use by interrogators in dozens of countries around the world. And methylenedioxymethamphetamine, MDMA. For years I experimented with these compounds in varying doses, with only moderate success. But then the government I was working for came into possession of a drug known only as SP-17. It was apparently developed by the KGB. I have tried for years to discover its active ingredients but unfortunately without much success. Its composition is for obvious reasons a closely guarded secret, and as the drug has neither taste, smell nor color it is hard to guess at its composition. SP-17 was much more effective, but the results still varied. It was only when I started to combine this new drug with the chemicals I had been using before that I started to achieve truly incredible results. It took me several more years of experimentation to arrive at what I believe to be the optimal ratio. Unfortunately the supply of SP-17 at the time was unreliable and sometimes months would pass when I had no access to the drug. Thankfully things have improved since the end of the Cold War and now I have several suppliers. The benefits of a free market economy.' He smiled.

'But I digress. What I learned was that, when combined with higher concentrations of MDMA and smaller amounts of barbiturates, SP-17 quickly renders a person incapable of withholding information. That information must be extracted quickly however. Despite its excellent performance my discovery has one significant disadvantage. Once the drug has been administered irreparable damage to the brain is unfortunately inevitable. The subject experiences only a limited period of lucidity before quickly becoming disorientated. First short term and then long term memory are lost. Speech quickly becomes impaired, followed by uncontrollable tremors and finally complete muscular paralysis. The drug can therefore only be used as a last resort, and when the interrogator believes he can extract the information he needs quickly. You will have noticed that I have prepared another syringe, in case I feel that more of the drug needs to be administered in the little time that we will have once I have given you the first injection. It is merely a precaution, however. I have never known a single dose to be insufficient.'

Alison listened, horrified, while the small man standing in front of her matter-of-factly described the devastating effects of the drug he was about to give her. She knew that barbiturates would suppress higher cortical functioning as well as depressing the cardiovascular and respiratory systems, but reasonable levels were unlikely to cause lasting damage. Higher doses of MDMA however had long been known to produce neurochemical damage, resulting in an impairment of learning and memory and other neurological dysfunctions. MDMA was structurally similar to a combination of methamphetamine – speed - and mescaline, a hallucinogen that acted on the brain's serotonin receptors. The drug forced unnaturally large amounts of serotonin to be released into the brain, causing the user to experience artificial feelings of empathy or well-being, which was why it had been used as a truth drug. Methamphetamine had been shown to cause degeneration of nerve cells containing the neurotransmitter dopamine, which could be responsible for the loss of control of motor functions, the tremors and paralysis, as well as the build up of neurofibrillary tangles inside the neurons of the hippocampus, the very symptoms that were characteristic of Alzheimer's and other chronic neurodegenerative disorders. But even concentrated doses shouldn't cause the effects he had described. There must be something within SP-17 that accelerated the effects of MDMA, temporarily enhancing its effectiveness as a truth serum, but at a terrible cost to the person to whom it had been administered. Alison realized that she was about to experience at first hand the horrors of the disease that had killed her father, that it would be the disease that she had been fighting all these years that would now strip her of everything that she was and then kill her.

She watched as de Souza prepared the injection, slowly drawing the pale yellow liquid up into the syringe before gently tapping the end to release any trapped bubbles. She tried to pull away as he approached but the restraints prevented her moving her arm. He quickly found a vein, and she felt the needle sink into her flesh. Then cold as he pushed the plunger, forcing the drug into her system. She tried to force herself to remain calm, to relax her breathing, anything to slow the passage of the drug through her system. But it was no use. Her heart was racing, pushing the chemicals through her bloodstream. It would be a matter of seconds before they reached her brain.

There.

Her nostrils flared as she detected the odor of garlic, faint at first, growing stronger with each breath. That was the sodium thiopental taking effect. The man with the white lab coat leaned in close, checking her pupils.

'*Qué buena*, Alison, that's good. I think we are ready to begin.'

Twenty minutes later it was over.

The small Honduran stood to one side as Friedrichs undid the straps around the woman's forearms and ankles. Her eyes were open but it was obvious that she was unaware of what was happening around her, her gaze blank, her mouth open, her jaw slack. She made no attempt to stand as he lifted her easily out of the chair and on to a gurney.

The information about her father's connection with Gant that she had initially fought so hard not to disclose was of little importance. The mother was already dead, the team he had left in Maryland would even now be preparing to leave the house, removing all evidence they had ever been there. It might be days before a neighbor would find her at the bottom of the stairs, the only sign of injury a broken neck and some bruises that would appear to have been sustained in the fall.

What they had learned about the adrenaline was much more interesting; *Der Eckzahn* would be pleased. Friedrichs had been impressed with how efficiently the Honduran had got the woman to talk. Having his men wear ski masks had been inspired. It was a shame that they wouldn't be able to use him again, but he already had his orders. *Der Eckzahn* wanted him to take care of it personally. A Lear jet had been waiting for him at Carroll County Regional Airport, and had taken off as soon as he was on board. As soon as they were in the air he had dispatched teams to each of the targets.

There could be no loose ends.

None at all.

31

THE GOLF CART'S motor hummed gently as it climbed the slope. He had played the course three times already that week, savoring the beautiful tree-lined fairways and mildly undulating greens. But this hole was his favorite. Surrounded by water, with winds whipping off the ocean that could send your tee shots drifting well offline, it demanded precise placement and a deft touch with the short game.

It had cost him a small fortune to join, but the course was limited to members and their guests and this early in the morning he would have it to himself. He looked around, savoring the moment. He could never have afforded this on an FBI agent's salary. The payoff he had received for the information about the sheriff in Hawthorne would be his last, but he had been paid enough over the years to enable him to retire, with enough money to ensure he would live out the rest of his days doing as he pleased, a wealthy man.

He parked on the green, spotting his ball as he stepped out of the cart. Not bad, closer than he had hoped. He rummaged in his golf bag and pulled out a putter. As he was walking to his ball he noticed one of the groundsmen coming up the fairway towards him.

Shit, he had driven onto the green again. It was the second time this week they had caught him. He held his hand up - *mea culpa* - gesturing that he would move on as soon as he had taken his shot, hoping it would be enough to convince the man to simply turn around and drive away. But the buggy kept coming, the groundsman showing no intention of deviating from his course.

DeWitty felt his good mood begin to evaporate. He watched the cart approach, finally coming to a halt just short of the green. The groundsman stepped out of his golf cart and started walking towards him.

As he approached the man slipped his hand into the pocket of his overalls. *Just a little closer.* The .22-calibre pistol with its tiny one-ounce slug was a gnat swatter, a gun for an old lady's handbag. If they had let him use a rifle he could just as easily have taken the shot from the tee, or anywhere else from within a five hundred yard range for that matter. But the Hi-Standard .22 auto was the only production-model handgun that could be effectively silenced and a result it was the weapon of choice for the mob's hit men.

The mark was walking towards him, a contrite expression on his face.

Close enough.

He pulled out the pistol, watching the man's expression change as he fired a single bullet into his chest. There was no sound other than the muted click as the mechanism cycled. The man dropped to his knees, hands clutching the front of his Argyle sweater. The putter slipped from his fingers.

He moved efficiently, quickly checking that the fairway was still deserted before stepping around to deliver the *coup de grâce*, a second shot just behind the right ear. The man slumped forward onto the green.

It went against his training not to collect the cases but those were his orders. He walked to the edge of the water and tossed the pistol into the lake. When they found the body the lake would be dredged and they would recover it. The gun would be traced to a Miami sporting-goods store known for supplying weapons to the Mafia.

He walked back to his golf cart and drove away.

32

THE RED LIGHT on the dashboard of the Volvo blinked gently, warning that a seatbelt was unbuckled. Fitzpatrick glanced over at his wife, already asleep in the passenger seat. He contemplated waking her but then thought better of it. The turn off US-95 was just up ahead, the base only another four miles, and there would be no traffic on Carson Road at this time in the morning. He would have her home soon.

He turned the station wagon off the highway. He had finally persuaded Carla that they should trade the Volvo in, and tomorrow, her week of night duty over, he would take it to the dealership and pick up the SUV they had ordered. He should have done it a long time ago. It worried him that his wife, who had never been the most attentive driver, used a car for her daily commute that had neither airbags nor anti-lock brakes.

The sun was rising over the mountains as he drove east towards the base and he flipped the visor down. Up ahead, still a mile or so in the distance he saw a truck pull off the hard shoulder and join the two-lane hardtop, slowly gathering speed as it lumbered towards them. He had noticed it parked by the side of the road as he'd made his way out to the hospital earlier that morning. US-95 was an important route for long-haul freight and big eighteen-wheeler semis were a common sight. He supposed the driver had pulled off the highway to find somewhere to park up for the night. Which was a little odd, now that he thought about it. There was a twenty-four hour truck stop only a couple of miles outside Fallon on US-50. But perhaps he'd missed it, or maybe he'd just preferred to spend the night out here by himself.

The truck was closer now, still some way off but closing the distance between them. With the sun in his eyes it was hard to tell, but it looked like the rig was still picking up speed. Every few seconds black smoke would belch from the exhaust pipe behind the cab as the driver shifted through the gears. Perhaps the guy had overslept and was now in a hurry to get back on the highway before the traffic started to build. Back roads like this weren't typically patrolled but he would need to watch himself when he turned onto 95. If he kept that speed up the highway patrol would be on him before he made it very far.

He looked past the truck to the base as a couple of F-5s took off, exhausts briefly flaring orange as their afterburners kicked in, the planes maintaining a tight formation as they banked to the right and started to climb. He leaned forward into the steering wheel, shielding his eyes against the morning sun to follow their progress a few seconds longer. They were old jets, only used by the Navy now as training planes, but the sharp needle-nosed design always reminded him of why he had wanted to be an aviator in the first place. Soon they were out of sight, disappearing over the mountains to the east.

His attention returned to the truck, still a couple of hundred yards away but bearing down on the Volvo at an impressive rate. The sound of its straining engine was now clearly audible above the gentle burble of the station wagon's, and he could see clouds of dust billowing behind in its wake as it forced its bulk through the still morning air. Without thinking he eased off the accelerator, inching towards the hard shoulder on his right. The truck had plenty of room to get past but he could already see the stones being kicked up by the rig's huge double wheels. It would be a nuisance if one were to crack the Volvo's windscreen the day before he was due to trade it in.

The truck was almost on them, the first rays of sunlight glinting off the chrome on the huge radiator, the sound of the protesting engine now drowning out the Volvo's. He had to be doing eighty miles an hour. Only a lunatic would drive a rig that big so hard on a road like this. For the first time Fitzpatrick wondered whether something had happened. Had the accelerator stuck open? Perhaps the driver was unconscious, his foot jammed on the gas. It was close enough that he could easily make out the letters in the grill – MACK - but with the sun behind it was harder to see up into the cab. He decided he would turn the Volvo around once the truck had passed them. If the driver didn't quickly show signs of slowing down he would call it in to the sheriff. Even at this time in the morning there would be carnage if the rig hit the junction where Carson joined the highway at anything like that speed.

No more than fifty feet away now, towering over the Volvo, the huge air deflector on top of the cab close enough to block out the sun behind, suddenly throwing the station wagon into shade. It took a fraction of a second for his eyes to adjust but now finally he could see up through the windshield. There were two men in the cab. The man on the left did indeed seem unconscious, slumped against the door on his side, his head resting against the passenger window. Fitzpatrick shifted his gaze quickly to the right. He suddenly felt a jolt of fear as he realized the man driving was wearing a crash helmet.

Everything happened at once.

He caught a glimpse of the driver pulling hard on the huge steering wheel and the rig suddenly swerved to the right, bearing straight for the Volvo, the huge chromed fender level with the top of his door, filling the windscreen and driver's side window.

Fitzpatrick knew that he was dead. Instinctively he braked, pulling the steering wheel hard to the right, trying desperately to get the side of the car where Carla was still sleeping out of the way of the mountain of steel that was now bearing down on them. There was no time to get to her seat belt. The old station wagon's wheels locked and it started to skid, bringing his seat directly into the path of the juggernaut. Without thinking he let go of the wheel, trying desperately to turn in his seat, to throw himself towards his wife in the second before the impact.

The Mack hit the left side of the Volvo squarely between the front and rear doors. The driver had braked before turning into the collision to avoid rolling the rig but nevertheless it was travelling at close to sixty miles an hour when it hit. Twenty tons of steel and cast iron engine block hit the station wagon with the force of a freight train, completely obliterating the body of the old car on the side where the base commander had been sitting, killing him instantly. Only the Volvo's reinforced chassis prevented the truck from cutting the car in half and continuing on. Instead the cab mounted the station wagon, the momentum driving both off the road and through a post fence, finally coming to rest in a cloud of dirt and debris two hundred yards from the road.

There were a few seconds of silence as the dust settled slowly around the wreckage. Inside the truck the driver took a moment to check he was uninjured before removing his crash helmet and placing it on the seat beside him. The airbag in the steering wheel had gone off and the air in the cab was thick with smoke and the acrid smell of the propellant. He ignored it. He needed to move quickly now.

He released his seat belt, reaching over to unbuckle his passenger's. His other hand pulled the latch to open his door and he kicked it open with his foot. The airbag hadn't fully deflated and it made his task difficult, but he moved efficiently. He slid out of the cab, balancing on the fuel tank housing beneath the driver's door, reaching across his seat to pull the unconscious man across to the driver's side. When he was in position he leaned over him, fed the seatbelt across his torso, then pushed the catch home. When he was satisfied that the man was in position he allowed him to fall forward, the seatbelt taking his weight. Then he placed his hands on either side of the man's neck, grabbed his jaw firmly then twisted sharply, hearing the vertebrae snap.

They had found the truck driver asleep in his cab at the Chevron truck stop on US-50 earlier that morning. He had been forced to drink most of a bottle of whisky while they drove his rig to the road that the spotters had identified as the route Fitzpatrick would take from the base that morning. Highway patrol would find the bottle under his seat. When they tested his blood they would discover that he was several times over the limit.

The man jumped off the rig, landing lightly on the ground. He reached up to grab the crash helmet, closing the driver's door behind him. A quick look into the station wagon told him that there was no chance that the base commander was still alive. He walked around to the passenger's side of the car to check on the man's wife. Incredibly the damage here was far less. The woman was unconscious, her head resting against the passenger window. He carefully opened the passenger door, placing three fingers under her chin. Her pulse was weak, but it was there. He quickly assessed her injuries. It was unlikely she would survive but his orders were clear. He placed the crash helmet on the ground and reached into the car, taking her head in his hands as he had the driver of the rig. His fingers covered her nose and mouth. Seconds passed, becoming minutes. When he was certain she was no longer breathing he closed the passenger door of the Volvo and picked up his helmet, taking one last second to survey the scene. Then he turned and walked away.

By the time he had reached the road a black van was pulling up, the door sliding open to let him in.

33

LARS CHECKED THE small clock on the nightstand. Almost dawn. He'd let Ellie sleep a few more minutes then he'd get up.

It was the dream that had woken him. In the dream it had been night and they had been coming for him, moving silently through the darkness, just as they had that night in the Laotian jungle. He had finally woken as the trip flares had gone off, pop-popping like fireworks, washing the vegetation in front of him in a sea of blinding white light. In that instant he had seen them clearly, scores of black shapes moving quickly up the trails, the jungle suddenly transformed into a moving wall of enemy assassins.

Now why in hell had he been dreaming about that? He hadn't had that dream since just after he'd gotten back, almost forty years ago now. Must have been what he'd told Doctor Stone about her father and Jackson, stirring up old memories.

Truth be told he hadn't had a good night's sleep all week, not since his conversation with DeWitty. The man had already called several times looking for the information he had promised on Emily Mortimer. He'd told Connie to run interference for him but the last time the FBI agent had called he'd been insistent, threatening to have her job if she didn't put him through immediately. Which was the last thing you wanted to try with Connie. It didn't matter if you were the Special Agent in Charge of Utah or the goddamned President of the United States of America, that particular brand of horseshit was unlikely to fly very far with her.

Nevertheless he could tell she'd been worried when she'd come into his office afterwards. He'd told her to put DeWitty through the next time the man called.

The FBI agent had been right about one thing though. He was well out of his league, and no mistake. But something had to be done, and soon. Brandt had already spent far too long rotting in that cell, and now he'd gone and put Emily Mortimer at risk as well. He told himself she should be safe for a little while, but he couldn't wait forever. If he had found her others could. And he still hadn't heard from Doctor Stone. He'd been trying her cell every hour for the last few days but it was constantly switched off. Something was wrong. He should never have let her convince him that she should meet Gant alone.

But who could he go to with what he knew? If the FBI's most senior agent in Utah was somehow involved in this then who was there to trust? Hell, who would even believe him? He wasn't even sure he believed it himself.

Well, lying around in bed sure wasn't going to solve his problems. He pulled his arm out from underneath his sleeping wife as gently as he could, sitting on the edge of the bed to stretch his leg. Goddamn if his knee wasn't getting worse each winter. He was just about to stand when he saw the bedroom door opening, the silenced barrel of a semi-automatic appearing behind it as the first of the men made their way into the room.

Lars was on his feet in an instant, his protesting knee forgotten. His service revolver slid easily from the worn holster in the gun belt draped over the chair beside his bed as he moved silently to the wall behind the opening door, out of sight of the men entering the room, flicking the switch on the wall that turned on the light in the bathroom as he passed. He had no idea how many of them there were. Best to let them all in before the fireworks started.

Lars was surprised to realize that he wasn't afraid. The gun in his hand was old but it worked just fine. Twice a year he brought Jed and Larry out to the desert behind Duke's place to get some practice in with tin cans. He wasn't a bad shot. Hell from this distance not even Ellie could miss.

The first man was making for the bed where his wife slept on, unawares. The second had seen the sliver of light under the bathroom door and was heading for it, assuming that was where he was. Good. He waited another second to see if anyone else was coming.

Just two of them for now then. If there were others he'd worry about them later.

When it was over, if he was still standing, he had some calls to make. There was a good chance men had been sent for all of them. He may not be able to get through to Alison but at least he could try and warn Fitzpatrick.

As he closed the bedroom door with his foot it occurred to Lars that he was supposed to give the men a warning.

He decided the same warning they were about to give Ellie should just about cover it.

34

HE WASN'T SURE how long he'd been out.

He'd come to in what looked like a room in a hospital, an IV hooked up to a cannula in his arm, various monitors on either side measuring his heart rate, blood pressure, respiration. There was a small camera high on the wall, pointed at where he lay. From the feeling in his stomach and the speed at which his heart was racing he assumed the drip contained an epinephrine solution.

Which meant Alison had told them everything.

That was to be expected; they had her mother. He had seen the look on her face when they had dragged him out of the motel room, had known then that she would do anything to prevent them harming her. But now she would no longer be of use to them. He still didn't know who these people were, but he had no doubt that they would want to dispose of her, and Fitzpatrick, and the sheriff, and else anyone they might suspect of knowing something about his secret. And they would want to do it as quickly as possible. They were all in grave danger and it was because of him, because he hadn't done what he should have and simply left. He needed to get out of here quickly, find Alison and get word to Fitzpatrick and Henrikssen.

That would be easier said than done however. Thick velcro straps across his chest pinned his arms to his sides, more across his legs. He tested the restraints, straining the muscles in his arms and legs. They wouldn't budge.

A moment later the door opened and a middle-aged man in a white lab coat entered. The man checked the monitors, ignoring his questions, then seemed to reach a decision. He disconnected the drip from the cannula. From a cabinet mounted on the wall he removed a couple of foil pouches, tearing open the first and removing a small clear bag with a plastic tube attached. Cody recognized the bags. Disposable PVC single blood bags, most likely prepped with anticoagulant, similar to the ones he carried in his CSAR medikit bag. The man removed the protective cap from the tube and connected it to the cannula in his arm. Immediately the bag began to fill, the bright red liquid flowing smoothly down the sides of the plastic, causing the bag to swell as it pooled at the bottom. After watching for a few moments the man hung the bag on the side of the table, out of sight, and then turned to close the cabinet. It took only a few minutes for the bag to fill and then he disconnected it, sealing the full bag before tearing the foil pouch and connecting a second.

It was unusual that they were taking a second unit immediately. There was a moderate risk of a person going into shock if they lost more than two pints of blood over a short period of time. Cody wasn't particularly concerned. He had donated more on occasion when it had been needed. His blood type meant that anyone could accept a transfusion from him without fear of rejection, and more often than not a single unit just wasn't enough. He would just feel light-headed for a little while.

When the second bag was full the man disconnected it. Then he picked up both bags and left the room.

Cody closed his eyes, analyzing the encounter to see whether he could learn anything about the people who were holding him. The man hadn't spoken, refusing to respond to any of his questions. But the speed with which he had entered the room once he had come around told him that they were watching him carefully. They wanted his blood, enough to take a greater amount than would normally be advisable. But he also knew they had gone to extraordinary lengths, taken incredible risks, to bring him here alive. They wouldn't want anything to happen to him, at least not yet.

Perhaps he could find a way to use that to his advantage.

35

DE SOUZA QUICKLY packed the few things he had brought, stuffing them into the canvas bag. His employer had explained that he no longer required his services and now he was anxious to be gone. They had paid him in cash just as he had requested. The tightly packed bundles of new notes filled the bag, leaving little room for the small number of personal items he had brought. It didn't matter. They would fly him back to San Diego and then he would disappear for a long while.

He had heard many secrets during his career, information that could destroy the careers of powerful men, information that could make him rich. But nothing he had come across had been as valuable, or as dangerous, as this. If what the young doctor had spoken of were true this man Gant would be truly priceless. He needed to get as far away from here as possible.

There was a knock on the door and he jumped. It was the large blonde man with the German accent who had brought him here, telling him the helicopter was on its way and that they were ready to take him back. De Souza nodded, picking up the canvas bag containing his cash, declining the man's offer of assistance. He followed him down the corridor, clutching the bag to his chest. As they approached the entrance to the facility he started to feel a little better. If they had wanted to kill him they would surely have done it by now. In a few short hours he would be gone. His services were always in demand, he lived a comfortable life. But with what he had earned over the last few days he would never again need to worry about money.

The German held the door open and he hurried through, gripping the bag tightly. It was the first time he had been outside, the first time he had even seen the sun, since he had arrived at the facility a week before. He looked around, squinting. So they were in the desert. He had been blindfolded when they had brought him here. Whoever his employer was he had certainly gone to considerable lengths to make sure the place didn't attract any attention. The small single story structure appeared derelict. The few windows were boarded up, the walls brown from the desert dust, the paint on the shutters faded and flaking. From the outside no-one could tell that there were further levels underground, that the facility housed a surgical theatre and an intensive care unit, as well as accommodation for those who worked there.

There was no sign of the helicopter. And something was nagging at him. Why had they not bothered to blindfold him this time? Behind him he heard a soft *snick-snick*, answering his silent question. De Souza froze. He had heard that sound a thousand times before. The sound of the slide being pulled back on a handgun, chambering the first round.

They had never intended to let him leave.

He started to turn to face the German, his mind racing to marshal his thoughts, to present the most compelling argument in the few seconds he had left. There was no reason to kill him. He had served their employer well and might be of use again at some point in the future. They didn't need to worry that he would be indiscreet. He had spent his whole life keeping secrets. He would never disclose what he had learned here.

Which was true.

Friedrichs aimed the Colt the moment the round was chambered, the tip of the silencer almost touching the back of the small man's bald head. He squeezed the trigger before the Honduran had even said a word. The silencer's baffles hid much of the sound. Nevertheless the *crack-snap* from the motion of the slide as the weapon cycled was surprisingly loud in the still of the desert.

Not that de Souza would have heard it, Friedrichs thought, looking down at the man's limp form. Blood was already spreading from where the bullet had exited, mixing with the dust to form a small dark brown puddle under the Honduran's head. *Der Eckzahn* had told him to kill the man inside. But that would just have caused a mess, and as there were only a couple of doctors at the facility apart from him that would have meant he would have had to clean it up. Besides, there was no one way out here in the desert to witness anything. He grabbed the man by the back of his jacket, lifting him easily with one hand, and dragged him over to the nearest outhouse. He might as well bring the woman out as well. He would fire up the incinerator and dispose of both bodies at the same time. But first he needed to report back that de Souza had been dealt with. He picked up the bag containing the money on his way back to the main building.

36

HE KEPT HIS eyes closed, controlling his breathing, forcing himself to remain still in spite of the commotion going on around him.

Once they had taken him off the epinephrine drip his body had quickly metabolized the adrenaline and he had started to concentrate on slowing his heart rate, using techniques he had learned in the mountain jungles of Thailand over thirty years before. He began by concentrating on his posture, on the alignment of his limbs, his torso, his head, becoming aware of everywhere his body was in contact with the thin mattress on which he was lying, every place the restraining straps touched his skin, relaxing each muscle in turn. When he was comfortable that he had released as much tension as he could he started to focus his mind on his breathing, examining each inward and outward breath, analyzing it as the air flowed into his body, deep into his lungs. Satisfied that his mind was in tune with his breathing he slowed it down, increasing the length of each inhalation and exhalation, lengthening the pause between. With each breath he felt his heart slowing in his chest, until he could count only an occasional pulse. Somewhere in the distance he heard an alarm sound, some part of his mind recognizing that it was the monitor in his room. He pushed the thought away. He needed to hold this state for as long as he could.

He was aware of other people in the room now, their voices excited but muffled. Someone was shaking his shoulder, leaning over to call his name. His mind wanted to go to the voice, to escape to consciousness, but he willed it to stay focused on his breathing, now almost imperceptible, on the occasional beating of his heart. The voices in the room receded, once again becoming distant. He felt a weight in the center of his chest, someone pushing hard, repeatedly, compressing his chest cavity in an attempt to force his heart to beat faster. On some level he realized that it hurt but he pushed the pain away, forcing his mind to remain where it was. He was waiting for something else.

The pressure on his chest suddenly stopped. Then he felt the straps across his arms and chest being loosened, his left arm being moved off to one side.

There.

That was what he had been waiting for.

He released his mind, willing it back to consciousness. He knew it would take a few seconds to come around, for his heart rate to return to normal after being that far under. He felt the cold of the pads, one in the center of his chest, the other on the left of his ribcage, the side he had gambled that they'd have to remove the restraining straps to expose. He wasn't certain now that he could come around quickly enough. Would the defibrillator work or would its sensors detect that his heartbeat was returning to normal? If it did work would the shock incapacitate him? He waited, bracing himself, forcing his mind back into the room. He could hear the activity around him more clearly now, the sounds from around him no longer muffled and distant. Just a few more seconds.

His eyes opened and suddenly he was back. His entire ribcage ached from the chest compressions but he ignored it, quickly looking around. To his left one of the men was leaning over the crash cart, his back to him while he frantically tried to get the defibrillator to activate. To his right the second man was simply staring at him, eyes wide, mouth open, for a moment too shocked to do anything.

Cody wasted no time. With one hand he grabbed the two wires lying across his chest and ripped the pads free, sitting up. With the other he struck out, hitting the doctor as hard as he could underneath his nose with the heel of his hand. The man howled in pain and grabbed his shattered nose. He collapsed to the floor, blood already pouring from between his fingers. Cody ignored him, bending forwards to release the straps that were still holding his feet to the tablet

The other doctor spun around when he heard the cry, finally noticing that the man on the table was no longer unconscious. He reacted faster than his colleague but it wasn't enough. His feet were finally free, and Cody swung them around, bending his knees and planting them in the center of the man's chest, pushing him backwards over the crash cart. The cart toppled backwards with a crash, the man landing awkwardly on top of it. He was on him in a second, knocking him out with a blow to the temple. He moved around the table where the other man was on his knees, whimpering as he held his broken nose. Soon he too was unconscious.

He rolled both men on to their sides, quickly binding their hands and feet with bandages he found in one of the drawers. When he was done he leaned back against the table, gathering his breath. He felt light-headed. Dealing with the doctors had been easy; it shouldn't have affected him that much. Maybe the effects of coming back that quickly from being so far under. Then he remembered that they had taken a couple of units of his blood. His body would replace the hemoglobin quickly, but it would take a little while longer for him to return to normal.

He certainly couldn't wait around for that. He glanced up at the camera on the wall. Whoever was watching would already have raised the alarm. He had no idea where he was, or how many other men, no doubt better trained than the two doctors, were already on their way. He needed to find Alison and get them both out of here. He had noticed a packet of disposable scalpels in one of the drawers while he had been looking for something with which to tie up the doctors and he took one, slipping it into the waistband of the pants he was wearing. Then he headed for the door. A quick look told him there was no one outside in the corridor. He closed the door behind him.

He made his way down the hallway, checking doors on both sides as he went. The place was like a small hospital. He passed an operating theatre and an ICU, as well as several other rooms with beds, medical supplies and monitoring equipment. None of the rooms on this floor had windows, which suggested he was underground. The last room contained a row of lockers and he found a pair of boots and some overalls that fit, but no weapons. He shoved the scalpel he had taken into the pocket of the overalls and moved on. So far his luck had held and he had encountered no one. The place, or at least this level, seemed eerily quiet.

There was a lift at the end of the corridor. The panel confirmed he was on the lower of two underground levels. He found the stairs and climbed quickly to the next level, checking carefully before emerging into a corridor similar to the one he had just come from a floor below. He crept forward, straining for any sounds that might alert him to the presence of anyone else in the facility.

Halfway down the corridor he opened a door to a small room similar to the one in which he had been held. Against one wall, lying on a gurney, he found her. He closed the door behind him, flicking the light switch, gently calling her name. Her eyes were open, as if she were staring at the ceiling, but she didn't respond, her jaw slack, mouth slightly open, her lips tinged with blue. Her breathing was labored, coming in irregular gasps. Occasionally her throat would convulse weakly, as if she were having trouble swallowing. He quickly checked her airway. She didn't resist. Her mouth dropped open as he rolled her onto her side, placing one arm under her head. Saliva slowly dripped from the corner of her mouth, running down her forearm, pooling on the gurney.

He didn't know what to do. He was used to dealing with battlefield traumas, with gunshot wounds, injuries caused by fire, by explosions, by shrapnel. He knew what to do to treat men who were bleeding profusely, who had spinal injuries, broken bones, even those who had lost limbs. But there were no external signs of trauma here. Whatever they had done to her seemed to have caused damage to her central nervous system that had impaired even her most basic functions.

And she was deteriorating rapidly. If he didn't find a way to help her soon she would simply stop breathing. He had no idea where this place was but he doubted it was anywhere near a population center. Assuming he could even get them out of here it could be hours before he might get her to a hospital. He looked at her again. It was time she didn't have. He could go back to the doctors he had left on the floor below, force them to help. But where would that get him? Whoever had brought him here had done this to her. He had to assume that person was already aware of his escape and would by now be sending others to make sure he was apprehended. He needed to get them out of this facility before they arrived.

The thought of the doctors in the room below gave him an idea. He had no way of knowing whether it would work, but he was out of options. He opened the door a crack, checking there was still no one outside, and wheeled the gurney into a room at the end of the corridor close to the stairwell, leaving her there while he ran back down the stairs. The two doctors were still lying on the floor, unconscious, as he had left them. He grabbed what he needed and sprinted back towards the room where he had left Alison, taking the stairs two at a time.

It took him less than a minute to set up, and then he stood, his right arm by his side, a tube snaking from the needle just above his elbow to the blood bag resting on the gurney, waiting for it to fill with his blood. Her breathing was getting more and more labored. He leaned over to check her pulse with his left hand, opening and closing his right, flexing and relaxing the muscles to increase the flow of blood, willing it to come more quickly. The bag was almost full. Just another minute.

As he waited for the bag to fill he looked around, noticing for the first time a chair in the corner of the room, bolted to the floor, thick velcro straps for wrists and ankles telling him that this was where they had interrogated her. On a bench opposite sat what looked like a defibrillator, next to it a small vial and two syringes, one full, one spent. Was this what they had given her? He grabbed the full syringe and the vial and placed both in the pocket of his overalls. Like all the other rooms he had been in there was a camera mounted high on the wall. With the door closed and the lights off the room was almost completely dark, but he had no idea whether they could see him. There was enough light for him to see well enough, which told him that if the cameras had image-enhancing capabilities his attempts to hide their position were probably in vain. He couldn't worry about that now. It was all he could do.

He sat in the darkness while the blood bag filled, listening for any sounds from outside the room. So far it seemed they were alone, but he knew others would be coming. How long they had simply depended on how far they had to travel to get here. If whoever had abducted them managed to get men to the building before he could get them out they were probably finished anyway.

At last the bag was full and he pulled out the needle. He worked quickly to set up the transfusion, placing the bag high on her shoulder, checking that the blood was flowing into her arm before taping it in place. Now he needed to get them out of here.

He opened the door a crack, checking the corridor was still empty. Satisfied, he returned to the gurney, gently taking Alison in his arms and carrying her out. The elevator was waiting, but if the lifts could be locked down remotely he would have delivered them back into the hands of their captors. He took the stairs, climbing as quickly as he could. When he reached the top he stopped, once again feeling light-headed. The weight of the woman wouldn't normally have bothered him but with what he had just given her he had lost three units of blood. He gave himself a second to rest and it passed.

The door at the top of the stairwell opened into another corridor, like the two below. But this time at the end of the corridor there was a door.

He made his way towards it.

37

FRIEDRICHS SAT ON the dusty ground, his back to the building, cupping his hand around the match as he held it to the end of his cigarette. He took a long drag, holding the smoke in his lungs for a moment before slowly exhaling.

His earpiece lay on the ground beside him, turned off. He had removed it after reporting back to *Der Eckzahn* that de Souza had been taken care of. Gant was secure and the woman, well after her last session with the Honduran she was a vegetable. She wouldn't even be able to lift herself off her gurney without help, let alone escape the facility. There was nothing left for him to do but dispose of the bodies. He checked his watch. Fifteen minutes since he had lit the burners. It required fourteen hundred degrees to properly dispose of a human body. By the time he got the woman the furnace would be up to temperature. He took a last drag on the cigarette and flicked the butt into the dust. He picked up the comms unit from where it lay on the ground, switched it on and placed it back in his ear.

He was almost at the door to the facility when the earpiece beeped, letting him know someone was trying to contact him. He tapped the side of the unit, opening the channel.

'*Where have you been? Gant has escaped!*'

It was *Der Eckzahn*.

Scheiße. Why had he removed the earpiece? If *Der Eckzahn* decided to blame him for this it could cost him dearly. He was about to respond when he saw the door to the facility opening.

He gently slid the Colt from the pocket of his flak vest and pressed himself up against the wall behind the door, waiting. *Der Eckzahn* would already have sent more men from Las Vegas; it would take them only minutes to arrive in the Lynx. He would have Gant back in custody before they got here.

Friedrichs waited, counting the seconds. If Gant would just take one more step he could take him. Why was he hesitating? He couldn't know anyone was behind the door. He was sure he hadn't made a sound, and as loud as *Der Eckzahn's* ranting sounded through the earpiece it wouldn't be audible to anyone else. The comms units they used were the best money could buy.

Gant was just being cautious.

38

HE HELD THE release down with his elbow, pushing the door open a fraction. It was bright outside, probably mid-morning. The ground was dry, dusty, like they were in the desert, possibly Nevada. He inched the door open a little further with his shoulder. He could see a couple of outbuildings, and beyond a chain-link fence. There didn't seem to be anyone out here.

He was about to step out when he heard a voice. Tinny, muted, almost inaudible.

But definitely there.

Cody froze, straining to hear. There it was again. Almost impossible to make out but definitely the sound of a voice, someone agitated.

It was coming from behind the door.

He didn't have time to put Alison down. Instead he threw all of his weight against the door, slamming his shoulder into it. He heard a grunt, felt the door connect with something on the other side, saw a gun flying off into the dirt. Without hesitating he stepped back, Alison still in his arms, and kicked as hard as he could. The door flew backwards and again he felt it slam into whoever was behind it. Hopefully that would give him a second. He stepped outside and knelt down quickly, lowering her to the ground as gently as he could.

The man who had been waiting behind the door appeared in an instant, rushing forward to tackle him, ignoring Alison, her vacant eyes telling him immediately that she was no threat. The man was huge, towering over him by five or six inches, grey eyes underneath a shock of white-blond hair betraying no fear.

Cody scrabbled backwards in the dirt, trying to get out of the way, but he was off balance and despite his size the man was quick, on him in a second. He lashed out with a boot, connecting with a huge ankle as the man advanced. His attacker fell forward, landing awkwardly on top of him and they grappled in the dirt. The blond man had to outweigh him by a hundred pounds, and he was immensely strong. Now he was using all of that weight to push the edge of one huge forearm down onto his windpipe, cutting off his air supply.

Then he heard it. Faint at first but unmistakable, the familiar *wop-wop-wop* of rotors. Still several miles away – his attacker hadn't yet noticed – but he knew the helicopter would be here in a minute, maybe less. He had no more time.

He twisted his body, pushing with every last ounce of his strength, throwing the man to one side, rolling clear. As he started to get to his feet he suddenly felt dizzy, the effort combined with the loss of blood causing his vision to grey momentarily. He looked up. Friedrichs was already on his feet, but for the first time the huge German hesitated, glancing up at the sky as now he too heard the helicopter. In a matter of moments his men would be here.

Cody knew he couldn't allow himself to be stalled for the few seconds it would take for reinforcements to arrive. The man was well trained, confident in his abilities. He had attacked without hesitation. He would have seen the bag taped to Alison's shoulder, would probably also know that the doctors had taken blood from him earlier. Another wave of light-headedness hit him and Cody staggered backwards, shaking his head to clear it. He saw the change in the German's expression and an instant later the man was lunging forward, feinting to the left before suddenly changing direction.

His attacker moved with incredible speed, but Cody had read the feint, had slipped the scalpel from his pocket as he stood. Now he stepped forward and grabbed one huge wrist, twisting it hard. Before he had time to react Cody yanked it forwards, at the same time stepping back slightly to pull the large man off balance. The hand that concealed the scalpel shot up to the man's neck. He had already slid his foot across in front of the German's right leg as he pivoted, continuing to pull the man's wrist down, locking it against his body. In one fluid motion he straightened his knees, lifting the large man off his feet. For an instant he felt the man's weight and then he was bending his own body forward, twisting his torso to the left, using his attacker's momentum to throw him over his shoulder.

Friedrichs lay flat on his back on the dusty ground, momentarily stunned. He tried to push himself up with his right hand but the wrist was broken, no longer able to bear his weight. With his left he reached for his throat, as if for the first time noticing something there. His fingers came away slick, a look of surprise on his face as he held them up. It had happened so fast he hadn't felt the scalpel entering his neck, slicing through the carotid artery. Bright red blood, a surprising amount of it, spilled from his lips and ran down his neck, pooling in the dirt underneath his head.

There was no time to waste. Cody grabbed the German by his flak jacket and dragged him into the facility. Once inside he pushed the call button for the lift, pulling the man in as the doors opened, an instant later closing silently behind him. As the lift descended he bent down to remove the comms unit from the man's ear. Friedrichs made no effort to resist. The lift stopped, the doors opening on the lowest level. He stepped over the man, and pulled him halfway out of the lift so that his body blocked the doors, preventing them from closing. Then he sprinted back up the stairs, pushing the comms unit into his ear as he went, tapping the earpiece to open the channel. He had to assume these men were professionals and would keep chatter to a minimum, even over a secure network. But he might be able to pick something up, at least until they realized he was listening in and switched frequencies.

He found Alison where he had left her, still staring blankly into nothing. He picked her up and carried her around to the side of the building, propping her against the wall. He crouched down to peer around the corner. He could make out the helicopter now, a Lynx, its nose pointed down, approaching fast. Had they seen him? He had to hope they hadn't been close enough. Everything depended on them coming straight in to land, on the men who were in the helicopter heading directly into the facility. There was a clear trail for them to follow. The blond man he had dragged back inside had left enough blood for them to spot even before they would touch down. But if the pilot decided to circle the compound before landing, or if whoever was in charge was smart enough to secure the perimeter before checking the buildings, they would be found. He had to assume eight or nine men in the Lynx. Armed, well trained, like the man he had already killed. He had retrieved the Colt he had knocked from the man's hand. He thumbed the release to eject the clip. Six rounds. He still had the scalpel. He might be able to take two of them, three if he were lucky. Probably no more. And he needed to do it without alerting the pilot.

The Lynx was only a few hundred yards away, still coming in fast, now starting to descend. He saw the landing gear drop from the fuselage. Through the comms unit he could hear someone trying to contact a man named Friedrichs, presumably the blond man whose body he had dragged back into the facility. If they didn't get a response would the pilot circle the compound first before landing? If they did he and Alison would be seen, and it would be over. He held his breath, watching as the pilot brought the helicopter straight in, choosing to land as close to the main building as possible. The pilot flared the Lynx at the last moment, the wash from the rotors kicking up clouds of dust. Before the wheels had touched the cargo doors slid open and men jump out of both sides, weapons drawn. He counted eight, waiting to see how they would disperse. The four who had exited the helicopter on the side nearest the entrance to the facility were already going through the door, stopping only briefly to examine the blood on the ground. He expected the other men to move out to positions around the compound, to begin searching the other buildings. If they split up he might be able to pick them off individually before he was noticed. Could he take all of them before the first group had completed their search of the facility? It was unlikely.

But after spending only a few seconds scanning the compound from where they stood the second group turned and followed the others inside.

He had no time to lose. It would take only minutes for them to sweep the building. By the time they came back out he and Alison had to be gone. He ran around the back so that he could approach the helicopter from behind, pausing for only a moment when he reached the other side to check that the men were still inside. The rotors were still spinning as he broke cover. He ran, crouching low, ducking under the tail boom, sliding in the dirt under the belly of the helicopter, emerging just behind the door on the other side. He needed to deal with the pilot before he had a chance to relay a warning to the team inside the building.

Through the perspex of the cockpit door Cody could see the man checking his instruments as the rotors slowed. He reached up and grasped the recessed door latch, turning it as gently as he could until he found the mechanism's biting point. Through the earpiece he could hear that they had found Friedrichs body. Then static as they switched channel, realizing he had taken the comms unit and was listening to them.

He was out of time. Even now they would be warning the pilot. He pulled the door open and reached in to grab the man's jacket, using the butt of the pistol to knock him out. He leaned over, quickly removed his headset and undid the harness. He pulled the unconscious man out of his seat, lifting him on to his shoulder. His luck had held this far but when the pilot didn't respond they would realize he was already outside. Even now they would be sprinting down the corridors, up the staircase, heading for the exit door. It would only be a matter of seconds before they would re-emerge from the building.

He ran around the nose of the helicopter and dumped the pilot in front of the entrance, wedging his unconscious body against the bottom of the metal door. The door only opened outwards. He had to hope it was the only way to exit the facility. It wouldn't take them long to push the pilot out of the way, but every second now might be vital.

Alison was where he had left her, lying in the dirt by the side of the building. He bent down to pick her up, then sprinted back to the helicopter, placing her on the floor in the load area, sliding the cargo door shut. Half a second later he was pulling himself up into the pilot's seat, not bothering with either the harness or the headset. He had never flown a Lynx before but it took him only a moment to scan the cockpit, pressing the ignition while he familiarized himself with the panels of dials and switches. He twisted the throttle grip on the collective to the start position and squeezed the starter trigger, listening to the shrill whine as the high-speed electric motors began to turn the blades, slowly at first, then faster. Then the flame caught in the turbine, and he opened the throttle to idle. Even inside the facility there would be no mistaking the sound of the helicopter's twin Rolls-Royce engines preparing for takeoff.

Above him through the canopy the four rotors were becoming a blur. He pulled the collective up, increasing the pitch to lift the nose. Through the perspex window to his left he noticed the door to the facility move a couple of inches as someone behind tried to open it, the pilot's unconscious body preventing it moving further. He twisted in power, raising the helicopter into a hover six feet from the ground. Beneath him he saw the door move again, opening further this time as whoever was behind it pushed harder against the obstruction.

He nudged the cyclic forward, tilting the spinning rotors down. The Lynx immediately obeyed, the nose dropping as it moved forwards. He could no longer see the door but he knew that one more push and they would be through. He pulled up on the collective, twisting in as much throttle as he dared. The helicopter lurched forward and upwards and he corrected with the pedals at his feet for drift. He was unfamiliar with the controls and for the first few seconds he overcompensated, the nose shifting to the left and then to the right, the helicopter waggling from side to side as it sped forward through the compound. Then he adjusted, correcting the pitch of the tail rotors and the nose came into line, pointing directly ahead. He pulled up on the collective, twisting the grip to add more power, and the Lynx accelerated smoothly across the compound. The chain-link fence passed beneath them as the rotors found undisturbed air, and the helicopter jumped into a climb. He looked over his shoulder in the direction of the facility. The last of the men were coming through the door, stepping over the pilot's body, each looking up as the helicopter they had arrived in climbed away from them. One of the men in front seemed to be talking, his head down, one finger to his ear, presumably relaying news of their escape.

But Cody knew they hadn't escaped yet. The Lynx would have a tracker. Once activated it would relay their position to whoever was responsible for their abduction. He needed to get Alison to somewhere that might be able to treat her. He switched on the helicopter's navigation system, reading their position. Nevada, just outside Las Vegas. Fallon was three hundred miles to the north. He checked the fuel gauges. They might just make it if he flew carefully, but he couldn't afford to do that. He needed to push as hard as he could. He had to assume that even now another helicopter, just as fast as this one, was being sent to intercept him. Fitzpatrick could scramble a team to meet them somewhere in the desert, before they ran out of fuel and had to ditch. He pulled on the headset and dialed in the secure frequency for the base tower, asking to be put through directly to the commander.

A moment later he switched off the comms unit, breaking the connection.

Fitzpatrick was dead.

If they could get to the commander at Fallon how could he be sure that they would be safe there?

He consulted the navigation unit again, looking for an alternative.

39

THE TWO DEAD men were laid out on the small patio behind his house. Ellie had refused to have them inside, not even for a minute. It was her home and he and his crime scene could go directly to hell in a hand basket. Besides, hadn't he been right there and seen what had happened? *Time to put away the notebook Lars. Looks like this one's all wrapped up. But first you can take the bodies out with the goddamned trash. They'd better not be in my house when I get back from taking Jake to the vet.*

Once Lars had removed their balaclavas he had recognized them immediately. The two men from the black Cadillac outside the Chevron on New Year's Eve. He'd met a third man on the stairs, had managed to get a couple of shots in before the man had turned and fled. Blood on the bannister, some more on the kitchen floor and on the driveway outside. Fresh, bright red. Looked like an arterial bleed. He wouldn't get far. Jed and Larry were out looking for him now.

No signs of forced entry. They must have picked the lock on the kitchen door. He'd found traces of hamburger on the kitchen floor. Most likely some sort of tranquilizer, crushed up and mixed in with the meat and shoved through the door. Jake would have wolfed it down and gone looking for seconds.

He looked over the equipment the men had been carrying while he waited for the coroner to send a van up from the mortuary. Gas masks, canisters of carbon monoxide, soft silicone facemasks attached to each small metal cylinder. Silenced automatics. But they hadn't planned to use those unless something went wrong. No, it was supposed to look like an accident. The silicone masks pressed to their faces, the gas inhaled while they slept, every lungful finding its way directly into their bloodstreams, the molecules binding to their red blood cells, starving their bodies of oxygen. He guessed it would have taken only minutes before they would have lost consciousness; death would have followed shortly afterwards. Afterwards they would have damaged the flue that vented gas from the house's hot water system. The Henrikssens. Just another tragic couple who had neglected to have their appliances serviced.

His cell phone rang and he dug it out of his pocket, checking the screen. Number withheld. Maybe it was Fitzpatrick, returning his call. He'd been trying to reach him ever since he'd dealt with the men who had broken into his house. If they were after him and Ellie they would surely be after the commander as well.

'Sheriff Henrikssen?'

A voice he didn't recognize. The accent neutral, perhaps British. Certainly not Nevada. Background noise. Regular, mechanical. Muted but familiar. A helicopter?

'Who is this?'

'Sheriff you need to listen, I don't have much time. My name is Cody. You may know me as Carl Gant or Luke Jackson.'

'Where are you, Cody? Is Doctor Stone with you?'

'I have Alison.'

'Is she alright?'

A pause.

'No. That's why I'm calling. We were taken by the people who were behind what happened at Mount Grant. Alison was tortured. It looks like she was given something that's caused some sort of brain damage. I'm flying her to the University Medical Center in Las

Vegas. It's a Level I trauma center, which means it will have neurosurgical capabilities, and a heliport. I need you to get in touch with them and tell them I'm on my way, and that I have a sample of whatever it is they've given her.'

'Okay.'

'But you need to tell them that no attempt is to be made to apprehend me.'

Lars paused.

'And why would I do that?'

'Because I'm not going to allow myself to be apprehended today, Sheriff, and if a couple of hospital security guards take it into their heads to try somebody might get hurt. Besides, there's something else I need to do as soon as I've dropped Alison off.'

'You know where he is don't you?'

'I think I do.'

'Then why don't you just tell me? Let the authorities handle this.'

'No disrespect, Sheriff, but I'm not sure that's a great idea. From what Alison's told me I think you may also have some idea how long this has been going on. I'm guessing to have avoided the attention of the FBI all these years he's probably got someone pretty high up on the inside.'

DeWitty. Maybe others.

'And he's used to covering his tracks. He got to Fitzpatrick this morning. Waited until he'd left the base to pick up his wife and then a truck ran his car off the road. Made to look like a DUI. There won't be a lot of evidence pointing to him.'

'How do you plan to stop him?'

A pause.

'Sheriff you don't want to know that.'

Lars considered what he was being told. Men had been sent for him and for Ellie as they slept in their beds.

Fitzpatrick and his wife, killed that morning. Alison Stone tortured. Joseph Brandt, thirty years in prison for a crime he hadn't committed. God knows how many others abducted for their blood, their organs. He heard Ellie's voice in his head.

Time to put away the notebook, Lars.

'Are you sure you're going to be able to handle whatever you find wherever you're going?'

Another pause, longer this time.

'I don't know. But none of us will be safe until whoever's behind this has been dealt with. He won't be expecting me and with eight of his men stranded in the desert it's the best chance I'm likely to get.'

'And assuming you get to him, whoever he is, will you be able to do it?'

'I've killed men before.'

'Like this?'

This time there was no answer.

'Alright, I'll put the call in to UMC. But first you need to listen to me for a moment.'

40

IT TOOK LESS than a minute to touch down on the helipad. He delivered Alison and one of the vials he had taken from the room where she had been interrogated, explaining briefly to the medics who met him on the roof what had happened to her. As the sheriff had promised there was no attempt to restrain him. Then he was taking off again, the navigation unit showing him his next destination. It was only a few miles to the south and would take less than a minute in the Lynx.

Suddenly it seemed like madness; he had no idea what he might face there. But he could see no other choice. When the Lynx's navigation system had displayed its recent flight history he had realized that this had to be the place. He had seen enough of the facility to know its purpose. Once the organs that were harvested there were out of the donors' bodies they would need to be transported quickly to the new host, which meant that whoever needed those organs had to be close by. And what he had said to Henrikssen was true: they would never be safe until the person who was behind all of this had been dealt with.

They wouldn't be expecting him. They would assume he would run for Fallon. With a bit of luck it would take them some time to enable the GPS tracker and lock on to the Lynx. Even if they had already acquired him there was a good chance they would think he was simply heading for one of the city's hospitals. By the time they realized he was coming for them he would already be there. There was bound to be a protection detail but they would have orders not to hurt him, and he could use that to his advantage. He felt inside the pocket of the overalls for the silenced Colt he had taken from the blond man outside the facility. Fitzpatrick and Carla had been murdered. He had seen the looks on the faces of the medics who had taken Alison from him. Whatever she had been given they hadn't held out much hope for her recovery. The sheriff was wrong. He had no reservations about dealing with whoever got in his way.

He brought the Lynx in to land, touching down lightly on the helipad of a twenty-storey building half a mile south of the Strip, the rotors still turning as he jumped out and ran for the only door that led off the rooftop.

The door was unlocked. It led to a half-flight of concrete stairs and another door. He drew the Colt from the pocket of his overalls and opened the door a crack, peering through to check there was no-one waiting for him.

He stepped through into a single wide, well-lit corridor. The place looked like a hospital, like the facility he had just escaped from. He moved swiftly, checking the doors as he went. An operating theatre, what looked like an intensive care unit, a storage room containing a crash cart and oxygen tanks. A security room. Banks of servers, green and red LEDs flickering intermittently in the darkness. A row of screens, showing feeds from various cameras. This was the place. Whoever had ordered his abduction had to be here.

At the end the corridor turned right. He inched up to the corner, peering around. A nurse's station, a nurse sitting in front of bank of monitors. A single guard standing in front of a door opposite, head bent forward, finger to one ear, speaking into his comms unit. He would have heard the helicopter land on the roof, would now be trying to contact the men who were still at the facility. There was no way to close the distance without being seen, but he couldn't afford to wait. Within seconds the man would realize what had happened.

Cody took a breath and stepped around the corner, gun drawn, leveled at the guard. The man was pre-occupied with his earpiece and it was the nurse who saw him first, her mouth dropping open as her eyes flicked to the Colt. The guard saw him an instant later, taking only a fraction of a second to register what was happening. The man was fast, his hand already halfway inside his jacket, instinctively reaching for the weapon holstered there, before he appreciated the reality of his situation. He raised both hands slowly, palms forward, to show the gun remained in its holster.

The nurse had not moved from her station. Cody moved forward, keeping the gun on the guard.

'On the floor, hands behind your head, interlace your fingers.'

The man hesitated a second. Cody raised the gun a fraction of an inch. The guard read the look in his eyes and complied.

He reached inside his jacket and withdrew a Colt similar to the one he had taken from the blond man outside the facility from the shoulder holster, shoving it into the pocket of his overalls. He also took the man's comms unit, removing the one he had taken from the blond man at the facility, placing the new unit in his ear. Then he marched them back along the corridor. There was duct tape in the storage room he had passed on his way and he used it to bind both of them securely. He stepped back into the corridor, locking the door from the outside. It should hold them long enough for what he needed to do.

So far he had been lucky. Whoever lived here was clearly conscious about security. A protection detail was normally stationed on the floor below but the nurse had told him that they had left in a hurry within the last hour, leaving only her and the guard in the penthouse. There was an elevator that operated by key card that went only to the lobby. With the guard's pass he was able to disable it. The only other way down was by the fire exit. The door that led to the stairwell was made of steel, several inches thick, the locking mechanism accessible only from the inside. It would take some time for anyone to break through.

Which only left the roof, and there was nothing he could do about that. He didn't have long. They might be only minutes away and he needed to make sure he was gone before they arrived. He took the comms unit he had taken from the blond man at the facility from his pocket, tapping it to check that the channel was still open. Satisfied, he reached for the handle of the door opposite the nurse's station that the man had been guarding. The door was unlocked and he stepped into a large, dimly lit room. His eyes adjusted quickly after the bright corridor.

In the middle of the room lay an old man, his shrunken frame lost in a large bed. A tube from a drip suspended above the bed snaked into a cannula embedded in a skeletal forearm resting above the bedcovers. The hands were twisted and arthritic, long fingers ending in thick, curved nails. He was peering up at several screens suspended from the ceiling.

It took a moment for the old man to realize someone had entered the room. He turned his head slowly, squinting in the darkness, trying to make out who might have entered his inner sanctum uninvited. His upper lip curled in preparation for the rebuke he would deliver.

Cody examined the face staring up at him from the bed. The man looked impossibly old, the skin liver-spotted, parchment thin. One eye was milky white, sightless, sunken in a rheumy, wrinkled socket. But the other, the one that now examined him, was shockingly green, even in the dim light. It betrayed a determination that the rest of his body seemed to lack.

For a long moment the old man said nothing, and then the eye opened a fraction wider as at last he realized who was standing over him.

'You!'

It came out as little more than a whisper. A trace of an accent, hard to place.

The old man struggled to sit up. His fingers scrabbled for the emergency call button tethered to the side of the bed. Cody held up the comms unit he had taken from his pocket, nodding to the door.

'He won't be coming to help you.'

The old man slowly released the call button and stared back at him.

Cody looked up at the images displayed on the screens suspended above the bed. Pictures of himself as Mitchell, Jackson, Kyle, Gant. Surveillance photographs of Fitzpatrick and Carla, a man wearing a sheriff's uniform who he realized must be Lars Henrikssen. Feeds from cameras at the facility. The room where Alison had been tortured. The evidence was all there, damning. He had found who he had been looking for. He reached into the pocket of his overalls, pulling out the silenced Colt.

The old man glanced briefly at the gun then returned his gaze to him.

'You won't do that.'

The vowels slightly clipped, a guttural edge to the consonants.

'What makes you so certain.'

'Because you need to know.'

Cody remained silent, finger curled around the trigger. Whatever game the old man was playing, he didn't have time for it. He had to get this over with.

'Know what?'

'Who you are. *What* you are.'

The old man was bluffing. He might know what Alison had uncovered but how could he possibly know more than that? He didn't know much more himself. The ploy was obvious. He was stalling, giving his men time to return from the facility. Maybe he even had other teams closer by, already on their way. He raised the Colt a fraction, flicking the safety with the side of his thumb.

'Go ahead, Codratus. If you do, you'll never find out.'

The old man waited, looking up him with his one good eye. After a few moments he smiled, sensing he had won some silent battle of wills, that he was back in control.

'He told me, before he died, that you might exist, but I never really believed him. Not until we analyzed a sample of your blood, that is. No agglutination. No clumping. Incredible. And to think you were out there all along.'

What was the old man talking about?

'What do you mean? Who told you I might exist?'

The old man waved the question away.

'All in good time, Codratus, all in good time. It's the blood. It's all in the blood.'

He smiled again, as if at a private joke that only he understood.

'My blood. That was why you brought me to the facility?'

The old man paused before answering, drawing out the seconds.

'Yes.'

'How did you find me? How did you know I possessed the *hh* blood type?'

'Datacore.'

'The company that maintains personnel records for the military? How do you have access to their records?'

'Datacore is mine. I own it. Finding donors with the *hh* blood type had always been the problem. So when I learned that the government was planning to outsource the maintenance of its personnel records it was an opportunity too good to pass up. Datacore was still just a tiny company back then, but it met the tender requirements. It never would have won, of course. But thanks to a senator on the Armed Forces Appropriations Committee who cost me almost as much as I paid for the company itself, Datacore ended up with the contract, and has held it ever since.'

'So you have access to the blood type of everyone serving in the armed forces.'

The old man shook his head.

'Not just the military, Codratus. Datacore now manages the records of most of the country's emergency services and law enforcement agencies as well. It even has a special division to advise the government on what information might usefully be stored about its servicemen and women.'

'So it was you who initiated testing for the *hh* blood group?'

A nod, yes. Cody thought the old man looked proud.

'The first of many initiatives. You may have heard of the genetic dog-tagging program? Another of my ideas. I now have access not just to the blood types but also to the genetic records of several million Americans.'

'So how many have you had abducted?'

'Over the years the information from Datacore has yielded several dozen candidates. We have to make sure of course that their records are altered before they're abducted, their blood types changed before the details can appear on the FBI's NCIC database. Otherwise people like the sheriff in Hawthorne start to notice. That was a lesson we learned after the first abductions.'

'Shilpa Desai, Cindy Rowe, Robin Taft?' Alison had told him what Henrikssen had uncovered.

The old man paused for a moment, as if considering. In the end he dismissed the question with a wave of his fingers.

'Perhaps. So long ago now, though. I forget the details.'

Not a trace of guilt; not a shred of remorse. He hadn't even remembered their names.

'But Lars Henrikssen figured out what you had done.'

'Yes, the sheriff proved unusually efficient in putting the pieces together. But ironically it was because of his meeting with Fitzpatrick that I came to you, Codratus. I could hardly believe it when I accessed the Datacore searches the commander carried out on Christmas Day.'

'And that was why you had Fitzpatrick killed.'

Cody's knuckles whitened, his finger involuntarily tightening around the Colt's trigger. The old man didn't seem to notice.

'Yes. You have been lucky to have kept what you are hidden for so long, Codratus. But it was foolish to confide in the Stone woman. Your secret is too valuable to share with anyone; you must realize that. Such potential. Doctor Stone was kind enough to tell us about the adrenaline trigger. I'm sure we would have figured it out sooner or later, but the information was very helpful. I have already had my first transfusion of your blood. This morning, the units my doctors took from you at the facility.'

That was when he heard it. The distant thrum of rotors. Still several miles out, but they would be here in minutes. The old man hadn't noticed yet, but Cody knew he was out of time. He needed to get him to talk. He raised the Colt again, pointing the barrel at the old man's head.

'Tell me what you know about me.'

'Not just yet, Codratus. Not just yet. I'm enjoying our conversation too much. Moments like this are rare. They need to be savored.'

Cody gripped the Colt tighter. He didn't have time for this. But Henrikssen had been right. In spite of what the old man had done to Fitzpatrick, to Carla, to Alison, now that he was here he found he couldn't shoot him in cold blood. And the old man knew it.

Then suddenly he remembered. He reached into the pocket of his overalls and pulled out the syringe he had taken from the facility, from the room where Alison had been tortured. He flicked off the plastic protective cap.

'What's that?'

For the first time the old man sounded worried. He tried to sit up, to back away but Cody leaned over the bed, taking hold of one skeletal forearm. The needle slid easily into the cannula already embedded there.

'It's what your men at the facility gave to Alison Stone to make her talk. I'm guessing you know what it did to her. One way or another you're going to tell me what I want to know.'

Cody placed his thumb over the plunger, pausing for a moment. When the old man said nothing he depressed it a fraction of an inch. Suddenly in a fit of rage the old man lunged forward, lips pulled back in a snarl, for an instant revealing a single long yellow curved canine. Their faces were only inches apart and his one good eye glared with such venom that for an instant Cody felt his blood run cold. But he kept his grip on the old man's forearm, his thumb on the syringe. After a moment the old man lay back, his rage spent.

'Wait. Wait. I'll tell you.'

The old man looked up at him from the bed with a look of utter malevolence, but Cody ignored it.

Go on.

272

The old man paused for a moment, wetting his lips.

'My name is Callum Newman. Heir to Henry Newman. Or Doctor Heinz Albrecht Neumann as he was known before we came to this country.'

Heinz Albrecht Neumann. The name meant nothing to him.

'Neumann was our father.'

The words hit him like a physical blow. He searched the old man's face for any evidence that he might be lying, concocting a story in order to buy time.

'*Our* father?'

He barely managed to stammer out the words.

'I say father, although I doubt either of us actually contain any of his genetic material. He never told me what he used to create us, even though I begged him, pleaded with him to know, right until the end. *Ein bißchen Bißchen über dieses ein bißchen Bißchen über jene* was all he would say. *A little bit of this, a little bit of that.* How it used to annoy me. From what Doctor Stone was able to tell us it seems that you've already guessed at some of your origins. A little more obvious in my case.' He pulled back his lips, with one long finger tapping the side of the curved, yellow canine he had flashed earlier.

'You're mistaken. I know I was born in London.'

'Yes, the center of the movement at the time. Neumann only returned home to continue his work later, when those ideas fell out of favor.'

'What ideas? What movement?'

'Eugenics. From the Greek. *Well-born.* The idea that a race of superhumans could be produced by selective breeding. Balfour, Churchill, Roosevelt: they all supported it. Neumann took it one step further. You were his only success, you know. He spent the rest of his life trying to recreate you. I was as close as he ever got. As you can see, not very close.' A bitter laugh.

So it was true, then.

Not born.

Created.

'It was his obsession with recreating you that destroyed him in the end. He became consumed by what he had done for the National Socialists at Ravensbrück, Auschwitz, a dozen other camps. All so that they would let him continue with his experiments.'

Cody's mind was still reeling, considering the possibilities.

'There...there are others then, like me?'

'It's possible, but I doubt it. I was the last of the *Lebensfähig*.'

'*Lebensfähig*?'

'The Viables. The term our father used to refer to those of his experiments that survived. Most didn't. And as you can see it wasn't always a blessing.'

The sound of the approaching helicopter was louder now. He needed to get out of here, before they arrived. His mind raced. He still had so many questions he wanted to ask.

'What about my mother?'

The old man waved his hand, dismissing the question.

'Before he had access to the camps our father used the homeless, the indigent, for his experiments. She was probably a prostitute, a young woman desperate for money. Who knows? Who cares? She was only an incubator.'

Suddenly the old man turned his head, straining to hear. A smile slowly crept across his face. He had finally heard the helicopter.

'Do you hear that Codratus? Within moments my men will be here. Even if you manage to get out of this building you won't escape me. It doesn't matter where you go, I will track you down. But this doesn't have to be unpleasant. All I need is access to your blood. I am a very wealthy man. I'll give you anything you want.'

'And all those people you killed?'

'Only because I needed to stay alive. You would have done the same if you were me. But if I have you, if I have your blood, the killing will stop. I won't need anyone else.'

Cody was out of time. He placed the comms unit he had been holding in his hand back in his ear.

'Did you get all that?'

'Yep, Connie's recorded it all. Feds are on their way, less than a minute out. You'd best get out of there. They've already secured the men at the facility.'

The old man stared up at him in disbelief.

'Who is that? Who are you talking to?'

'That was the sheriff in Hawthorne you tried to have killed this morning. He's recorded our conversation.'

The old man stared up at him, his face contorted in a mask of rage.

'You fool. Do you think the sheriff can protect you? He'll be dead before the day is through. And you, all I need is your blood. I can keep you in a box if I choose.'

'That helicopter you hear isn't your men returning. It's the FBI. You'll spend whatever time you have left in a cell.'

Cody pointed down at the syringe he had inserted in the cannula in the old man's arm.

'I'm going to leave you with that.'

He looked down at the old man for a moment longer. Then he turned and walked out of the room, closing the door behind him.

Moments later from the roof the sound of the helicopter's Rolls-Royce engines preparing for takeoff, and then it was gone, replaced by the sound of another helicopter, closer now, coming in to land.

The old man stared at the syringe for a long moment. He heard the door from the roof open, the sounds of boots in the corridor outside. Then he was pressing the plunger, pushing the pale yellow liquid into his veins.

As the door to his room burst open the old man thought he detected the first faint odor of garlic.

Epilogue

ALISON WALKED BACK from the lecture theatre to her lab. The fog that had settled in from the bay to the east that morning, blanketing the campus, was slowly burning off. It had been a long, grey winter. She was ready for spring to begin.

It had been her first lecture since Christmas, and she had been a little nervous, but she thought it had gone well. Physically she had recovered quickly, but it had taken a long time for her memory to return. The first few weeks after she had regained consciousness had been the worst. She hadn't even been able to remember her name. But it had come back, slowly, frustratingly slowly at first, and then faster. As far as she could tell she was now largely back to normal, although she still had no recollection of anything that had happened in the fortnight prior to her admission to UMC. The neurologists there had told her that she might get fragments back as time went on, but it was also possible that she would simply never remember what had happened to her. Those few weeks might remain a mystery forever.

She had learned from the hospital that she had arrived by helicopter, but they had been able to tell her little else. The sheriff from Hawthorne, Henrikssen, had visited her in hospital, and again a few weeks after she had been discharged, at her lab. She had no memory of ever having met him. He had explained that he had come to see her just before Christmas and asked her to look at blood samples related to a crime that had occurred in his town. That visit had led to her having been targeted by

Callum Newman, a reclusive billionaire, one of the most prolific serial killers in U.S. history, who had somehow managed to evade detection for almost half a century. Even now, three months later, the story was still all over the news. Alison had no idea whether she had ever even met the man, or what he might have done to her to cause the neurological trauma she had suffered. She would probably never find out - Newman had taken the information with him to the grave. When the FBI had finally tracked him down they had found him in a coma. He had died shortly after they had taken him into custody and his body had immediately been cremated. She didn't even know what he looked like. Not a single picture had ever been released of the man responsible for at least two dozen deaths over a period of over fifty years.

The sheriff had explained that she had been taken to the hospital by someone called Carl Gant. Newman had targeted him because of his rare blood type. It was Gant's blood the sheriff had brought to her and asked her to analyze. She didn't remember Gant's name but she had recognized him from a photograph the sheriff had shown her. It was the young man who had visited her on campus just after term had begun the previous fall to talk about some screenplay he had been working on. When she had asked the sheriff whether she could contact him to express her gratitude he had told her that Gant had since disappeared. She thought the sheriff had looked awkward, as if he were holding something back, but she hadn't pursued it. She had had other things on her mind.

A few weeks after she had regained consciousness, when her memories had started to return in earnest, the doctors had broken the news. One of her neighbors had found her mother, maybe a week after it must have happened. She had tripped and fallen down the stairs, and had broken her neck. A random, senseless accident.

Alison knew she had been home for Christmas – she had checked her credit card statement for details of the flights she had booked and then called the airline to verify that she had actually flown. It had become important to her to prove that she had seen her mother before she had died, even though she knew it was unlikely she would ever remember what they might have talked about during her final visit. She hadn't even been at the funeral; she still had not regained consciousness by the time they had buried her. Sometimes when she thought about it she just felt like crying.

The faculty had been incredibly supportive, the dean particularly so. Alison remembered his interest in her research before whatever had happened to her. Now he seemed more curious about her recovery, whether her memory of those missing weeks had returned. Whenever he asked her about it she couldn't shake the feeling that he was relieved when she told him it hadn't.

The tall hardwoods opened above her as she made for the entrance to the Life Sciences building. As she walked through the lobby, Ryan, the security guard, stood up, calling her over. A package had been delivered for her while she was giving her lecture. He reached under his desk and handed her a cardboard box, about a foot square, heavily wrapped in packing tape. It was marked for her attention, with instructions that only she should open it. As she rode up in the elevator she examined the label. Austin, Texas. Strange. She wasn't expecting anything from there.

In the lab she set the box on the table while she went in search of box cutters. Once she had cut her way through the tape she lifted the flaps. Inside was a small cooler box. She lifted it out, setting it on the table. A card was taped to the lid, on which was printed a single word.

Adrenaline.

What could that mean?

She turned the card over, looking for any clue as to who might have sent it, but the back was blank. She released the clasps that held the lid in place. Wisps of vapor snaked out as she lifted it free.

Inside the box, packed in dry ice, were three vials of blood.

*

HE PULLED THE bike to the side of the road and turned the key in the ignition to kill the engine, removing his helmet. Brushy Creek, just north of Austin. A nice neighborhood. Wide, tree-lined streets, manicured lawns. He checked the mailboxes. There it was. A handsome two story, directly ahead.

For the first time he felt nervous.

He could just keep going. It was only two hundred miles to the border; he could be there in three hours. He planned to cross the Rio Grande at Laredo. Eagle Pass was closer but it was a smaller town, and he was more likely to be noticed. After three months he didn't think anybody would still be checking for him at the borders but it was hard to be sure.

Datacore had been shut down, its records transferred back to the government, the various initiatives it had enacted, including the genetic tagging program, suspended. He had pulled the motherboards from the servers he had found at Newman's penthouse on his way back to the roof, carefully removing all references to himself before handing the files over to Lars to give to the FBI. But for him it was too late. The military already had his DNA on record. Besides, all the information that linked the various lives he had led was still out there, just waiting for someone to look in the right places and put it all together. There was nothing he could do about that.

A nationwide manhunt had been launched for the men who had worked for Newman, and was still under way. Given that he had been operating for almost half a century the FBI had anticipated having to track down scores of former operatives. But once the search had begun it quickly became apparent that there would be no need. None of the men who had left Newman's service had survived more than a few months beyond their retirement, each dying shortly afterwards in a variety of accidents. Some of the active teams had been apprehended, but most were still at large. They were all well-trained, experienced operatives, practiced at avoiding detection by law enforcement. He suspected that by now most of those who had not already been arrested had left the country.

He had seen to it that the teams responsible for Fitzpatrick's and Carla's deaths and for the death of Alison's mother had not escaped, however. He had not been prepared to leave their fate to chance. Each deserved the end they would ultimately have received at Newman's hand, but he had spared them that. The files on the motherboards had divulged their locations and he had left each of the men outside the nearest FBI office, bound and gagged, a little the worse for wear but otherwise unharmed.

He had met with Henrikssen only once since. The sheriff had managed to recover the St. Christopher medal from the items the highway patrol had found scattered in the desert near Salt Wells, after Newman's men had first tried to abduct him. Henrikssen had told him that Joseph Brandt had been released from prison and was likely to receive a record settlement for the time he had spent in jail. Not that it would matter. He might be out of prison but Brandt was likely to remain in an institution of some sort for the rest of his life.

At least Alison seemed to have recovered well. The sheriff was keeping an eye on her. She still didn't remember anything of her ordeal, which was probably for the best. He hoped the blood he had sent would lead to the breakthrough with her research she had been hoping for.

So it was time. He wasn't sure how long he might be gone. He wasn't even sure if he was ever coming back.

But there was one thing he needed to do before he left. How often had he placed his life in the hands of the men he had served with, and asked them in turn to place their lives in his? It had been a mistake to walk away from all of those lives afterwards. Nevertheless he sat on his bike in front of the house for a long time. Finally he kicked the stand down and climbed off. As he approached the house he saw an old Ford Bronco sitting in the driveway, its bright red paintwork freshly waxed, its chrome glinting in the afternoon sun.

Life was too short.

At least for some.

THERE'S ONLY ONE PLACE LEFT THAT'S
SAFE...

IT'S THE LAST PLACE YOU SHOULD BE.

Printed in Great Britain
by Amazon